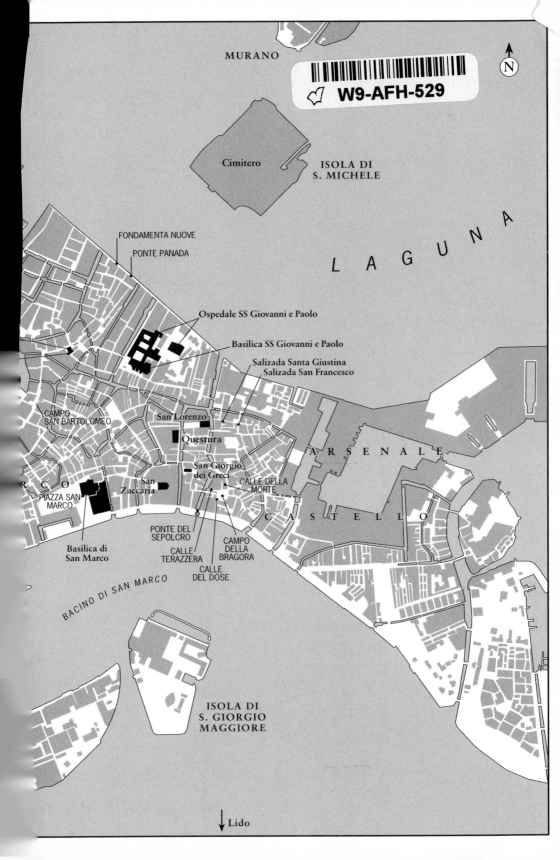

# A Refiner's Fire

## Also by Donna Leon

# Donna Leon

# A Refiner's Fire

Atlantic Monthly Press
*New York*

Originally published in Great Britain in 2024
by Hutchinson Heinemann, an imprint of Penguin Random House.

*Published simultaneously in Canada*
*Printed in the United States of America*

First Grove Atlantic hardcover edition: July 2024

Library of Congress Cataloging-in-Publication data is available for this title.

ISBN 978-0-8021-6254-0
eISBN 978-0-8021-6255-7

Atlantic Monthly Press
an imprint of Grove Atlantic
154 West 14th Street
New York, NY 10011

Distributed by Publishers Group West

groveatlantic.com

24 25 26 27   10 9 8 7 6 5 4 3 2 1

For Christine Stemmermann

See, the raging flames arise.
Hear, the dismal groans and cries.

*Joshua*, Part II, 29
Handel

# A Refiner's Fire

# 1

The first few times, the messages on Instagram gave no certainty of their numbers, nor did the participants have a specific target, but tonight they had agreed on la Fondamenta della Misericordia, only to have someone down in Castello complain that it was too far for them, so how about Santa Giustina? Only to have the decision changed by the person who wrote that Santa Giustina wasn't worth the time to cause trouble, so why not try the Piazzetta dei Leoncini? It was closer, and what they did would not pass unobserved.

In less than ten minutes, both groups were running into the Piazza, one from Calle de la Canonica, the other from under the Orologio. They crashed into one another, silent but for grunts and the sound a fist makes when it hits a shoulder or a head. They quickly coalesced into a mass of moving body parts: they fell, they got to their knees, were knocked back to the ground, got up and landed a punch on someone's neck, then had their feet kicked out from under them and fell again.

One gang was larger than usual: surveillance cameras later individuated twelve, six of whom were identified for the first time; the other six were already known. The other gang had ten members, one of whom carried a piece of metal pipe with which he had already smashed a display window; he and two friends stuffed the pockets of their jackets with eyeglass frames.

As bad luck would have it, their changes of destination, disputes about the better way to get there once they'd finally decided, and their general desire to enjoy and exult in the anticipation of violence caused them to arrive at Piazza San Marco three minutes after the change of squad at the police station not far from Caffè Florian. Thus a double squad of officers was in the station when they heard the shouts and screams from the direction of the Basilica, and it was five officers who ran into the piazza, drawn by the sound until they could follow their sight.

Two more officers, on special duty from eleven until five in the morning as part of a police decision to keep the city safe at night, happened to be entering the Piazza, and so the boys, some of them already uncomfortable at the realization that both the bruising and the punching they had given and taken had not been as much fun as playing basketball, found themselves unarmed and undefended against seven police officers.

The number of officers and the sight of the clubs and pistols hanging from their belts changed the adrenaline of combat into fear at the sight of a greater force. The weapons the police carried nullified the boys' numerical advantage and burst the bubble of their valour. The youngest wet his pants, another put his hands over his face and bent over to pretend he wasn't there, another took two steps and lowered himself to one of the *passarelle*, stacked there to be used in the event of *acqua alta*.

Seeing the uneasiness their mere presence caused the boys, the officers hardened their faces and raised their voices, forcing the boys towards the police station. At no time did the policemen touch them: like cowboys, they herded with changes of voice and one-word commands. Instead of cow patties, two of the boys left behind them a trail of discreetly discarded eyeglass frames.

Macaluso, the sergeant who had remained behind and who had observed the round-up from the steps leading to the station, went back inside, pulled out a number of forms from the drawer of his desk and set a dozen or so pencils on top of them.

When the first few came in, he pointed to the papers and said, 'Take a pencil and a form, fill it out. Give it to me when you're finished.'

The smallest of the boys said, 'Please, Signore, may I make a phone call?' His voice held the promise of tears, but still the officer, who had three children, stood and shouted '*Silenzio*' at the group. When the talking stopped, he added, 'No, you cannot make any phone calls. Not until you fill out the form. Then you can each make one call.' He saw one of the boys at the back of the group raise his phone in front of him and start to touch the keys.

'Andolfatto, take his phone,' the sergeant ordered, pointing towards the boy with the phone in his hand. The officer walked over and snatched the phone before the boy could try to lower it.

'That's my—' he started to say, but the officer who had taken it turned and gave him a look so cold it turned the boy to ice. The officer walked back to the desk at the front of the room and tossed the boy's phone carelessly on the surface.

While this was happening, another boy cupped his phone in his hand and started to tap in a text, but the light reflected off the glasses of the boy standing beside him. The sergeant saw the flicker and got to his feet. The phone disappeared. The sergeant bent over and picked up the waste-paper basket beside his desk and emptied it on the floor. Ripped forms, used Kleenex, three or four crumpled maps of Venice, and six or seven cardboard cups that had contained coffee fell to the floor. The sergeant looked into it and, seeing it was clean, took two steps towards the boys.

'All right. Pay attention. All of you. Two of you do something wrong, the rest of you pay the price.' He shoved the basket into the hands of the boy nearest him and raised his voice to address them all. 'When your friend here walks by you, put your phone in.' There was a collective gasp, after which came an indignant 'But . . .'

The sergeant moved as quickly as a snake, and in less than a second stood in front of a boy in his mid-teens, taller than he and far more muscular. 'You have something to say, sonny?' the sergeant asked in a neutral voice. 'You couldn't wait to call Mummy and Daddy, could you? Well, now you're all going to have to use my phone and call them, one by one.'

He turned and looked at the standing boys. 'This causes you trouble, talk to your friend here,' and went back to his seat.

The boy with the waste-paper basket came up to the desk and set it down. Before the sergeant could ask, he reached into the side pocket of his jacket, pulled out his own phone, and set it gently on top of the other phones.

'They all there?' he asked the boy.

'Yes, sir.'

'How many?'

'Twenty-two, sir,' he said, lowering his head. In a softer voice, he added, 'Galvani had two.' The sergeant looked at the boy in front of him, only now seeing the boy's fear that he'd somehow be held responsible for this.

The sergeant leaned over the desk and said softly, so only the boy would hear, 'You think he's schizophrenic?' and smiled. When the boy did not react, the sergeant clarified things by saying, 'So he'd need two different telephones?'

It took the boy a moment to understand what the sergeant had said. When he finally understood, he tried not to smile. 'Yes, sir,' he said.

Before the sergeant could respond, a voice came from the back of the group. 'Officer?'

'What?'

'Is there a toilet here?'

There followed a few snickers, after which the sergeant said, 'And if I told you it was out of order for anyone who just laughed, and it will be a few more hours before anyone comes to get you, would you still laugh?'

Then, turning his attention to the boy who had asked the question, he said, 'Down the end of the corridor on your right.'

He took the completed forms and arranged them in alphabetical order, then called each boy's parents, identified himself, said that their son was in police custody at the station in Piazza San Marco and asked them to come and take him home. Some were stunned, some were angry, and some were frightened; some protested, but all of them, in the face of Macaluso's refusal to give more information, agreed to come. By this time, the boys occupied all of the chairs and a good deal of the floor. Once all of the parents had been called, and all but one found at home, Macaluso made a call to the Questura to ask them to contact the commissario on night duty, then busied himself entering the boys' full names, birth dates, and addresses into the computer.

Commissario Claudia Griffoni, on duty that night, arrived at the police station at eleven minutes before two. The Commissario wore beige trousers, a pair of tennis shoes, a beige suede jacket, and had a red cashmere scarf around her neck. The sergeant got to his feet when she arrived but did not salute. 'These are the members of the gangs,' he said neutrally. 'They were in the Piazzetta.'

She looked out over the somnolent group.

Two of them raised their heads and looked at Griffoni, then one of them let out his variant of the wolf whistle.

Commissario Griffoni looked up slowly and glanced at the
two boys. Then, turning to the sergeant, she said in her most
dispassionate voice, 'Article 341 *bis* of the *codice penale*: Insult to
a public official in the performance of their duty. Damage to
their reputation. If committed publicly . . .' here, she paused a
moment and waved her arm in a wide circle '. . . there is the
chance of a sentence of from six months to three years.'

Griffoni put her palm to her forehead, as one does when
trying to see a long distance in very bright light. 'Young man,'
she said to the one who had whistled, 'was there something you
wanted to say to me?'

'No.'

'No? No, who? My name is Claudia Griffoni, and I am a commissario of police in this city.'

The boy was confused by the message Griffoni was sending
him.

After waiting for him and hearing only silence, she said, 'Let
me ask you – what is your name?'

'Alessandro Berti.'

'And so, Signor Berti, what is mine?'

'Claudia Griffoni.'

'Have you perhaps forgotten something, Signor Berti?'

It took him a long time to accept the situation, but Griffoni
had all night and was ready to wait for him.

'Commissario Griffoni,' he said.

Griffoni's smile was minimal, but it was a smile.

After some more time, the parents who had been called first
began to arrive. Griffoni left it to the sergeant to examine their
identification, answer their questions, and deal with the paperwork. The sergeant took care to ask each boy to find his own
phone in the waste-paper basket.

It wasn't until well after four that all of the boys, save one,
had been collected by parents in various stages of disbelief or

disinterest. Some of the mothers seemed disturbed to be told what their son had done or at least what charges might be recorded against him; others seemed not at all surprised.

When only one of them remained, Griffoni handed him the remaining phone and asked if he'd like to try his parents again, then asked his name.

'Orlando Monforte, Dottoressa,' the boy answered, and told her he lived in Castello with his father. He held up his phone and explained that his father turned off his at eleven at night. 'There's no chance he'll answer it,' he said apologetically. Looking around the room, he asked Griffoni, 'Could I stay here, Dottoressa?'

He was small, shorter than Griffoni, with broad shoulders that suggested they were waiting for the rest of his scrawny body to do its part and make him as tall and broad as he was meant to be. His eyes were brown, his nose short, his ears close to his head: he would have looked average, had it not been for his gaze, always curious, always quick. He reminded her of her nephew, Antonio.

'And sleep on the floor?' Griffoni asked.

'In a chair. There's no more competition for seats,' he said and smiled. He looked younger when he smiled, more like a child, and somehow frailer.

His was the only form left on the sergeant's table, so Griffoni went over and looked at it. 'Is this the right address, Castello 3165?'

'Yes, Commissario.'

'In Salizada San Francesco, near La Beppa?' she asked, naming a store in deepest Castello that sold hardware, underwear, shoes, shirts, sweaters, just about anything you asked for.

'How do you know where that is?' he asked. 'We're the only people who go there.'

'We?' she asked.

'People from the neighbourhood.' When Griffoni said nothing, he added, 'I was surprised when you knew it because
you're not from the neighbourhood.'

'Why do you say that?'

'With all respect, Commissario, not with your accent.' He
bent down to tie his sneakers.

'Does that mean only Veneziani live in Venice?'

'Would be nice, wouldn't it?' he asked, speaking with the certainty that anyone he asked would agree with him.

'I live here, and I'm not Veneziana.'

He smiled again to prepare her for the joke and said, 'I think
you didn't have to tell me that,' and a second later, he added,
'Commissario.'

She laughed. Then she asked, 'Do you have a key?'

'Yes, Dottoressa.'

Griffoni looked at the sergeant, who had ignored their conversation in favour of yesterday's *Gazzettino*. 'Do you think I
could serve in loco parentis, Sergeant?'

Lowering the paper, he looked from her to the boy and back
again. Apparently having decided that neither posed a serious
risk to the other, he said, 'If that means you'll walk him home,
Commissario, I think it's a good idea.' He freed one hand from
the *Gazzettino* and waved it around the room, saying, 'This is no
place for a young man like him to spend a night.'

Turning to the boy, she asked, 'Is that all right with you,
Orlando?'

'Yes, Dottoressa. I agree with the sergeant – it's a good idea.'

That was enough to get them out of the office and into the
Piazza, empty now save for two garbage men slowly sweeping
the pavement.

Griffoni looked at her watch: it had somehow become 05:32.
Today was Tuesday, so he would be going to school. 'What time
is your first class?'

'Eight.'

'You'll have time to go home, then. What will your father say when you come in so late?'

Casually, as though the subject didn't interest him, Orlando said, 'He'll still be asleep.' Then, voice full of false bravado, he added, 'I can come home any time I want.'

She waited a bit before asking, sounding both surprised and concerned, 'Do you like that?'

Orlando shoved his hands into the pockets of his jeans and consulted with his feet. After some time, a conclusion was reached, and he looked up at her and said, 'Not particularly, no. It would be nice if he paid more attention to me.'

'Is that why . . . ?' but before she could finish, Orlando had hopped down the three steps to the pavement and turned to the right. He looked back and waved his arm in a broad arc, summoning her to join him.

# 2

While he waited for Griffoni, the boy ran in place, arms pumping in the cool morning air. When Griffoni came down the last step, he glanced towards her. She noticed, but ignored, him and continued walking out into the *Piazza*. He launched himself towards her, flat out, and only at the last step veered around her predictable saunter, continued to the other side of the Piazza, disappeared in the underpass, sped past a few columns, then targeted her again at increased speed.

This time, he slowed, slowed again, then came up beside her and stopped. Like a professional runner, he bent over and braced his palms against his knees and gasped in air.

As if they'd been in conversation and could resume it now, Griffoni said, 'After I moved to Venice, I used to come here about this time, a couple of times a week.'

Still breathing heavily and staring at the pavement, he said, 'Why?'

She glanced down at him, apparently enough to encourage him to stand upright. 'Why what?'

'Why did you come here?'

She stared at him. After some time, she said, 'Did you leave your eyes back in the police station?'

He wrapped his arms around himself, as if only now aware of the chill of the early morning. He was wearing jeans and a denim jacket, with only a cotton T-shirt under that.

'Other people do notice it too, you know,' Griffoni said cheerfully, as though she were pointing out some great fortune that was being given away free. She shrugged and started walking again, heading towards Ponte della Paglia and Castello. There was a more direct way, but Griffoni preferred to walk with the *bacino* on one side, waterspace open to endlessness.

She walked at her normal pace, the area in front of her broad enough to give her sight lines to everything and everyone approaching her. And if she chose to stop and look behind her, there was more than enough beauty to justify her turning around. She'd learned his footsteps, so she knew when he came from behind her, on the left, choosing to allow her the freedom of the water view.

'I was curious about the time you went,' he said. 'Not about why you'd go there. Anyone in their right mind would want to see it.' He spoke with quiet urgency, as if the thought she had misunderstood him would somehow work against him, diminish him in her eyes.

'I went because, that early, it was still possible to be alone.'

He laughed and tossed away any shyness, as Griffoni knew children did at his age. He walked off first this time. The light had turned itself up while he was running, although there was no sign of the sun for them to know where it came from yet. Although it was lighter, it was definitely not warmer: this was to be one of those spring days when the sun, its warmth exhausted by so much exercise in the last few days, decided to stay in bed until noon.

At the bottom of the next bridge, Griffoni turned into the underpass and stopped at a bar on the right side of the *calle*. She remembered it opened at six for the first people on their way to work. She called to the barman and asked for a coffee, then turned back to the boy, who nodded. She caught the barman's eye and, pointing her chin towards the brioche inside the plastic display case, said, '*Due*,' quickly amended to '*Tre*.'

While the barman was making the coffee, he nodded at a small round table in the back of the room. 'It's warmer there,' he said, then pushed the button on the machine.

They were both happy for the promised warmth. The boy's coffee and two of the brioche were gone before she had finished her coffee. She shoved her plate in front of him and asked the barman for another brioche. He brought it over and set it in front of Griffoni, who passed it to Orlando. Both of them asked for another coffee and, as they drank them, talked about how cold it still was outside, and when would spring ever get here, any banality that would allow them to linger in the warm corner. The barman ignored them.

A few people came in, barely glancing at them, and drank coffee without testing its temperature, so desperate was their need. Two old men, one fat and one thin, entered and asked for a Fernet-Branca *con* grappa, which they downed as though it were life itself.

When the men left, Griffoni stood and started for the bar, pushing back the boy's attempt to pay as they went out to the *riva*. If anything, perhaps because they'd had the coffee, it felt warmer, warm enough to sit side by side facing the water and be silent with one another and the world. Neither spoke, but occasionally one would point to something, poking the other into noticing and paying attention to it.

After what was either a short time or a long time, Griffoni unwrapped her scarf and handed it to Orlando, who had begun to shake with the cold. He tried to push it back, but she put it around his neck, got to her feet, and started walking again, her attention entirely devoted to the arrival of a vaporetto, something she must have seen a few hundred times.

Griffoni quickened her pace and maintained it until the third bridge, when Orlando pulled up beside her, the scarf wrapped around his neck, the ends tucked into the front of his jacket. The red looked very good, especially now that some colour had come into his face.

There were some people on the *riva* now: joggers, more male than female, a third of them accompanied by dogs. Early tourists came off the boats from the littoral, Phone Photos already at work, showing them what Venice looked like. The sellers of the worst sort of tourist tat pushed their disassembled stalls out to their rented spaces and started to arrange the souvenirs. Behind them stretched fenced-off areas where the crews busy rebuilding the *riva* stored their material; they would not arrive before eight, surely.

'What class are you in?' she asked.

'Second year of the Superiore.'

'Anything worth studying?'

Her question surprised him, and he gave it some consideration before he said, 'Only maths.'

That stopped Griffoni in her tracks. 'Maths?' When Orlando nodded, she asked, 'Why?'

With no hesitation, he said, 'Because it's so clean.'

She turned away from looking across at San Giorgio, then looked at him. 'What's that supposed to mean?'

Perhaps no one had ever asked him; he certainly seemed unprepared. He looked out to San Lazzaro: maybe the monks on the island could help him find an explanation. He put his hands in his pockets and raised and lowered himself on his toes a few times before saying, 'It's not like history, or Italian literature, or religion, or any of the other things we study. It's just *there*. You ask it a question and it gives you the answer. It shows you a rule, and that won't change, no matter how much someone prays about it or threatens you if you don't change the answer to the one he wants.' He pushed himself up a few more times, then got tired of doing it and let himself down with a thud.

'Probably why I never liked it very much,' Griffoni said. Then, roughening her voice and speaking in quasi-understandable Napolitano, she said, 'We don't like rules very much.'

When he heard her say this, his head swung round towards her and he took a longer look. 'You sure you work for the police?'

'My shift ended at six, so I'm free to say anything I want.'

At a certain point, she asked him to take over navigation, admitting that he would get them to his home faster than she could. Two *calli* later, he cut to the left and moved away from the water. She didn't bother to pay attention to where they were going so much as to the ease with which he slithered through the groups of people they now began to meet – workers getting the vaporetti that would take them to the train station or to the buses at Piazzale Roma, and from there to wherever on the mainland they had found work.

She'd read that only fifty years ago, Venice had had a population of nearly 150,000 inhabitants; a third of that remained. There was little work, there was little work, there was little work. As simple as that. So they went off to *terraferma* for the day, while people from the mainland came into the city to work. Many of the other officers lived in Dolo, Noale, Quarto d'Altino, Mestre, Marghera, the small towns, not really cities, that had turned the land into a parking lot.

She wanted to lose no time thinking about this, since Orlando and his generation had known no other Venice than the one they were born into. It came to her that she had arrived to work in the city – being a tourist didn't really count – after he had been born. So she knew no more than he did about the Serenissima, had no right to complain or to be grumpy about the tourists.

Considering all this, she had slowed her pace and now, looking ahead, saw no sign of him. She sped up, but when the *calle* led into a small *campo* with three other exits, she had no idea which way to turn, and stopped. On one corner was a butcher; facing him, a cheap jewellery shop. On the next corner was a bar. Well, she told herself, it wasn't only a bar, but also a place where you could get a pre-cooked slice of pizza, standing at the counter to eat it while drinking a beer or a glass of wine from a plastic cup, or go to a small table and see what was on the menu.

Looking around, she saw a white wall plaque with the name 'Salizada S. Francesco'. She checked the photo she had made of his form – 'Castello 3165', almost as if Orlando were a package to be delivered – glanced up and saw that she was still short of the number. Meaningless. Hopeless. No one understood the system, except perhaps the *postini*, and then only if they'd had the route for a long time and had learned how the numbers ambled wherever they wanted to. His address, Castello 3165, need not be next door to Castello 3164, nor to 3166. It could be down the street, around the corner, back three or four houses. She'd lived in Venice for how many years? And never been asked for her address; didn't know anyone else's.

Lowering her gaze from the plaque, she saw her scarf; it had worked its way free from his jacket. The boy was in the pizza place, standing at the counter, eating a piece of pizza covered with many small pieces of meat and vegetables, too many for Griffoni to identify. She went in and stood next to him at the bar. Five adult male heads turned to observe her arrival: they paused in place when she came up to him and said, 'Ah, there you are.'

'May I offer you something, Dottoressa?' he asked, no doubt having decided it was wiser than calling her 'Commissario'. He was careful, as well, to continue to address her, as he had from the beginning, with the respectful '*Lei*'.

'That's very kind of you,' she answered with the same formality, 'but I'm not in the habit of eating pizza for breakfast.'

One of the men who belonged to the five heads at the bar, eating a slice of pizza with onion and salami and half finished with his beer, said, 'Orlando will eat anything you give him, any time of the day.'

Another, patting Orlando's shoulder with an affection so strong it would have knocked Griffoni to the ground, added, 'Lives in that house right over there,' pointing to a door a bit to the left of the plaque. 'People in the neighbourhood see that he gets to school on time and keep an eye on what he eats.'

Orlando looked away, but when he saw himself in the mirror, he looked at the floor instead. Griffoni put a hand on his arm and said, obviously including all the men at the bar, 'And all of you picked at your food like little birds when you were his age.'

The man with the pizza put his hand over his mouth and began to cough. The man behind him whacked him on the back until he stopped, then he picked up his plastic cup and drained it of the remaining beer but not before tipping it as a compliment to Griffoni's retort.

He smiled at her and said, 'Well done, Signora. Put us all in our place.' Then, taking a closer look at her and seeming not to find it at all strange that she was standing there with them, he said, 'You wouldn't happen to be a teacher, would you, Signora?'

'Dottoressa,' Orlando quickly corrected him.

'Of course. Dottoressa.'

'Oh, good heavens,' said an embarrassed Griffoni. 'I didn't realize it was so obvious.' She looked across at the boy and said, 'Yes, as a matter of fact, I am. I'm Orlando's mathematics teacher.' Then she turned to him and said, in a parody of sternness, 'Don't forget your homework, Orlando.' She smiled at the circle of men, said goodbye to all of them and went outside, leaving it to the boy to explain.

# 3

Griffoni realized she would have to go to the Questura to file a report, even though she was not on duty that day, and decided to spend some time with another round of Flight School, a game she had invented years ago, two weeks after she'd found an apartment to rent in Venice. Early one morning in late October, she had left her apartment at five-thirty. More importantly, she'd left behind her map, which she had bought in her second week, tired of being perpetually lost.

The street number of her apartment had been no help, although she knew it was in Dorsoduro, only one bridge from Tonolo. The *pasticceria* was so famous that she had soon come to trust it as she would a lighthouse: it was enough to name it, no matter how far she had wandered, and any Venetian would direct her home. Her investigation had also confirmed the testimony of people in the neighbourhood: both the coffee and the pastries were excellent, among the best in the city.

She knew that she would get lost by crossing Campo Santa Margherita and following the canal that ran in front of the church of the Carmini. Flight School started after walking for twenty minutes from that point, at which time she had to stop, turn around, and find her way back home without asking for any help. For a month, she had used the first half of one of her days off to play at being lost, sometimes actually getting lost. She had never asked for directions or help, nor had she accepted it, unless it came from old women with walking sticks, who took great joy from being of help to another woman who looked entirely lost.

Standing now in Salizada San Francesco, she remembered that she had, on one of those mornings, stood in this same place and told herself she was a Venetian housewife in search of kitchen tools: garlic presses, *parmigiano* graters, corkscrews, funnels. Now, years later, with most of these items still visible in the window, she had no doubts about where she was. Barely thinking, she turned to the left, then to the right, over the bridge, over the next one, and straight on down to the hospital and to Rosa Salva, already open.

Once there, she allowed herself another coffee; this time she got to eat the brioche. The boy already forgotten, she decided to head back towards the Questura, as sure now of the way as a Native American hunter following the hoof prints of a deer.

It was only a little after eight, but she went up to her office and wrote her report on the events of the previous night, explaining that she had taken the decision to accompany the one boy remaining at the police station and see him safely home. She gave his name, found the photo she had made of his form, and sent it along with her report, adding that the report from the supervising sergeant at San Marco would contain copies of the forms filled out by all the boys involved in the incident.

A half-hour later, when the officer at the door phoned to tell her that Commissario Brunetti had arrived about five minutes before, Griffoni walked downstairs and went towards his office.

'*Avanti*,' he called when she knocked. Inside, she found

Brunetti at the window, leaning out, arms braced to keep himself from falling, head turned to the right as he studied the empty garden on the other side of the canal.

'What are you doing, Guido?' she asked when she saw him.

He pulled himself back and closed the window. 'Trying to see the flowers,' he said as he dusted his hands together.

'Are there any yet?'

'There were a lot of buds yesterday. I was curious.'

'Changes things, doesn't it?' Griffoni commented, then explained, 'When they start blossoming.'

Without thinking, Brunetti said, 'Springtime always gives me the sense, or the hope, that we're being given another chance.'

'A chance for what?' Griffoni asked, going to the chair she usually used while they talked.

He came back to his desk, then moved some papers and a notebook and that day's copy of *Il Gazzettino* a bit to the left. 'Would you laugh if I said a chance to make it better?'

' "It" being?'

'Oh, I don't know. The broken people we have to deal with and the bad things we see and that people do.'

It took Griffoni a long time to respond, but finally she said, 'No, I wouldn't laugh.' Brunetti waited for the 'but' he suspected would be coming, and she did not disappoint. 'But blossoms and flowers don't make people act any differently than they usually do.'

'Are you talking about those kids last night?' he asked, pointing to some other papers on his desk.

'They're a good place to begin.'

'What did you think of them?' Brunetti asked.

'I spent time with them, Guido. And they frightened me.'

'Why? How?'

'If there hadn't been two armed policemen –' remembering her own pistol, she changed the number, '– three armed police officers there, I have no idea what could have happened if we had lost our nerve.'

'Don't you think you're exaggerating, Claudia?'

'Probably,' she admitted with a smile. 'But it could have grown violent. They were pumped up with testosterone. The air smelled of it.'

'But nothing happened,' Brunetti said, placing a hand on the papers on his desk, as if they were a talisman as well as communications. 'You write your report yet?'

'Yes. I even reread it before I sent it.'

'I've read Macaluso's,' Brunetti said. 'He and Andolfatto were on duty, and after the parents had all left with their sons, he wrote and sent it.' Before she could ask, Brunetti added, 'It sounds like he gave the boys a hard time before you got there.'

'Physically?' she asked in open astonishment.

'No, of course not. He wouldn't do that. He simply drew the line at what they could and could not do, could and could not say.'

'And?'

'And they became a flock of lambs. Or at least that's what he wrote.'

Griffoni nodded. 'How does he do it?'

'He told me once he looks at lots of cops and robbers films from America, the ones from the forties and fifties. Tough-guy stuff.'

'Oh my God,' she exclaimed. 'If only I'd known about this before I went to that workshop.'

'Which one?' Brunetti asked.

'The one in Parma.'

'About how to treat people during their first interrogation?'

'Yes,' she said, digging her fingers into the hair on both sides of her head.

But then she smiled and gave a snort that might have begun

as a laugh. 'It was all about being certain that the rights of arrested people are respected,' she said, 'and that we never express, in word or deed, a negative opinion of their crime. Or crimes.'

Brunetti opened his mouth, preparing to say something, but he stopped, aware that he had nothing worth saying. He shifted the subject and said, 'Let's go back to last night. Tell me what happened.'

'It's probably all in the sergeant's report,' she said, pointing to the papers on Brunetti's desk.

'Tell me anyway.'

The right corner of her mouth pulled up impatiently as she said, 'There were twenty-two of them, all from the city. Nothing much to do after dinner. Nothing good to watch. So why not a little violence and maybe some robbery, if there's anything they want?'

'There'll be a recording on their phones or in the Cloud of everything they said to one another,' Brunetti said, casting his eyes towards heaven at the very thought of such sloppiness. 'The planning?'

'None, of course.' After saying this, she patted her palms on her thighs a few times and said, 'They're hopeless.'

Her voice grew a bit louder, her accent perhaps a bit stronger. 'They've bonded with their phones and can't take five steps without them. But they still don't have the sense to be careful about what they write, the messages they send.' She shook her head in exasperation at their carelessness.

'What do you want them to learn to do?'

She raised a hand in the air but brought it back before it got out of control. She saw his expression and stopped, then fixed her gaze on him and said, 'Guido, you've known me long enough to know I'm not a hysteric.' He nodded. 'So please believe me when I tell you that I was afraid of that mass of boys.'

She paused a long time before speaking again, 'I'm a woman. That makes a difference in how the threat of violence affects a person. You might think you know it. But you don't *feel* it, not the way women do.'

He nodded again, either in agreement or to acknowledge having heard her. Finally he said, 'All right, we're dangerous in groups.'

She leaned back in her chair and said, her surprise audible, 'That's the first time I've ever heard a man admit that.'

'Young men will,' Brunetti said.

She smiled and nodded, 'But they don't understand it, not really.'

'And older men?' Brunetti asked.

Griffoni could not stop herself from smiling. 'They understand it. But they won't admit it.'

Brunetti's lips moved; it might have been a smile but probably wasn't. 'I'm not sure I really understand what makes us – men, almost always – put violence on the list of possible choices when we have to respond to something.'

Griffoni sat quietly, interested in what he had to say.

'You know the domestics are always the worst,' he continued. 'It's almost as if our heads – men's heads – are too small to allow love and anger to fit into a space together. So if a baby cries for a long time, or a woman says she thinks a man drinks too much, love gets dumped and anger takes over.'

'Not always,' Griffoni objected.

'I know that. What I'm trying to say is that not many women are brought in here because they hurt their child or their partner.'

Griffoni moved nervously in her seat, as though it had decided it didn't want her sitting there any more. 'Can we talk about something else?' she asked.

'About what?'

'About why a bright, decent boy of fifteen would have been prowling with that pack last night?'

'You mean the one you so rashly took home?' Before she could ask, he said, 'Macaluso mentioned it in his report.'

'Yes,' she said, and added, 'so did I, and explained that it was impossible to find his father. So perhaps my action wasn't so rash.'

'This thing is already complicated.'

'What's hidden behind your voice?'

'It's not what but who,' Brunetti answered.

'Uh-oh. That sounds like trouble.'

'It could well be,' Brunetti said.

'Tell me.'

'Retired Judge Alfonso Berti.'

Her face tightened and her eyes narrowed. He watched her try to find an answer with no more information than a name, and he watched her face when she found it.

'The boy who whistled at me is named Berti.' After saying that, Griffoni shook her head, as one does upon discovering that the vase casually knocked over in the antique shop was made in Constantinople in the ninth century.

'And his grandfather is known to be a very unpleasant man.'

'Where does that leave me?' she asked.

'That probably depends on your report,' Brunetti said, then asked, pointing towards his computer, 'Is it in there?'

'I came in this morning to write it. None of the boys can be mentioned by name, but you know that.'

He nodded.

Griffoni waved a hand towards his computer, closed her eyes and rested her head against the back of the chair. 'As my cleaning lady never tires of telling me,' she began, sending her voice towards the inactive ceiling fan, '*siamo nelle mani del Signore.*' So, if you don't mind, I'll just keep sitting here in the hands of God.'

Brunetti tapped his computer into life and typed in the address of the online version of *Il Gazzettino.*

The only public reference to the incident in San Marco was to be found at the very end of the 'Venezia' section, in competition with a story about the closing of a veterinary clinic on the Lido, 'a sad blow to the residents, both four-legged and two-'. The second story explained that a group of at least a dozen young people had met in the Piazza and had begun to argue about the recent performance of the local soccer team. From there it had descended into shouting and name-calling until a squad from the police command station had rounded them up and sent them home, thus putting an end to the disturbance they were causing people still in the Piazza.

Brunetti found himself making up a list of those who could have been responsible for the airbrushing of the behaviour of the gang. Only intervention from above could so effectively have removed any hint of danger in the boys' behaviour, for the *Gazzettino* was usually eager to sink its teeth into crime and shake it around until there was some blood on the walls. A semi-brawl in Piazza San Marco could possibly have vibrated its way as far as the *New York Times*, yet here it had died the death with only a whimper.

Could the story have been treated as barely significant and slid to the bottom because of the latest *femminicidio*, in Spinea, not far from Mestre? This article got the day's ration of blood onto the front by reporting that the suspect had stabbed his wife thirteen times, after which he drove to the local Carabinieri station and gave himself up.

Aside from this, the only explanation Brunetti could find was that a parent or relative of one of the boys had called in a favour from someone at the paper who had the power to adjust the story that was finally published. The most likely was retired Judge Berti, who could certainly have done it with a phone call.

Brunetti turned to his colleague, who appeared still to be in communication with the ceiling fan.

'We might well all be in God's hands,' Brunetti said, 'while you, unfortunately, might be in those of retired Judge Alfonso Berti as well.' He returned his attention to the computer.

# 4

'Very little in there,' Brunetti said, closing the *Gazzettino*'s online edition. 'What time did you file your report?'

'Before nine, so it has to be in there,' Griffoni said, pointing to his computer.

Brunetti grunted and switched to the internal system used by the Questura, opening the file for 'Civic disturbances'. Within seconds, he had her report in front of him and read of her 'desire to enforce upon the suspects the seriousness of the law and the need to show it every respect.' She had addressed all of the young men brought in for questioning with 'the same respect for their persons' and had been careful to address them as '"Signore", followed by their surname'. They, in their turn, had been equally formal when addressing her.

As soon as they were aware of the legal basis of her authority, all of the young men had proved fully cooperative with the measures imposed by the law. Further, they seemed pleased that their parents had been informed of their situation and thus could become participant in assuring their sons' well-being by coming to the station to see that they got home safely. The parent of one of the boys proved unreachable, and so Dottoressa, Commissario Claudia Griffoni, having informed the officer on duty that she was acting in loco parentis, accompanied the boy to his home, where five of his neighbours welcomed him and assured Dottoressa, Commissario Griffoni that they would see him safely into the care of his father, who was certain to ensure that his son got to school on time.

When Brunetti finished reading her report, he turned to her and said, his voice rich with admiration and something close to awe, 'Oh, you are a snake. You don't even know Judge Berti, but you've certainly poured sugar into the fuel tank of any war machine he would happily have used against you, perhaps even turned the old bastard into an admirer.'

Griffoni pushed herself upright in the chair and raised her arms above her head, joined hands, and waved them from right to left a few times, then let them fall into her lap. 'You're always so mealy-mouthed, Guido. Why don't you just say that you don't like ex-Judge Berti and have done with it?' Then, suddenly serious, she said, 'I told you. His grandson whistled at me when I came in.'

Brunetti was about to say that this seemed a perfectly natural male response, but he feared his clumsy compliment would be misinterpreted, so he merely asked, 'Whistled?'

'The usual noise they pick up from the movies. So I asked him what his name was and gave him a spontaneous lesson in how to address a person politely.'

'I'm sure he was impressed.'

'Not until I cited the law about disrespect to civil servants in the performance of their work.'

'Ah,' Brunetti said. 'I wondered what you were up to in your report. All that bowing and scraping to the law.'

'It's not like me, is it?' she asked with a smile.

'Did you have to pistol-whip any of the others?'

'No. Once they realized that Macaluso and Andolfatto and I weren't kidding, a lot of their courage – no, that's the wrong word. None of them has any courage. They need a gang around them to have that, and then it's not courage, just testosterone. Anyway, they quietened down. A few of them even fell asleep while they were waiting for their parents to show up to get them.'

'Do you want to talk about that?'

'No, not really. They were parents, afraid for their kids.' She thought about that, then added, 'I imagine they'll need to think about this for a while, now that they know what little Giovanni is doing when he asks to go and do his Latin homework at a friend's house.'

Griffoni grew thoughtful. 'There were some couples who seemed shell-shocked, as though the world had changed in some terrible way. And then there were others who merely looked irritated at having been got out of bed and made to come and pick up their son.' She let a long time pass before she continued, 'Three women came alone.'

'And the boy you took home?'

Griffoni smiled. 'Nice kid.' Before he could object, she said, 'I mean it, Guido.' She tried to find something that would persuade a person that Orlando was a 'nice kid', and came up with little more than that he was polite, intelligent, and had a sense of humour. It was with not a little embarrassment that she realized these had for some time been her requisites for a lover.

She decided to backtrack. 'Maybe I was judging him in contrast to the others.'

'In which case?' Brunetti asked.

'He'd be Prince Charming.' She let that lie there for a moment, then added, 'Of course, there was little competition.'

Dropping this, she squirmed around in the chair until she found a more comfortable position. 'Why do they do it?' she asked. 'Some of the parents were really upset. I'd guess they had no idea, or didn't want to have an idea. But some of them must have known. If you suspect your son is out knocking other kids around, you do something, for God's sake.'

Brunetti turned off the screen on his computer and rested his chin in the palm of his right hand, elbow propped on his desk. Discussions of young people who committed crimes always left him with a kind of hangover. Any serious conversation about it troubled him for days. Chicken or egg? Which influenced their behaviour more, parents or friends? Or the society in which they lived?

To change the subject and, he hoped, the mood, Brunetti said, 'Patta wants to see me.'

'When?'

'When he gets back from Treviso.'

She seemed confused by his answer, so he said, 'I told you, Claudia, he has a class there.'

'He's still going?' she asked, sounding honestly surprised. 'The attack was months ago.'

Brunetti could do no more than shrug, not wanting to enter into a discussion with her, for it always led him into the uncomfortable position of defending Patta.

Some months ago, returning home after work, Patta had been set upon while only metres from his door by two young men who had been standing in conversation at the bottom of the bridge in front of his home. Busy searching in his jacket pocket for his keys, Patta had paid no attention to them until one of the men grabbed him from behind while the other reached for his back pocket and had his wallet in his hand in a second.

Patta had broken free and turned to slam his fist into the stomach of the one who had been holding him. The second one, much bigger and much faster than Patta, used his shoulder to slam the Vice-Questore against the parapet of the bridge. Patta tripped on the steps, failed to grab the railing, and fell, banging his head against the top of the parapet.

By the time he hauled himself to his feet, they were gone, leaving behind only the sound of their running footsteps.

Patta had not been seriously hurt, but he had been shaken. When he went inside and told his wife what had happened, she insisted they go to the hospital to have his head X-rayed. Perhaps a mild concussion. There was a bad scrape on his right temple; the skin had been ripped, and the area slowly turned blue and then black.

To let the public know that the Vice-Questore of the city had been assaulted, robbed, and knocked to the ground in front of his own home would probably have driven the *Gazzettino* into printing the front page in red, so Patta did as his wife suggested and said only that he'd tripped on a bridge and hit his temple against the handrail.

Patta's self-esteem was injured far more than his body: how could he have failed to defend himself? What would have happened if his wife had been with him? To prevent a repeat, Patta decided to prepare himself by taking a class in martial arts. Because he was taking the class at the better-equipped police headquarters in Treviso, he was taken there every Tuesday during his lunch break and brought back to the Questura by car and boat, as he would be for any police business carried out on the mainland. Over the weeks and then months of the class, as the weight disappeared from Patta, the truth seeped out through the porous root system of the city, for there was an open information conduit between workers at the hospital, where Patta had gone after the attack, and workers at the Questura.

The evidence of the good it was doing the Vice-Questore – weight loss, a more even temper, the occasional exercise of patience – was so obvious that no one begrudged him the freedom to take the class, while yet another Patta story was added to the legends pertaining to his stay at the Questura di Venezia.

'He's lost more than five kilos,' Griffoni said.

'How do you know that?' Brunetti asked.

'He told Signorina Elettra.'

Surprised by this unusual familiarity between Patta and his secretary, Brunetti asked, 'Do you know how the topic came up?'

'He wore a new suit one day and she admired it, said it was bolder than what he usually wore.'

Brunetti took some time to respond but finally said, 'A compliment from her is like being on the cover of *L'Uomo Vogue*.'

Griffoni crossed her legs, then looked at her shoes, as if to be sure she was still wearing the same pair she'd put on that morning. She shrugged, like someone who had nothing to lose, and said, 'Because it was single-breasted and thus more ... revealing.' Perhaps because Brunetti still looked puzzled, she added, 'She also complimented him on his dedication to his vitality programme.'

The last words fell like blossoms on Brunetti's upturned face. 'The Vice-Questore's "vitality programme",' he whispered, then his lips silently sounded the word 'sublime'. He shook his head a few times, marvelling at Signorina Elettra's ability to seduce people with a few kind words. 'Vitality,' he whispered again, then looked at Griffoni, and smiled.

Brunetti's phone rang. Probably Patta, wanting to talk about the baby gangs and the bad image it would give of the city, and what's wrong with these kids, anyhow? They have everything they want, go to good schools, have enough to eat, take summer vacations, and here they are causing trouble and doing it in Piazza San Marco, when they could just as easily go down to Castello, where no one would be much bothered by them or their noise. More importantly, there were few tourists to be disturbed.

'Brunetti,' Patta said when he picked up the phone. He was one of the few people in the Questura who first tried the old landline system. Brunetti believed he did so because he could then know who was working in their office and not out on some errand when they should be at their desk.

'Could you come down here, Brunetti?' Patta asked. The easy almost-warmth of his voice made Brunetti uneasy. Patta hadn't said 'please', but the word was tapping on the window of his question.

'Certainly, Dottore,' Brunetti said. 'A few minutes.'

Patta made a polite noise that sounded very much like *'Grazie'* and hung up, leaving Brunetti with the phone in his hand, staring at the place from which Patta's last words had come.

'What's wrong?' Griffoni asked.

Brunetti shrugged.

'He probably wants,' Griffoni suggested, 'to continue the official policy that they were groups of young boys on their way home from soccer practice and made all that noise because of their enthusiasm for clean, healthy sports.'

'My very thought,' Brunetti said, getting to his feet. 'But let me go and listen to how he phrases it.'

Signorina Elettra was not at her desk, so he crossed her office and knocked on Vice-Questore Patta's door.

*'Avanti.'*

Brunetti found, to his surprise, that Patta was standing by the open window, hands in his pockets. He could have looked no more casual if he had come to work in his pyjamas. His superior's hair, Brunetti noted, was cut shorter than it had been the last time and made him look like a young man trying for a more adult look, rather than a man in his fifties striving after those earlier, better days.

'Ah, Brunetti, glad to see you.'

Brunetti nodded and smiled, came closer to Patta's desk and, without being asked to, took a place in one of the chairs.

Patta, hands still in his pockets, ambled over to his desk. He sat and folded his hands together, a well-known Patta gesture, usually an indication that he was going to make a request of some sort.

What could he possibly want? Brunetti mused. He knew himself to be in no way involved with the baby gangs, had not exceeded his legal powers, at least not recently. He had not worn his dark grey suit with the red lining, nor had any member of the press asked to interview him. Deciding that silence would help this end sooner, Brunetti smiled amiably and looked down at his own folded hands.

'I have to ask you a favour, Brunetti,' Patta said with no introduction. 'Or perhaps it's better to say I'd like to make a suggestion.'

At least he did not say he was going to *do* Brunetti a favour. The last time he had done this, it was to allow Brunetti to attend, in his place, a weekend conference on criminal penetration into the world of cryptocurrency, to be held in, of all places, Taranto.

Years had passed, and Brunetti had forgotten if Taranto was the most polluted city in Europe or merely the most polluted city in Italy. In either case, the Taranto steelworks were the beating heart of the city, the chief employer in southern Italy, and the probable source of the red dust that filled the minds – not to mention the lungs – of many of the residents.

Brunetti had spent a day and a half in Taranto, had opted to leave half a day early and had himself paid for a seat on the plane that took him to Milano, along with two other police officers who had fled the place after little more than a day.

He nodded and smiled, thinking that it would be better to do a favour for Patta than to receive another one. 'If I can, Vice-Questore.' Hearing how paltry that sounded, Brunetti quickly added, 'Gladly.'

'Good.' Without prelude, Patta said, 'I've had a number of phone calls.'

'Ah . . .' escaped Brunetti's lips. It seemed a safer response than asking anything. This way, Patta could continue with his vague generalities and never be heard referring to a particular person. Or to a particular judge.

'The person who called me – who is very well connected in the city – was concerned that the episode of high spirits near the Basilica might be misinterpreted or the events somehow exaggerated.'

Brunetti put on his most serious face and said, 'The two reports I read of the events, sir, suggest no more than the bois-terous behaviour of those who are not of legal age.' He paused, looked at Patta and said, 'There were, of course, two broken windows.'

Patta smiled and waved a hand. 'That's already been taken care of, Brunetti.'

'Ah, I see,' said Brunetti. In ordinary circumstances, he might have offered some opposition or pointed out that this 'episode' had not been the first. Instead, he said, 'I'm glad it's been so easily settled.'

'Nothing but high spirits, Brunetti,' his superior confirmed. 'I'm glad you agree with me.'

Brunetti was incapable of doing anything other than nod.

'The oldest is only sixteen,' Patta added, and Brunetti under-stood that it would not be necessary to consult the criminal code to translate that into 'No chance of a criminal case.' The Vice-Questore paused only a moment, then continued, 'So I think we can best leave it like that.'

Brunetti resisted the temptation to repeat 'high spirits'.

Instead, banishing all emotion from his voice, he said, 'I understand, Vice-Questore,' and then, in a neutral tone, enquired,
'Will that be all, Dottore?'

Patta produced a small slice of smile and held up his right
hand, as though interested in preventing Brunetti from bolting
from the office. 'I'd simply like to enforce upon you the delicacy
with which this is to be treated.' He repeated his smile.

Brunetti returned it with the blandest of the smiles he used
when dealing with his superior. He nodded, put his hands on
his knees and pushed himself to his feet. He reminded himself
that he and Paola were having dinner at her parents' that evening, and the thought gave him whatever comfort he needed to
walk across the room and let himself out. He closed the door
quietly behind him.

# 5

The thought that he was to have dinner with Paola's parents that evening helped Brunetti put aside the memory of his conversation with Patta. In recent years, he had come to prize the company of both his parents-in-law and wished them ever more sincerely continued good health. The Conte had begun to ask Brunetti to speak a bit louder, and the Contessa had given in to reading glasses, but both of them remained quick-witted and well informed about the world. The Conte continued in complete control over his business affairs, while the Contessa remained a serious reader.

They were having dinner in the family dining room, which looked across the Grand Canal and was used, as the name stated, only for meals with members of the family. Often, they were served something the Contessa had overseen or that she and Paola had cooked together. The table seated four perfectly, six with a bit of moving closer. That evening all of them were there, Chiara and Raffi sitting in their seats, the best, which looked across the Canal into the front rooms of a *palazzo* about which they knew nothing beyond the name.

As they were finishing the main course, a *gallina faraona ripiena*, and the meal was coming to an end, the Contessa, in response to a question from Paola, said that she was reading the *Aeneid* for the first time. 'I don't know how it slipped past me,' she said. 'At school they drummed what they considered the classics into our heads, but somehow they overlooked the *Aeneid*.'

'In an Italian school?' Brunetti asked, unable to hide his surprise.

'Swiss,' she answered after a moment's hesitation. 'In Lausanne.'

'French-speaking?' Brunetti asked, thinking this might have had something to do with the absence of Virgil from the curriculum.

The Contessa smiled, perhaps at the memory of former days, and said, in that language, 'English, darling.'

'Oh, Mamma,' Paola broke in, her hand suspended in surprise above her plate as she continued, 'you always made it sound like all they taught you was how to crochet tablecloths and walk in a straight line while balancing a morally bracing book on your head.' This was certainly the version Paola had given Brunetti of her mother's schooling, although he had never been able to make it fit with the Contessa's obvious familiarity with literature in at least three languages. Had she not, some years ago, made a reference to *Beowulf*?

Paola set down her fork and asked, with real curiosity, 'Was it considered a good school?'

'I believe so,' the Contessa said.

Before anyone else could speak, il Conte turned towards his wife and asked, 'Then how could they not have you read the *Aeneid*?' Then, sounding indignant, 'How else was a man supposed to learn to behave?'

'I beg your pardon,' Paola said. 'Learn to what?'

'As I said, how to behave.'

'Behave how? Where?' Paola asked, her fork and plate forgotten in front of her.

Her father's response was instant. 'As Romans were supposed to behave. At least in Virgil's time.'

'When was that?' Chiara interrupted to ask.

After a long, speculative look at her and making no attempt to disguise his astonishment that she didn't know, her grandfather answered. 'About the time of the birth of Christ.'

'What was he told, and who told him?' Chiara asked, her interest palpable, quite unconscious of the fact that she had interrupted her grandfather, something that would no doubt rank high on il Conte's list of how *not* to behave.

'He'd have had a private tutor,' il Conte answered, quite as casually as if he had said that he would wear sandals.

'And he'd believe what the tutor told him?' Chiara asked. 'Even if a friend's tutor told him something entirely different?'

'That was the problem,' il Conte replied, and smiled as he always did when either of the children asked an intelligent question. 'Every one of them might have a different set of rules or values.'

'Weren't a lot of the tutors slaves?' Raffi asked, having dipped back into the conversation. Then, not bothering to wait for anyone to answer, he continued: 'Captured in war, and since the Romans fought wars everywhere, he could be from anywhere, and have his own ideas and opinions.'

'And whole moral system,' Chiara added. She noticed that Raffi's attention had been diverted by the arrival of the almond cake, leaving her to play with the idea. 'Today it's the same thing. Everyone's got an influencer to listen to, so they don't have to think about what they like or don't like, because there's someone to tell them what to choose.'

None of the other people at the table thought of a remark that could follow this, so Paola said something about it being late, tomorrow was a school day, and they should be on their way.

Outside, in the *calle*, Brunetti suggested that they all go home the long way, over the Accademia Bridge. The kids had no need of an influencer to tell them they preferred the shorter walk that saved them from having to climb both the Accademia and the Rialto bridges. They separated in Campo San Barnaba.

Brunetti and Paola walked back towards the Accademia, both of them silent, content with that. The night-time boat schedule was in force at this hour, but given the chance to walk home arm in arm, they didn't bother to check the time of the next vaporetto. Tacit agreement led them to pause at the top of the Accademia, where the moon awaited, no longer bothering to try to hide itself behind anything. Neither of them could find something to say about the perfection spread out for them on both sides of the bridge. Brunetti often succumbed to the temptation to joke about the excessive beauty of the city, but tonight he was silenced by it and could do no more than look upon it with wild surmise and turn towards home again.

Although Paola had seemed interested in what her father had to say about teachers and how it was that children learned to behave, she had not joined in, nor did she make any attempt to resurrect the subject now. For his part, Brunetti had already decided he had no desire to return to a discussion of children and how their minds and spirits were formed. It had been decades since he'd read the *Aeneid*, and he knew he would not read it again. His only hope was that his children would be drawn to *pietas* and not *furore* and would be spared the weight of living always in service to some high ideal.

As they reached the bottom of the bridge, Brunetti lightened his hold on Paola's arm, but kept it in his care. They turned into Campo Santo Stefano. Ahead of him stood the statue of a thickly bearded Niccolò Tommaseo, a writer Brunetti had never read. In his worst moments, Brunetti saw the statue as one of the high points of the vulgarization of the city. Leaning back against a pile of books, Tommaseo had quickly been given the nickname 'Cagalibri' and was thus destined to be pointed out to every passing tourist. He served the city not as a writer but as a source of mockery, perhaps as the source of a tip at the end of the tour.

Neither of them spoke, both taking advantage of the possibility of seeing an empty city, the one they'd both grown up in. They continued, up and down the bridge and into Campo Sant'Angelo. All the restaurants were closed, and they encountered very few people.

Paola drew to a halt and turned to look at the windows of one of the top-floor apartments on their left. Freeing her arm, she pointed towards the one illuminated window in the row. Behind it hung a large portrait of a woman, so far away that there was no telling the epoch or the style. Neither mattered.

'That's beautiful, isn't it?' Paola asked. 'The way you can't know anything about her?'

Recognizing a rhetorical question when he heard it, Brunetti squeezed her arm and said, 'Think of the view they have.' He waved his arm in a circle around the *campo*. 'I love it because there are almost no shops. All you can do is look at how beautiful it is. Or buy a newspaper.' When necessary, Brunetti was capable of ignoring the wheeled mobile souvenir stands that got rolled to and fro all over the city every day; tonight he decided not to remember them. Ugliness annoyed him less in the absence of daylight.

Paola nodded and they continued walking, starting down Calle della Mandola. Both remained silent as they crossed Campo Manin and then, on their left, walked alongside the ugliest building in the city and emerged into Campo San Luca.

'Remember when . . .' Paola began and patted his arm with her free hand. 'Remember when there was a Standa over there?' She stopped then and turned to him, her surprise visible. '*Oddio*,

I don't remember how many floors there were – four or five.' Wistfully, she added, 'They sold everything.'

Brunetti stared blankly at her for a moment and then laughed, and when she gave him a puzzled look, he said, patting her arm, 'Then take a look at the building, my dear. There are likely to be as many floors now as there were then.'

He saw her face change from confusion, understanding, embarrassment to laughter. She tapped the side of her head a few times but did not look at the building again. Neither of them spoke until Paola looked at the clock above the entrance to the bank in Campo San Luca and said, 'It's after one, Guido,' acknowledging that they could continue.

Brunetti, enraptured by the silence and the solitude, made no move towards home. He walked over and looked into the show window of a clothing store; it had once sold books. At least the *pasticceria* was still there, although the travel agency had given up and closed. He tapped on the window to get Paola's attention and said, 'When you can buy a ticket for a flight to Bali on your *telefonino*, you hardly need a travel agent, do you?' Paola did not bother to comment.

Brunetti looked from window to window, door to door. If memory served, the office of *Il Gazzettino* had once been over here – perhaps even still was – to the left of the *pasticceria*. He paused to take a closer look at the door: if he'd had a bouquet of flowers with him, he'd go to the door, kneel, and leave them there in praise of a newspaper that never failed to amuse him, to anger him, and, not uncommonly, to inform him. Over the years, he'd learned how to read the faces in the photos on the opening pages. An attractive woman, especially if she had long hair, had certainly been murdered, usually by her husband or companion. Most robust men in casual clothing had died of a sudden *'malore'*, while younger ones had been the victims of

'*una lunga malattia*', unless they'd died in an automobile accident returning from a disco at three in the morning, in which
case the cause of the accident was the inevitable '*colpo di sonno*'.
Only sleepiness, never alcohol or drugs.

'Are you coming?' Paola called to him and started towards
Rialto. It struck Brunetti then that they had seen almost no people
since leaving the Accademia. Paola slowed her steps and he
came up on her right side and took her arm. They passed through
an empty Campo San Bortolo and turned towards the equally
empty bridge. At the top, they moved over to the left side and
rested their forearms on the low parapet. They looked off in the
distance to where the Canal curved to the left. There was almost
no motion on the water, and there were no boats in sight.

They stood and looked at the water, the façades, the flickering
lights of the one restaurant still open, the flags in front of the
Comune fluttering in a paltry breeze.

From ahead of them, both heard voices coming from Campo
San Giacometo, the murmur of many voices, not unlike the low
hum of the sea, rising up, drawing back, then going silent for a
moment until someone shouted out and the cycle began again.

At the bottom of the bridge, they would ordinarily have gone
straight ahead until they got to the cheese stand, turned left,
and continued. But Brunetti was enjoying the absence of human
contact and the sound of human voices, so he suggested they
turn now and continue along the Riva del Vin: if nothing else,
they could stop now and again and look back at what they both
thought was the most beautiful bridge in the world. Thus, arm
in arm, they made their way to their home.

Brunetti woke early. He glanced at Paola, who lay beside him in
a position much reminiscent of one of the residents of Pompeii
killed in the eruption of Vesuvius. She wore a loose garment
and was bent at the waist, her head resting on one arm, the other

thrust uselessly ahead of her. He watched her sleep for a moment, saw her shoulder rise and fall, rise and fall. Reaching over, he covered her with the blanket and turned onto his back in order to let things run around in his imagination.

Because he was not yet fully awake, Brunetti's mind drifted to the conversation about the *Aeneid* from the night before. Certainly, books were no longer the sacred touchstones of any culture, any society, and surely not of the one in which he and Paola lived. When had he last heard a reference to a book as part of normal conversation? When had he last heard a character from a book – much less from a classic – used as a measure of good or bad for human behaviour? Harry Potter had provided that, but Harry was surely a father by now, perhaps even a grandfather, and magic had been replaced by . . .

Thinking of books, he drifted back towards sleep, and memory brought him the horrible photos of the museum in Baghdad and the looting that had gone on for days while the library burned to the ground. He could still remember the front-page photo in one of the national newspapers – did it matter which? – of an open courtyard, a man standing ankle-deep in what appeared to be still-smouldering manuscripts. There had been articles in magazines by outraged academics, mourning librarians, comments by simple, sometimes illiterate Iraqis who mourned the murder of their culture.

He stopped himself there, opened his eyes and saw that Paola was standing beside the bed. With coffee. She set the cups down and pushed herself in beside him. 'Where were you?' she asked and handed him his coffee.

He remained where he was, looking at the clouds rolling over the city. 'Nowhere, really. Just thinking.'

'About what?'

'Books.'

'Books,' she repeated. 'A particular book or books in general?'

'In general.'

'And thinking what about them?'

'Only vague things.'

'Tell me one.'

'We have to protect them.'

She turned from him and stared across the room, saying nothing. She reached beside her and picked up her cup.

'Tell me,' she said and took a sip of her coffee.

With no attempt to make a connection, Brunetti asked, 'Do you remember reading – it was during the war in Iraq – about the director of a museum, I don't even remember where it was, who refused to tell the people who'd taken over the city where they'd hidden the best objects?'

He paused, wishing that Paola, with her flawless memory, would help and tell him where it had happened, but she didn't speak.

'He'd hidden them somewhere in the desert, had the workers bury them before they fled. When they captured him, they said they'd kill him unless he told them where the things were. And he refused. I think I read that they tortured him, but when he still refused to tell them where things were buried, they killed him.'

Paola put her cup and saucer on the table beside the bed. She pressed her lips together, then asked, 'You believed this story?'

'As much as I believe stories about virtues that most of us don't have,' Brunetti answered.

'What's that mean?'

'I'm not sure I know,' he said, taking the last sip of his coffee. He went on: 'I think most of us would be ready to die for the people we love – our kids, our family. But *things*?'

Paola grinned and said, 'This sounds like one of those sneak quizzes professors give in philosophy class.'

'The ethical equivalent of "How many cats can you see in this tree?" ' he asked.

'Something like that,' Paola said, nodding. 'And in the end it's just a set-up so that people can proclaim their moral courage. But no one knows what they'd do in a real situation. Most of us can't even decide how much to tip the waiter. Imagine knowing beforehand what we'd do with guns and blood all over the floor.' She held up her hand and asked, 'How'd this conversation get here?'

He shrugged. 'No idea,' then went on. 'He was willing to give his life for objects. I can't understand how a person finds the courage to do that.'

Paola rubbed her fingers across the linen bedcover, back and forth a few times, then looked up at him and said, 'Maybe he was thinking about his children, at least in part.'

Brunetti didn't understand but didn't interrupt her.

'Maybe he thought they had a right to their culture.' There was no surprise in her voice when she said that, but it was clearly a question.

He answered. 'And he thought their culture was more important than his single life?' Brunetti asked.

'Isn't it?' Paola asked, and then went on: 'The *Epic of Gilgamesh*, their temples and palaces, their music, their food, all the things that proved that they were – what were we taught to call it when we were in school? – the Cradle of Civilization.'

Seeing the look he gave her, Paola said, 'I couldn't make that choice. I don't have the courage. But I certainly understand it.'

As if her thought led to his, Brunetti added, 'And we have the influence of a culture that supposedly puts human life above material things.'

She sat up straight on the edge of the bed and gave him a sudden look, as if she needed him somehow to signal to her whether he was serious or not. To test this, she said, 'I'm glad you put in that "supposedly". I like that.'

# 6

What Brunetti and Paola had heard from the bridge was another eruption of the baby gangs, this time near Rialto, in Campo San Giacometo. It had begun a bit before midnight, when two gangs began to dispute each other's right to stand in a public space. The usual escalation of tone and volume followed until their noise began to irritate a much larger group of university students gathered in the nearby Erberia for the peaceful consumption of alcohol and drugs. Voices rose, then tempers, and then someone from the baby gangs made the mistake of throwing a bottle at the students, hitting a girl on the shoulder. The young men near her formed a protective line, which quickly became an aggressive line that used the weight of its advancing bodies to push the badly outnumbered baby gang to the *riva* and then three of them into the Grand Canal. At this, the others ran and quiet was restored. No one offered to help the three gang members out of the water, so they had to doggy-paddle their way to the dock of the *traghetto* and stumble up the steps that led to Campo della Pescaria, from where they could ignominiously make their escape.

When the police foot patrol – alerted by passers-by and certainly not by the students – arrived fifteen minutes later, things
had returned to noisy normal and there was no sign of trouble.
Of course, none of the students knew what the police were talking about when they asked what was going on. Brunetti learned
what had provoked the noise only the morning after the fight,
when it was discussed with great glee by the people having
coffee in Caffè del Doge.

When Brunetti entered his office, the phone was ringing. He
picked it up on the seventh ring. 'Brunetti.'

'Ah, Commissario Brunetti,' a woman with an American
accent began. Speaking slowly in very careful Italian, she went
on, 'My name is Marylou Wilson, and your *capo*, Vice-Questore
Patta, suggested I call you.'

An American woman speaking cautious Italian and given
his name by Patta. It didn't take Brunetti long to suspect that
his services or his time had been offered to Signora Wilson,
which meant she was either rich or well connected, or both,
but not to such a degree that Patta had to bother himself
with whatever it was she wanted, not when the Vice-Questore
thought he could pass her along to Brunetti. Help with a residence permit? A parking place for her boat? Trouble with a
neighbour?

Brunetti chose to respond in English, thinking this might
make it easier for her to explain precisely why she had called.
'In what way may I be of help, Signora?'

She paused for some time before answering, as if considering
whether to accept the help offered by the change of language.
Finally, she said, in English, 'I met the Vice-Questore only last
evening, Commissario. I don't want you to think I'm an old
friend of his, wanting special treatment.'

It hadn't taken her very long to understand how some things
worked. Or perhaps the process was international. It must be, if

she thought her being an old friend of Patta's would impose a greater obligation on Brunetti.

'I'll gladly help you, Signora. But first I must know what it is.'

'Only information.'

'Of what sort?' he asked, careful to show no impatience.

'About a man who has been recommended to me as a possible employee.' After a brief pause, she said, 'Dottor Patta told me he had heard the name, but couldn't remember the context, so he suggested I speak with you, Commissario.'

'What would his position be, Signora?' Brunetti asked, realizing how abrupt he must sound. Perhaps that came with the English.

'Helping me settle into my new home – all those administrative procedures like getting gas and electricity changed to my name. Seeing that papers are sent to the correct office, finding someone who could check the heating system and the air conditioning and find me a trustworthy maid and a cook.'

Brunetti knew no one who worked in the growing business of providing personal services to foreigners and told her that, adding, 'I think you said someone has already been recommended.'

'Yes, he has. The Vice-Questore said he recognized the name, although he had never met him,' then quickly she added, 'Nor heard anything bad about him.' Brunetti noticed her failure to name the person who had made the recommendation.

'Could you tell me his name, Signora?'

'Dario Monforte.'

The name sounded familiar to Brunetti, as well, familiar in a positive way, as though he'd risked his life to stop a robbery or had talked a potential suicide down from the roof. He recalled Griffoni's story of the boy she'd taken home; his father's name had been Monforte. But then it came to him that his own father had made the sign against the Evil One the only time Brunetti had heard the man's name spoken in front of him.

'Are you in a hurry, Signora?'

It took her some time to answer his question. 'No, not really. I could wait another month. But I'd prefer to find someone soon.'

'I could ask around today,' Brunetti said, although the name and his automatic positive response to it kept spinning through his head. 'Is there some way I can reach you?' he asked.

She gave him her *telefonino* number and thanked him both for listening to her and for agreeing to help. Then, switching back to Italian, she said, '*È stato un piacere*, Commissario.'

Remembering the occasional verbal elegance of his father when receiving a request of any sort, Brunetti replied, '*Dovere*,' as though a request that passed through Patta's care became a duty.

Brunetti entered the name 'Dario Monforte' and Google took temporary leave of its senses. He scrolled to the bottom of the page and discovered that there were more than ten pages of articles about him, and then more and then more, with no end in sight. He went back to the first page and ran his eye down the titles. He read the word 'Nasiriyah' – spelled in any one of a number of ways – and the illumination of memory almost knocked him from his chair. Of course, of course. He whispered the name so softly that even a person sitting next to him would not have heard: 'The Hero of Nasiriyah.' He marvelled that even an uncommon name such as Monforte should have been buried in the common memory by the place, and by the infamy of the place. He continued, reading only the headlines, and each time he came upon the word 'Nasiriyah', more pieces fit themselves together.

More than twenty years ago, the fireball of the suicide bombing at Nasiriyah had erupted into the skies above that city,
wreaking fiery havoc among the Italian troops who were there
on a peacekeeping mission, an oxymoron that Brunetti had
never managed to let himself understand.

Although the explosion took place in Iraq, south of Baghdad,
within hours the cloud of horror it created had covered all of
Italy and then spread and dissipated over many other countries
of the world.

Mid-morning, one temperate November day, a truck filled
with three hundred and more kilos of explosives had exploded
just at the entrance to the Italian headquarters in Nasiriyah,
blasting out walls and windows even on the other side of the
Euphrates, sending to their graves nineteen Italians, as well as
nine Iraqis, and wounding others so severely as to fill the burn
centres of Europe for years.

The country gasped, then wept. It was the worst military disaster since the end of the Second World War. The papers wrote
of little else for days. The photos were standard disaster photos
and seemed peculiarly horrible to anyone who read that the
truck had been a tank truck.

The bodies were brought back to Italy on military transports;
flags were lowered in respect and remembrance. The joint
funeral was held at San Paolo Fuori le Mura in Rome, the coffins
were draped in flags, and the President of the Republic was
photographed at the side of the bed of one of the survivors. Italy
is thought by some to be a heartless country, but no one can
deny that Italians, for whatever it is worth, honour their dead.

It was only after the first days that some journalists stuck
their heads out of the foxhole and mentioned that there had
been insufficient protection – no cement blocks or barrels filled
with sand – between the road outside and the courtyard of the
headquarters. Luckily, at that very moment, a Venetian was

reported to have rescued two of his comrades from the inferno. He had left the safety of one of the buildings that survived the explosion and had run across the still-apocalyptic courtyard to save one of his fellows and carry him to safety, then returned amid the flames to drag back a second, only then giving in to the pain that had burned through the small protection of his uniform and seared him for life.

For almost a week, Dario Monforte might as well have been a soccer star, so much was he the subject of interest, articles, admiration, and love. His photo in full uniform, handsome and proud, was on the cover of the major weekly magazines, and it seemed that *Il Gazzettino* could not go to press happily until a photo of him appeared somewhere amongst its pages. His bravery had shown it to be a lie that Italians were cowards, that they ran from danger and lacked manly courage. The day after shaking the hand of the President of Italy, Monforte was sent to the burn centre in Barcelona and then, more or less, disappeared from the public eye.

After his time spent on the front pages of *Il Corriere*, *La Repubblica*, and *Il Gazzettino*, the man who returned to Venice after an absence of more than six months at the burn centres in Barcelona and Copenhagen barely made it to the fifteenth page of *La Nuova Venezia*.

There had been a resurrection of interest in Nasiriyah for the tenth anniversary of the massacre. Brunetti found the use of 'anniversary' in this context so grotesque that he was forced to look away from the page. Ten years on, the 'commemoration' passed almost unnoticed. Assuming that he had come to the end of the useful information, Brunetti told himself it was time to go home for lunch.

When he closed the main door to his home and started up the five flights of steps, Brunetti pulled out his phone and called

Patta. After six rings and two more flights of steps, Patta answered, saying, 'Ah, Brunetti, I was just about to call you.'

Brunetti resisted the temptation to say, 'And I'm the Queen of Sheba,' but instead said, 'Signora Wilson called me.' He paused long enough to allow Patta to speak and when he did not, asked, 'Do you know anything about this Monforte she wants to interview, Vice-Questore?' then added, 'I've read about his heroism in Iraq, so there's no doubt about his bravery.' When Patta still failed to speak, Brunetti said, 'So he should be acceptable to her.'

When Patta finally said, 'She wants me to come and see him in person,' Brunetti searched for a way to refuse the request he knew was coming, but no idea presented itself. Patta, certainly, would tell him something vitally important had just come up that prevented his going, and since Brunetti had already spoken to Signora Wilson, he was the obvious person to go and meet her in Patta's place.

Suddenly Brunetti was tired of it all: the charade of politeness and amiability, the predictable outcome of every scene. Patta was still in costume, but Brunetti was fed up with the script. 'One moment,' he said, no 'please', no title of address. Just an order: straight, flat, unadorned.

Patta stopped talking long enough for Brunetti to shut the door and walk down to Paola's study. He slid a piece of paper across her desk and said, 'What's her address?' and waited while Patta gave it to him. 'What time?' He wrote that down too, said, 'I'll be there,' and ended the call.

A few minutes after four, Brunetti rang the doorbell in Fondamenta Venier; after some time, the door snapped open. He found himself inside a building the form of which he had been seeing for much of his life: a long, beamed hall with heavily grated windows looking onto the canal on one side and along the other canal at the end of the building. Large, thick wooden doors gave access to both canals; they were open now to allow the delivery of boxes and furniture, suitcases, and more boxes. An enormous mirror was swaddled in what seemed like hundreds of metres of plastic bubble wrap. Had it been a person similarly wrapped, they would have long since given up the ghost. Brunetti saw abandoned cartons, a pair of brown rubber boots, and some electric cables that slithered from one side of the room to the other.

The afternoon light flowed in from the barred leaded windows in the left wall. Brunetti saw the usual huge chandeliers hanging from the central beam, probably original to the time of construction, and the six flowery metal wall stanchions that had been converted to electricity sometime in the past, three on either wall. Light splashed everywhere, but the room still seemed dim and faintly ominous.

Brunetti crossed the atrium and paused to turn and see if his shoes had left marks on the floor. None.

He turned right at the end of the room and took the steps to the first and then to the second floor. The door was open and just behind it stood a tall woman wearing a thick lapis-blue cardigan, the same colour as her eyes. Behind her invisible make-up, she was evidently somewhere between fifty and seventy. Her steel-grey hair, cut into a boyish cap, fell forward to cover her ears. She stood so straight she could have found a job as a palace guard in any European country that still had a reigning monarch.

'Commissario Brunetti?' she asked in a voice he recognized. After he nodded, she pulled the cardigan tighter around herself. 'No one told me how cold these places are,' she said in English, shaking his hand and stepping back so that he could enter. Inside, he knew, it was likely to be colder than it was outside. And it was.

'Come into my study. I have an electric heater in there.' As he followed her into the room, Brunetti saw the six red bars glowing unsuccessfully against the cold. She paused and waved her hand at the heater, then looked at Brunetti and gave him a wide smile. 'This is why I want to hire someone who will know what to do about the heating system.'

Brunetti nodded in agreement but did not move closer to the glowing bars. Curious about how word passed around in Venice, he asked, 'Would you tell me, Signora, how you found Signor Monforte?'

'A French friend who's lived here for years mentioned him.'

The bell rang. Telling him to stay there and keep warm, she left the room to go back to the speakerphone. 'Second floor,' Brunetti heard her say from the end of the corridor, followed by the click that opened the door downstairs.

A few minutes later, she came back into the room with a man dressed in black: black sports shoes, black cotton trousers with cuffs buttoned at the ankle, a red stripe on the outside of both legs, and a zippered black bomber jacket with many pockets. He was somewhere in his fifties, thick and solid. He wasn't tall, but the bulk of him took up a lot of space and much of the air around him.

From across the room, Brunetti saw a trail of button-sized red marks running across his forehead before sneaking into his hair, where three bald spots could be seen disappearing amidst his thick dark brown hair.

Monforte greeted the woman in Italian, bowing a bit as she gave him her hand. Brunetti could see that she was not displeased with his gesture. He then walked over to Brunetti and extended his right hand, saying, 'Dario Monforte.'

Monforte's eyes were a very pale grey and looked even lighter in contrast to his boatman's complexion. One of his eyes was a bit tight at the outer edge, where the skin had contracted around another red spot, although this was smaller than the others on his face.

Brunetti took the extended hand and started to introduce himself when Signora Wilson interrupted and said, 'Signor Monforte, this is a friend of mine, Guido Brunetti. He agreed when I asked him to come and . . . well, help me remember the things I would like to ask you but might overlook.'

Signora Wilson continued. 'I'd like you to have a look at the entire place for any improvements you can think of.'

Monforte nodded and asked, 'Would you like me to do that now?'

'Could you?' she asked. 'I'm afraid I have a painter coming in half an hour, so perhaps you could have a look around, then make your rough calculations.'

Monforte gave her a long look, and Brunetti saw the moment when the man decided not to work for this woman, not for someone who treated him like a common workman. But he nodded, no doubt giving in to any Venetian's curiosity to see the *palazzo*. When he did not respond, she said, 'I'd like you to point out everything you find.'

Monforte gave a small smile before asking, in Italian, but pronouncing every word clearly, 'Like the locks on the door to the street?' He paused to see how she responded to this and then added, 'And the rust on the bars on the ground-floor windows? I could push them out of the way if I wanted to, push them back with my hand.' His accent was pure Veneto. Brunetti suspected he would feel more comfortable speaking in dialect.

Brunetti nodded and asked Monforte, 'What's wrong with the locks?'

Monforte considered the question for a few seconds, then answered in a level voice: 'I think it was probably once a very good lock, but from the outside, you can see rust running down the door below it. That's an invitation to trouble.' Silence spread.

Monforte changed tone and said, 'Once you've got a good one in place, and maybe an expandable vertical iron rod that slips into metal cups on the top and bottom of the frame, then no one is coming in unless they have a key or you open the door for them.' The smile Monforte made after saying this seemed forced to Brunetti.

While Signora Wilson considered what to say next, Brunetti studied the back of the other man's hands; they looked like they'd been badly scratched by a cat, except that the scars were darker than blood, almost black.

Monforte asked Signora Wilson if she would show him the rest of this floor, then asked if the two floors above would also be hers and seemed content when she said she was renting the entire *palazzo*. 'Good. That makes it easier for you,' he said.

'Easier to do what?' she asked.

'To know who comes in.' Seeing her expression, Monforte explained. 'You have no neighbours in the building to let in their friends, so there should be no strangers on the staircase.'

Brunetti, who had lived his entire life in Venice, had met a stranger on the stairs only once, and he had turned out to be the electrician who was returning from having placed a communal television antenna on the roof of the building.

Signora Wilson nodded and said, 'And thus less need for security.' Her tone surprised Brunetti: ironic, almost provocative.

Monforte seemed offended by her remark but did not respond. He glanced at Brunetti, and when Brunetti said nothing, Monforte turned back to Signora Wilson.

The Signora suggested she show the rest of the rooms to Monforte and asked Brunetti if he'd like to come along. Brunetti gave in to his curiosity and they started up. The rooms on the third and fourth floors were little more than windowed rectangles filled with cardboard boxes and more furniture protected by plastic sheeting. Four or five unwrapped paintings leaned against the walls, a pile of neatly folded strips of plastic bubble packaging to their right. On one side of the third floor, the windows showed only the building across the *calle*; the three other sides showed more windows and walls, but at greater distances. Brunetti cast off shame and leaned out of one of them and saw gardens below.

The building had the luxury of an *altana*, that essential railed and roofless room raised on pillars above the roof itself. It was believed that, centuries ago, the women of the house went up to sit in the sun and bleach their hair.

Brunetti had always been of a mind that the owners wanted no more than to stand, look around, and marvel at what they saw. When he stepped out onto the *altana*, he was immediately intoxicated by the view. He thought for a moment that he could reach out, pick up the cupolas of la Salute, and slip them quietly into his pocket. He toyed with the idea of putting the bell tower in beside them, but he feared it would be too long and stick out, so he turned around and decided he'd settle on taking San Francesco della Vigna's instead.

Monforte, on the other hand, snapped the handle on the glass door leading to the altana up and down a few times, examined the hinges that attached it to the frame, and shook his head in theatrical displeasure when he turned the key in the lock. At no time did he display any interest in the view.

Signora Wilson asked what he thought should be done, and Monforte, almost defiant, said it should all be replaced to prevent water damage.

As they stood there, Signora Wilson asked Monforte, who had said nothing about the rooms, what he could suggest. He replied that, aside from what he had already said, there was a serious sound problem because of the nearby church bell tower. The single-glazed windows would be little help against the noise.

'But that's part of the charm of living in Venice, I would think,' Signora Wilson protested.

Brunetti knew that his own face fell into a particularly hostile expression every time he saw tourists picnicking on bridges, and he thought he saw a similar look cross Monforte's at the word 'charm'.

'That charming bell tower you saw, Signora,' Monforte began, in a voice usually employed with children, 'is less than ten metres from the back rooms. That's why I mentioned it to you.'

Signora Wilson raised a hand in the air to catch his attention and said, 'My architect says we cannot change the windows without paying for a very expensive special permission.'

Nodding to show he had heard her, Monforte said, 'There are no such permits, Signora. You apply, you pay for the application, and you pay the architect and his office for making both the design and the application, and after some months, or years, the Sopraintendenza rejects your request because there is a law against double-glazed windows in certain buildings. Like this one.'

He put his hands up in the air as though in surrender, walked to the top of the stairs, and then put out a hand and took her arm as they started down. When they reached the door to her apartment, Signora Wilson asked Monforte if he would be kind enough to submit a written summary of his ideas and suggestions and an estimate of the entire cost. It took Brunetti some time to translate her Italian, even to himself. He had also heard enough of the unspoken antagonism between them and so suspected that the plan, no matter what it entailed, was not going to be accepted.

Failing to register the tone of Signora Wilson's question, Monforte suggested she should start with the minimum necessary – change most of the locks, install the metal pole and the cups above and below it, and commission an ironsmith to make new gratings for the ground-floor windows. After telling her this, Monforte continued, one hand raised to pat the air between them, 'There's no charge for the estimate, Signora,' quite as though he were dealing with a poor widow who needed to save money wherever she could.

Seemingly deaf to the sarcastic provocation in Monforte's voice, she said, 'You have my email address, Signor Monforte. You can send it to me.'

'I have to wait for the estimate to be calculated by the mathematician,' he said. 'He's very good, very efficient, and he's only fifteen.'

'I hope you pay him enough,' Signora Wilson said, trying to make it sound like a joke. Her phone pinged, and she looked down to read the message that had arrived.

Monforte, Brunetti noticed, gave her a long look: milder than previously, but definitely not mild. Had Signora Wilson seen it, Brunetti was sure she would have told him not to bother sending the estimate.

After tapping a short response into her phone, Signora Wilson put it back in her pocket and returned her attention to Signor Monforte. She thanked him for coming and walked with him to the door.

When he was gone, Signora Wilson came back to Brunetti.

'What do you think?' she asked.

'He seems honest and conscientious,' Brunetti said, wondering if the presence of another man had affected Monforte's behaviour.

'Yes,' she said. She walked over to a window that looked across the canal and stared at the boat traffic for some time. It occurred to Brunetti that as far as Signora Wilson was concerned, he, like Monforte, was no longer of any use to her and she was considering how best to get rid of him.

Turning to him, she asked, 'Is this mathematician meant to be his son?'

Brunetti shrugged and said only, 'I don't know. Perhaps.' He let more time pass, and when it was evident that neither had anything further to say, added, 'I'm sure you'll make the right decision,' and started towards the door.

Surprised that he was giving himself permission to leave, Signora Wilson had time to say no more than 'Ah, yes,' but Brunetti was already at the door. He paused, pasted on his best smile, and waited to allow her to open the door. He thanked her for the chance to see the *palazzo,* gave her a polite farewell, and started back to the Questura.

# 7

On the way to work the next morning, Brunetti was accompanied by the memory of what he had read about Dario Monforte and what he had seen of him in the short time they were together in Signora Wilson's home. He considered the step-by-step account of Monforte's rise to fame and his equally fast disappearance from it once the President had shaken his hand.

As he walked, Brunetti attempted to reconstruct the chronology. The Americans, unhappy about the state of things in the Middle East, blew the whistle of war, and the Italians sent a few hundred men to do what was considered a safe job in what they considered a safe place. And it had been, for a few months. And then it wasn't.

He started towards the squad room, hoping to find Vianello, but then he remembered that the Ispettore was still not back from vacation and continued up two more flights and went directly to Griffoni's office and knocked on the door. '*Avanti*,' she called. In the past, he had developed the habit of taking a deep breath before entering the tiny space, as though it were best to take sufficient oxygen to last the entire visit. But ever since she had managed to fit her desk into the closet, two people could fit into the space without thinking immediately of caves and mines and prison cells.

Griffoni was seated in her chair, her computer on her lap, so he could not see what she was looking at. Noticing his glance, she pulled the second chair up beside her and patted it. He sat, and she put the computer on the desk in front of them, turning the screen to make it easier for him to watch.

He saw a long corridor, new wooden flooring, an open doorway to the right of whoever was recording the video. A brown animal appeared at the end of the corridor, a furry thing hanging from its jaws. The focus was not very sharp, and Brunetti wondered for a moment what kind of animal it was: a giant rat, perhaps, or one of those South American capybara things, or a small brown dog that had turned on its owner and killed him in his sleep and scalped him.

He bent closer and watched the animal advance to deposit what turned out to be a furry toy rabbit between an equally fake grey squirrel and a black and white badger that were already on the floor. He turned to Griffoni, searching for words. She held up her hand, saying nothing.

The animal went back down the corridor and entered another room, soon emerging pulling a pink sweater behind it, which it brought to the mound and stuffed carefully between the squirrel and the badger.

It backed away a few steps, moved forward to poke the sweater deeper into place with its nose, then returned to the room at the end of the corridor. As it walked away, Brunetti noticed the paddle-like flat tail and whispered, 'It's a beaver.'

The beaver emerged, this time holding a long strip of wrapping paper. It took the animal some time to find the right place.

Finally, the shoved-together paper served as a buttress for the toy squirrel.

Brunetti looked at Griffoni, who was still paying attention to the screen. 'Claudia, we've probably had enough for today.'

She touched a key, and the animal disappeared. 'A friend of mine – he works in the anti-Mafia squad in Messina – sent it to me to show himself at work under the new government.' She paused, and Brunetti gave her the nod of understanding she – or perhaps her friend in Messina – probably wanted.

'And that's us?' Brunetti asked, pointing at the now empty screen, 'still trying to build dams and plug holes?'

She leaned forward and closed her computer. 'Something like that, I suppose. Us, and the magistrates who know which dams are at risk.'

She started to say more, but Brunetti cut her off.

'I think I don't want to talk about this government.'

'All right,' she said. 'Then tell me more about this American woman Patta sent you to see.'

'So much for the secrets of the Questura,' Brunetti said dryly, but he smiled as he did so. Instead of answering her, he asked a question of his own. 'Do you remember Nasiriyah?'

After only a moment's hesitation, she said, 'Of course. I even remember where I was when I heard about it.'

'He's living here now,' Brunetti said.

'The one who saved them?' When Brunetti nodded, she said, almost in apology, 'I've forgotten his name.'

'Dario Monforte.'

He watched her face change and her posture become more alert when she recognized the name. 'The father who turns his phone off when he goes to bed?'

'The very same. He has a son he referred to as "the mathematician".'

'How . . . ?' she began to ask, but lost hold of the question.

'Someone recommended him to the American.'

'As what?'

'Someone who can help her settle in – forms and paperwork and finding a maid and a cook.'

'Not given to stinting themselves, are they, the Americans?' she asked with a smile.

Ignoring her joke, Brunetti said, 'What I don't understand is how a person finds the courage to do what he did.' He stared at the back of his hands, fingers spread wide. 'I kept thinking that when the American woman was talking to Monforte. He's got what I think are burn marks on his face and hands.' Brunetti shook his head. 'No one made him do it; no one gave him an order. He was safe. And then – at least this is what I remember reading at the time – he went back to . . .' He rubbed one hand with the other, then changed them and rubbed the other hand, and finally said, 'He didn't seem very heroic to me.'

If Griffoni was surprised by this, she hid it well by saying, 'They don't wear signs.'

'Huh?' Brunetti asked, returning from wherever his memory of the meeting at Signora Wilson's house had taken him. 'Who?'

'Heroes,' Griffoni said. 'They don't wear signs.'

Whatever explanation Brunetti was going to give was broken off by a peep from Griffoni's phone, announcing the arrival of a message. She glanced at it, looked away for a moment, then looked at it again before sliding the phone over to Brunetti.

*I have your scarf and want to talk to you,* he read. *OK? When? Same place?*

Brunetti looked up, his face asking the question.

'It's from Orlando,' she said. 'The boy I took home the other morning.' There was no disguising the pleasure in her voice, at least no disguising it from Brunetti.

Neither of them said anything for some time, and then Brunetti asked, ' "Same place"?'

'The bar near his home.'

' "Scarf"?'

'I told you. It was cold. He was wearing a denim jacket and a T-shirt.' Then, more forcefully, 'A scarf.'

'I see. You have any idea why he wants to talk to you?'

'It could be anything,' she said, as though talking were something she'd heard about but didn't quite understand.

She reread the message, studied Brunetti's face for a few seconds, then tapped a response and pushed the arrow, whizzing the message into the empyrean.

# 8

Reading the question on Brunetti's face, she said, 'I explained this in the report. He said his father turns his phone off at eleven, so making sure he got home seemed the best choice. It was nearly morning by then, and I didn't know what else to do with him, and I certainly didn't want to leave him in a police station.' She paused here, and Brunetti nodded that he understood.

'He got ahead of me and arrived there earlier. For all I know, he might have switched roles and gone in and checked on his father to see he was all right.'

Brunetti gave a nod of parental understanding and then shook his head. 'I still do it when we come home very late.'

Griffoni smiled as though she'd recognized an old friend and said, 'I remember that, even opening the door again to be sure, sure, sure that no one had slipped in and taken her.' Here it was again, a reference to Griffoni's daughter. When she'd first been posted to Venice, she had said she had no children, but once or twice she had let slip mention of her.

Brunetti said nothing, but he stole a glance at her and saw how lovely she'd become, remembering a fear she'd outgrown.

She stopped and shook her head as if at a list of numbers that would not add up correctly. 'Now kids are checking on their parents.' After a moment, she asked, 'Is this going to turn into a sermon blaming the parents?'

Brunetti smiled at her. 'There's a long list of things that get blamed for why kids are the way they are, not only parents.'

Griffoni started listing them before he did. 'School and teachers, the kids themselves, the internet. Lack of corporal punishment, the use of corporal punishment, the removal of the crucifix from classrooms.'

While Griffoni tried to think of more, Brunetti put on his most serious face and voice and tried to top her by suggesting a few scientific explanations: 'High-tension wires, PFAS in drinking water, global warming, slowing of the Gulf Stream, pesticides and chemical fertilizers.'

She started to laugh and abandoned the search for more likely causes. 'Maybe it's a fashion, like tattoos.'

'Let's hope,' Brunetti said, 'that in a year or so they'll stop doing it.'

'At a certain age, they usually do,' Griffoni said.

She considered the matter for a while and finally said, 'His father and another boy's parents are the only ones who haven't responded to the invitation to consult social services.'

'Then perhaps someone from social services should get in touch with them,' Brunetti suggested.

'I see two ways,' she answered instantly: 'with the first, we can make a request to social services that we be allowed to talk to him, and, after a few weeks, perhaps they'll say we can do it, but only if someone from their agency is there to assure that the child is not intimidated by our questions, even by our mere presence in the room with him. We can start leading delicately to the subject of the baby gangs, but the instant those words are spoken, the social worker will take out his blue whistle, blow it and call "Foul!" And if we try again, or if the boy shows any strong reaction to anything we say, then the whole thing will be cancelled, and we will be banned from speaking to him.'

Brunetti seldom had to deal with social services, for which he now gave thanks. Griffoni, however, was a woman of imagination and exaggeration, so he thought it best to find out, now, how much of what she'd just said was legend and how much was direct experience.

'Might I ask for a footnote here?'

'Footnote?' she asked, but it was evident she understood what he meant.

'What specific social worker said and did those things, and to whom were they said and done?'

Instead of answering, Griffoni hunted through her handbag until she found a much-used red notebook. She opened it and began to page through it slowly, not hesitating to lick her finger when necessary.

Finally, she made a satisfied noise, flipped ahead a few pages and then back to where her left hand was anchoring her place. In a neutral voice, she said,

'I'll spare you the worst and let you hear what the chief of juvenile services had to say.' She turned a page and ran her eye down it, then another, and then stopped, muttering only, 'Here.

'"I'm afraid, Commissario, that we can't continue with this. The suspect is obviously deeply upset by your use of the word 'attack'. No judgement has been made that an attack, in fact, took place, or that, in that circumstance, the suspect was the attacker."'

She turned a page and then another and continued. '"Though he was seen in the company of the complainant, there is no physical evidence to prove that he was the attacker."' Griffoni looked up at Brunetti and gave an enormous smile, then said, 'There are six more pages of the same.'

She flipped ahead and stopped at a dog-eared page. '"I'm

afraid I have to interrupt you here, Commissario. As you can see, male suspect is deeply upset by your reading of the statement made by female complainant and asks that this interview be brought to an end." '

She closed the notebook and tossed it back into her handbag. Soft-voiced, she added, 'Guido, if you want to speak to the boy in the presence of someone from social services, you are perfectly free to do so, but if so, you should limit your questions to his name, perhaps his middle name, his age, and perhaps the name of the school he is attending. If you feel like taking a risk, you might think of asking him which class he's in and what grades he gets. But even that is a tremendous risk, I assure you.' Seeing Brunetti's persisting confusion, she added, 'You're invading his privacy.'

Brunetti was silent for some time, trying to remember the emails from the Ministry of the Interior concerning the 'respectful treatment' of those being questioned. He did recall one that advised him always to use the formal '*Lei*' when interviewing a suspect, regardless of age.

'What do you suggest, then?' he asked.

'That we have something to eat in the place around the corner from Salizada San Francesco where I left Orlando with his neighbours. I told him we'd meet him there.' Then, absolutely straight-faced, she added, 'Besides, their sliced egg and red pepper is sensational, and we might be lucky and have interesting gossip for dessert.'

As they walked, Brunetti realized how comfortable it was to work with a colleague who, while keeping her own life private, judged gossip as an invaluable asset in the gathering of information. It was certainly a feminine behaviour – he said this only to himself – but he wondered if a fondness for gossip might also be part of the Neapolitan character. If he knew more about Griffoni, he might be able to answer this question.

Neither of them spoke for a long time, and then it came to Brunetti from nowhere to fill the silence by asking, 'Did you work while you were at university? To have some money for books, at least?'

She looked at him, then appeared to look at something standing in the past, and said, 'I was a tour guide in Napoli. A kind of a private guide.'

'Meaning?'

'Who gets a job as a tour guide is determined by . . . well, by other factors than how well you know the city or its history or what you might have studied at university.' She paused and he watched her look back at her earlier self. 'I love the city, so it was always a pleasure to get paid for walking around, seeing the things I loved, and telling people about them.'

'But why "private"?' Brunetti asked.

She stopped in front of a *gelateria* not yet open for the season, appeared to give his question some thought, and then resumed walking.

'There's a union, well, a group of people who have the training and the municipality's licence to be tour guides.' She paused again, perhaps for effect, and then said, 'I had both.'

'Training?' he asked.

'Of course. Growing up in Naples means listening to the stories your family and friends tell. It makes everything sound more official if you call it "training".'

'And the licence?'

Griffoni banished that with a wave of her hand. She tended to use wider gestures when speaking of Naples.

'It wasn't necessary. The man who ran the travel agency I was working for had a friend who owed him a favour, and this man spoke to someone who had a cousin who was in charge of membership in the union. So I was given a union identity card with my photo on it, and I started working.'

'As a guide?'

She nodded. 'I did it until I was finished with my studies and decided to join the police.'

'And then?'

'I called my friend and said I wanted to retire from the union.'

'What did he say?'

'That he'd take care of it and that he was very glad I had been using a fake identity card when I was working because it would be so easy to change the photo and let someone else use it. He said it saved a lot of paperwork.'

Brunetti missed a step but corrected it and said nothing. They turned left and she slowed, looking into the windows of the stores that lined both sides of the street. She stopped in front of one that sold light bulbs, small appliances, and one would have to enter to know what else.

After inspecting them all, she turned to Brunetti and said, 'Naples is a different . . .'

'Planet?' Brunetti enquired in his sweetest voice. He thought of telling her about his summer jobs while at university but decided not to. During the summer of his second year, Brunetti had had a series, often simultaneously, of odd jobs. He delivered packages for the local butcher, not at all ashamed to be paid in meat. He worked for two weeks with a city crew of labourers who were cleaning a canal; it was hard, filthy, back-breaking work, and it was early August. The canal had been drained, and their job was to dig out the years of muck that had accumulated on the bottom, shovel it into wheelbarrows, push them up the temporary wooden ramps. After that, they pushed them along the *riva* of the canal, and dumped them into the large boats floating on the other side of the temporary wall that blocked off part of the *rio*. No one had bothered to ask to see his identity card, and he was paid in cash. He had not needed a licence.

# 9

They got to Salizada San Francesco a bit before two, both of them having accepted the idea of *tramezzini* for lunch, he more reluctantly than she. Brunetti had called Paola and apologized, resisting the temptation to ask what he was missing for lunch that day. He followed Griffoni into the bar; she went to the counter to see what was on offer. Brunetti came up behind her, muttered something about the sandwiches to the barman, then went to a table at the back, looking grumpy. No matter how miserable a thing it was, Brunetti would not abandon lunch, even if he knew he would not enjoy it.

There were three men at the bar, all elderly; having lost the ease of command, they were talking among themselves in the softer voices of the retired.

Griffoni discussed options with the barman, ordered the *tramezzini* and a litre of still water, room temperature, and went back to join Brunetti. If he wanted wine, he could go to the bar and order it himself; she never drank at lunch.

The barman came to the table and set down two empty plates and another with the piled *tramezzini*. He went back to the counter, then returned with a bottle of mineral water and two glasses and set them down.

As he walked away, he said, '*Buon appetito*, Professoressa.' He gave a special emphasis to the last word, but not one of respect.

Brunetti poured them both some water, gave her first choice of the sandwiches, then set the bottle down and put a ham and egg on his plate. 'Professoressa?' he asked.

She took a small bite of peppers, eggplant, and egg, and smiled. 'I told them I was his mathematics teacher when I was here the other day. I didn't think Orlando would want them to know he was being brought home by the police.'

'From what you've said, he doesn't sound like the kind of kid the police would have to bring home.' Then, in a lower voice, 'Did you check the juvenile files?'

'I haven't had time,' she said nervously, embarrassed to admit this, then explained, 'I'm no good at getting into heavily protected sites, so I risk doing it only if it's absolutely necessary.'

'Did he say anything else about his father?'

'No. There seems to be no mother, at least none living with them.'

Brunetti looked out of the window, ignoring the sandwiches on the table, then glanced down at the platter and saw that most of the *tramezzini* were still there.

'What do we do now?' he asked.

'We wait for him to show up.'

'You sound certain that he will.' Brunetti tilted his head to one side and raised his eyebrows. 'The fact that the barista here recognized you,' he said, 'and seemed delighted to be able to call the word "professoressa" into question, suggests he knows who we are and whom we're waiting for.'

'One of the great pleasures of living in a small town, I suppose,' Griffoni said.

Suddenly the door of the bar banged open and a few boys

wearing backpacks pushed their way inside, all talking very loudly. Griffoni had her back to the door, so it fell to Brunetti to watch their arrival. The tallest, whose hair was cut in the current style of short back and sides with a longer extension protruding forward above the forehead in the fashion of a searchlight, ordered a beer; the others, after a minor hesitation, asked for a Gingerino. They did a bit of shoving and poking while removing their backpacks and setting them on the floor; the barman opened and poured the beer, then got the three small bottles and set them beside the three glasses on the counter. They took their drinks and turned to survey the other customers in the bar, moving in the same cocky-aggressive manner common to actors in bad Western films.

One of them looked towards the back of the room and, seeing Griffoni, let out a startled 'Oh,' but quickly erased it with an uninterested 'Dottoressa' barely louder than his speaking voice, then reached and took a sip of his drink.

He set his glass on the counter and walked towards Griffoni and Brunetti. His jacket was unzipped, so one saw how narrow he was; his jeans reached only the middle of his socks, but that might as easily have been a fashion statement as a sign of growth. The red scarf was nowhere in evidence.

Three lines of text were printed on the T-shirt, but because of the jacket only the four middle letters were visible. Brunetti could read 'I', below it, 'm' and at the bottom 'me'. The 'I' was capitalized, so it was the first word of a sentence, probably '*Io*', preceding a personal assertion. These declarations usually spoke of love. So the 'm' in '*amo*' would be perfect for the second line. But what was it that he loved? The middle letters were 'm' and 'e'.

All of this went through Brunetti's mind in the time it took the boy to reach the table. Brunetti stood and waited while Griffoni and the boy shook hands, then he introduced himself as a colleague of Griffoni's. He extended his hand and, while still holding the boy's, took a step to the right, supposing the boy would turn. But he freed his hand and, at Griffoni's invitation, took a seat at the table. The only word that came to Brunetti now was 'caramelle', which was probably not right because candies didn't need publicity.

The boy was too thin and thus seemed shorter than he was. His eyes were brown and, at the moment, capable of seeing nothing more than Griffoni.

The waiter looked over; Orlando walked back to the bar and, without a word to his friends, retrieved his backpack and glass and returned to the table.

With no hesitation, he sat and, careful to speak softly, said, 'I'm glad you came.' He looked at Griffoni, his glance a mixture of longing and uncertainty.

'You said you'd go to school, but I left you in here, so it's reassuring to come back and see you survived the experience.'

'I'm never late for school,' Orlando said seriously.

Recalling their conversation, Griffoni asked, 'Even for the boring classes?'

The boy's face flowered, perhaps at the realization that she'd remembered what he'd said. 'No, no, it's not that. Maths class is always the first class.' He bowed his head and said, 'I've even been known to be early.'

Brunetti, while appearing to follow their conversation, kept his eyes on the boys and the old men. The boys had turned away from them: what's less interesting than adults? The old men, however, stared at them openly.

Griffoni smiled and said, 'Your secret rests with me, and I'm sure Commissario Brunetti feels himself bound the same way.'

Brunetti nodded. He'd play the silent cop.

'Did you bring a witness because I said I wanted to talk to you?' the boy asked with a note of jealousy or suspicion in his voice.

'He didn't come as a witness, but maybe it's not a bad idea that I bring one,' Griffoni answered.

'To protect me because I'm still a minor?'

Griffoni couldn't stop herself from laughing out loud. 'If anyone's in danger here, Orlando, it's not you.'

'Who do you mean?' he asked.

'Me. I shouldn't talk to you without witnesses,' she said. She saw his surprise and added, 'Or without a serious reason.' Brunetti watched the boy's face respond to the coolness of her voice.

'You mean about the episode the other night?' Orlando asked.

Griffoni swallowed a laugh and repeated 'episode' as though it were something on television.

Orlando gave in, 'All right, that's a stupid thing to call it.'

Neither of them spoke for some time, and when Brunetti looked around again, he saw that three or four people were sitting at the tables around theirs, and a few men were standing at the bar with glasses of white wine in front of them. One of them was observing them while speaking on his phone.

Griffoni, sounding faintly impatient, said, 'Orlando, we shouldn't be here. You're a minor and we're police officers. There is no one from social services present as a witness, so there is no use that can be made of anything we say. No legal use, that is.'

The boy's face grew tighter as he digested all of this.

Brunetti interrupted to say, 'Because the Commissario is involved in this, she's vulnerable if she speaks to you other than in a monitored situation.'

He explained a bit more. 'When she told me about the message you sent her, I volunteered to come along.' Then, before Orlando could interrupt, he said, 'So she wouldn't be talking to you alone.'

The boy pushed down on the table in an attempt to stand, but his sleeve caught on the chair and he failed. He thrashed at it, trapped. Brunetti leaned forward and released his sleeve, but Orlando had stopped pushing himself up and so sat there, unmoving.

His voice grew urgent. 'But I'm the one who asked to talk to you.' Clearly eager to prove his good faith, he grabbed his phone from his pocket and put it on the table. He snatched it over and started pressing keys, scrolling up and scrolling down.

At last he found the message he had sent her and stuck a stiff arm in front of Griffoni's face, the phone close enough to read. 'Look, look,' he said, his hands shaking with nervousness. 'I asked you to come. You didn't ask me. Anyone can see that.' He stared at her with complete attention. 'I'd never put you at risk, not with anything.'

Griffoni said, 'That's why we're here, Orlando.' Brunetti, who had known her for years, had never heard her use that voice, nor had he seen such softness in her face. 'I thought we might both need some help, so I asked Commissario Brunetti to come along.' After she said this, her voice changed and retreated to the one he was accustomed to hearing. The serious, emotional part was gone: now it would be ordinary talk, but Brunetti could see its effect in Orlando's eyes.

The boy stared across the table at her, confronted with the power in her voice. Brunetti made fists of his hands and told himself he'd keep them like that until one of the others spoke. After what seemed a long time, Orlando said, speaking at just above a whisper, 'Something's happening. Something big. I don't know what it is or when it will be, but Gianpaolo is wild with it. He says that once we take care of the Lido, we'll be the best in the city, tougher than Mestre, and bigger than Marghera.'

'Gianpaolo?' Griffoni enquired, as though she'd been introduced to someone and wasn't sure she'd heard the name correctly. Her audible disregard cut at least ten centimetres from Gianpaolo's height and at least as much from his importance.

Griffoni's tone had been so dismissive that even Brunetti felt the desire to defend Gianpaolo.

Instead, Orlando tried to do it himself. 'He's at school with me, but he's in the class above me, and his teachers leave him alone because they know he's not afraid of anyone.' To Orlando, this was obviously meant as a compliment.

'What's he like?' Griffoni asked.

'Oh, he's tough. He's the one who decides.'

'Ah, I see,' Griffoni said. 'That's a good thing.'

Brunetti, who had been watching Orlando, turned to Griffoni, who asked the boy, 'Did he tell you anything about it?'

Orlando closed his eyes and shook his head, as if this double show of ignorance would be convincing. 'I have no idea. No one does, except that it will be big.' Brunetti was struck by the change in his voice when he said these last words, as though a man were speaking. Orlando had said 'best' and 'tougher' and 'bigger', yet was so thin a medium wave would knock him over.

As though the room had suddenly become too hot for him, Orlando pulled open his jacket. Brunetti saw his T-shirt and read the message *Io amo i numeri*, but for the life of him, he could not understand why someone would advertise a love for numbers.

The boy looked across at Griffoni and blushed. He brought his hands up from where they'd been under the table and looked at them. Finally, he said, 'Even if I knew, I couldn't tell you. I think. Because this time it will be troub—'Then, as though he'd sent himself into a trance, Orlando appeared to levitate in his chair, rising up slowly yet keeping his seated position with his legs still bent at the knee. The chair was at least a metre above the floor, blotting out the form behind it. Orlando's face was tight and without colour, his hands splotched pink and white on the arms of his chair, his eyes tightened in fear.

The cause was not far to find: a looming presence stood a bit behind the boy, silent, holding the chair suspended in the air by its arms as though it were weightless, joggling it up and down, blocking and then uncovering the side of his face that Brunetti could see. The man had reached the table without having been noticed by any of them, no mean feat for someone of his bulk. He wasn't tall, but the volume of him took up all of the space around him.

Brunetti looked at the man's one visible hand and saw the thin scars that ran its length. It was only then that he realized it was Dario Monforte and realized how the aura about him had become palpably dangerous.

Brunetti saw metal flash at Monforte's wrist, light reflecting off what he suspected was a Rolex. This indeed proved to be the case, he observed when Monforte lowered the chair to the floor. He was right: it was indeed a Submariner, but where would someone find a place to dive a thousand metres deep with it on his wrist to test it? Surely not in the Laguna, probably not in the Adriatic.

Orlando's hands were locked to the seat of the chair, his head bent forward. After some time, he raised his head and turned in the chair to look at his father, but he made no attempt to pretend that what had happened was an old family game, a bit of rough play between males.

Brunetti got to his feet slowly. 'I'm surprised to see you again so soon, Signor Monforte,' he said, quite as if it were completely normal that they should meet in this bar, of all places. 'This is my colleague, Claudia Griffoni.' She nodded but remained in her seat. Then, with exaggerated friendliness, Brunetti said, 'Such a small city. We're always running into people we've just seen.'

Taking one step towards Brunetti, the other man said, 'I'm not here by accident. I had a call from a friend, telling me my son was being interrogated by the police.'

Brunetti allowed a few beats to pass and then asked, making his surprise audible, 'Interrogated?'

He looked at Griffoni, who shrugged and raised her eyebrows. She glanced up at Monforte and said, 'We were trying to decide which sandwich to have. I'd almost decided on the egg and tuna when suddenly this young man – who invited us here – rose up in the air in front of us.' Then, almost contritely, she said, 'I'm sorry. I'm a police officer as well, and I'm trying to have lunch, not carry out an interrogation.'

The man's smile was a stiff and formal thing. He held his fists closed tightly and a bit away from his hips, as though he might want to use them soon. He did, however, have the strength of will to step back from the chair and let his hands fall to his sides. Griffoni offered her hand, and Monforte took it as though it were a piece of gossamer he might damage were he to hold it too long. He released it but kept his attention on her.

'Signora,' he said, 'it was very kind of you to see that Orlando got home the other night.' Then, before Griffoni could respond, he added, 'And to have fed him all the way.'

Griffoni gave a quick laugh at that and said, 'I'm glad his school starts so early. If I'd had him all day, I'd have to have mortgaged my home.'

She slipped out of her chair and stood behind it. The boy scrambled to his feet. It occurred to Brunetti that, could she and the boy somehow be fused together, they would not occupy as much space as Monforte.

The man put his arm around the boy's shoulders. He glanced at his watch and said, 'Lunch is ready, Orlando.'

Orlando turned to his father and began to say something, but Monforte stopped him. 'Not now.'

'All right,' Orlando agreed and stepped away from the table. He nodded to Brunetti and then to Griffoni. He bent and picked up the backpack, opened it, and pulled out Griffoni's red scarf, washed, neatly folded, and freshly ironed. 'I washed it for you,' he said as he handed it to her. 'Thank you for coming to get it.'

Griffoni flashed him a smile, and holding the scarf by a corner, let it open and cascade in centurion red towards the floor. She folded it lengthwise with old familiarity and wrapped it twice around her neck.

Without another word, Monforte, arm around his son's shoulders, led Orlando to the door and out into the *calle*, where they quickly disappeared.

Griffoni reached down to pick up her bag. She nodded to Brunetti and started towards the door. Just then, a group of giggly girls pushed it open, one holding it for Griffoni, then they all crowded in and blocked the door until they managed to line up along the counter.

By the time Brunetti edged past the girls, paid for lunch, and got outside, Griffoni was halfway down the street. He caught up with her and, silent, they started back to the Questura together.

# 10

They doubled back on Salizada Santa Giustina and Calle Zorzi, then back to San Lorenzo. They stopped by unspoken agreement on the bridge in front of the Questura. Brunetti had always found it a troubled spot: the closed church behind him offered no comfort, nor did the old people's home on his right, even less the Questura at the bottom of the bridge. All three worlds – spiritual, physical, and legal – offered little solace to those who sought help or peace from them. The church had not functioned as a church for decades; the rest home kept people quiet, and the Questura wanted them to speak, but always at the expense of some other person or themselves.

He turned to Griffoni and said, 'Clever boy.'

'For bringing the scarf?'

'It's the perfect explanation to assure his father we weren't there to talk about what the boy was doing in San Marco.'

Griffoni pushed herself to and fro on the railing a few more times, then tired of it and stopped.

He turned and looked off at the blue sky over the *bacino* and said, 'I wonder what Monforte is concerned about. There was no need for him to come to talk to us.'

'It's natural to be concerned if the police want to speak to your child,' Griffoni countered. 'Everyone within a radius of five hundred metres knew we were police. You can be sure of that.'

Brunetti was forced to agree.

He smiled. 'His behaviour seemed odd, as if he needed to show us both his strength and his amiability. If one wouldn't make us leave him alone, the other would.' Hearing how vague this was, Brunetti could do no more than shrug.

'Maybe it's a holdover from being a Carabiniere,' Griffoni said. 'Acts like he thinks he's smart, but he's really not. After all, it takes three Carabinieri to change a light bulb, doesn't it?'

If she'd expected Brunetti to say, 'One to hold the light bulb and two to turn the ladder,' she was mistaken. Brunetti looked at her in surprise and said, 'That's it. He was a Carabiniere. It was the Carabinieri who were in Nasiriyah, not the army, and the Medal of Valour is given to the Carabinieri.'

Griffoni whispered, 'Of course, the Carabinieri.'

Monforte had been stationed abroad as a peacekeeper, then, after Nasiriyah, had spent long periods of time in foreign hospitals and had, for a while, been a national hero, and all of these things had happened when he wore the uniform of the Carabinieri. After this, he had slowly disappeared. Was catering to the wishes of wealthy foreigners sufficient to permit a Rolex?

A tourist group crossed the bridge, led by a guide holding up a small Greek flag, and followed their leader onto the *riva* leading to the Greek church.

Two seagulls landed on the roof of the house to their left and set up a terrible back-and-forth shrieking. It kept on for what seemed a long time, until one of them thrust himself into flight, followed by the other, both now silent.

Brunetti turned to look in the direction of the empty church: perhaps San Lorenzo could be of help. Perhaps not. In the absence of his help, there was always a higher power.

'Shall we ask her?' suggested Griffoni.

'Yes.'

Signorina Elettra was, not to put too fine a point on it, a push-over, but because there was information to convey, and her open door was on the main thoroughfare of the Questura, Brunetti thought it best that they move to Griffoni's office: very few people had need to go to the fourth floor of the Questura, and its long, dreary corridor was certainly never on the itinerary of the Vice-Questore.

Although they were the only people on the staircase, they spoke in soft voices as they made their way to Griffoni's office. 'The last time I entered the Carabinieri's system, I had no trouble whatsoever,' Signorina Elettra said in response to Brunetti's question about the scope of her powers. 'Their protection is much better now, I must say, but as soon as I speak to my friend in Caltanissetta, I'll surely find my way in.'

'Caltanissetta?' Brunetti said, asking for confirmation. This being one of the strongholds of the Mafia, he spoke the name softly, and with a certain trepidation.

'Caltanissetta,' she repeated with effortless certainty.

They continued to the fourth floor and paused while Griffoni unlocked the door. She pulled it back, revealing the changes she had made. 'Oh, lovely,' Signorina Elettra said. 'So cosy. And the idea of putting the desk into the closet – how very clever. Think of how much space we'd save if everyone did it.'

The problem of the seating was quickly solved, even though there was barely room for two people. Brunetti offered the women the two chairs and then, closing the door to the room, pulled Griffoni's desk backwards out of the closet. He could use the now exposed half as a seat, and did. If performed in the proper order, this procedure created both sufficient seating and sufficient privacy.

With no preface, Griffoni explained to Signorina Elettra what they would like to see happen: the investigation of the baby gangs would continue under their care and – perhaps with her help – they could have a look into the juvenile files.

There was one other search they would like her to make: a retired Carabiniere named Dario Monforte, who had been injured during the massacre at Nasiriyah.

'Good heavens,' Signorina Elettra could not stop herself from exclaiming. 'He was one of my heroes when I was younger.' She remained silent for a while, her thoughts perhaps returned to those more innocent times. 'I believed more then than I do now, I fear, so it was some years before I began to take a closer look at the story.'

Because this seemed an odd thing to say about a hero, Brunetti asked, 'And what did you find?'

Signorina Elettra shifted her chair back a millimetre or two, then said, 'One of those figures my history teacher always referred to as "convenient heroes".'

Brunetti waited, but nothing more came. 'What did he mean by that?'

'The ones who arrived just at the right time, like that Russian boy – what was his name, Stak . . . something or other? – who dug tons and tons of coal, just when production was failing. Nothing better to boost public morale.'

Both Griffoni and Brunetti sat silently, waiting, their silence urging her to continue, encouraging her to explain, which she finally began to do. 'I haven't thought about it in years. The massacre was terrible. So many dead boys, so many dead Iraqis.

It was a disaster that could have been avoided – they'd had at least three warnings from the secret service that an attack was planned. But they ignored the warnings and didn't bother with barriers to slow down the entering traffic.

'But once we had our hero, everything changed, and the debacle was turned into a case of extraordinary heroism. Did he not risk his life and suffer terribly to save his colleagues?'

Brunetti was never to grasp the extent of Signorina Elettra's access to privileged information and had come to think of her computer as a half-living creature, able to slip down any tunnel, unravel any knot, but only if she were in command. Its vision of events and opinions about people were often similar to her own, but in some matters they varied widely in the faith they put in the sources available.

'Did you doubt the heroism?' Brunetti asked.

'No, not really,' she answered quietly. 'But I found it very convenient.'

Both Brunetti and Griffoni shrugged as a sign of their not remembering the chronology of events.

Brunetti turned a bit to face the two women and noticed that even though they were about the same height and size, Signorina Elettra seemed to take up significantly less space on one of two identical chairs. Her legs were turned primly to the left, as if to allow more room for Griffoni's, and her hands were folded modestly – the word surprised him with its accuracy – in her lap. He realized only then how much her sense of decorum rendered her virtually invisible; he'd been watching it deceive people for years.

Griffoni had pushed herself back in the other chair and crossed her legs. The anchored foot tapped up and down, up and down, as if searching for a place to go.

Signorina Elettra looked back and forth between the two of

them, cleared her throat, and said, 'I don't mean to be impertinent, believe me, but in order for us to have any freedom in looking into this matter of the Carabinieri, we need the Vice-Questore's approval, otherwise we'll have no authority at all.'

She brushed a vagrant strand of hair behind her ear. Over the years, Brunetti had learned to distinguish the various smiles that could be made manifest upon the face of Signorina Elettra. There was the everyday smile for simple pleasures, used after returning from the flower market every Tuesday morning; there was the smile of triumph, when someone she liked was proven right in an idea or suspicion; a rather enigmatic smile he'd sometimes seen her using while talking on her *telefonino*, usually late in the afternoon; and there was this, the small, half-guilty smile she used when given rein to abuse rules, traditions, or laws, all for the greater good of her friends and thus, by extension, humankind.

'But I think that might be arranged,' she said simply, as though she'd been asked to call a restaurant and ask if there would be a problem if a fourth person came to dinner. 'We can count on his dislike of the Carabinieri.'

After a pause, no doubt observed to allow both Brunetti and Griffoni to catch their breath, she continued, 'There is very seldom much to be found online, even in our files, about minors, not unless they're chess champions or have helped save a person's life.' She paused again, then added another possibility, 'Or killed their parents.'

She gave them the chance to speak, but neither took it. 'But certainly there's got to be information, somewhere. And about Signor Monforte, there will be an abundance,' she added.

Having said that, Signorina Elettra folded her arms across her chest and gazed again at the tiny window high on the wall of Griffoni's office. Unmoving, ignoring them, in the manner of an oracle, she said, 'I'd like to point out, if I've understood what you've just told me, that we are involving ourselves' – Brunetti was elated to hear her use the plural – 'in an investigation of events that took place more than twenty years ago, in a country that's now engaged in violence at times at the level of civil war, involving people unknown to us.' She stopped speaking, but both of them knew she was not finished, merely pausing to introduce an idea or point to an interesting fact.

'And, so far as I can see, you have no more complicated reason than simple human curiosity.'

That silenced them. But only for a moment. Brunetti smiled across at her and, in an entirely normal voice, asked, 'Is there a better reason?'

Signorina Elettra nodded. Then she stood, again complimented Griffoni on so intelligently having solved the problem of her office, and said, 'I'll give some thought about how to approach the Vice-Questore.'

She navigated her way from her chair, past Griffoni's, in front of Brunetti's legs, and let herself out of the office, closing the door quietly behind her.

The silence in the room was such that they both heard the smooth slither of Griffoni's stockings as she uncrossed her legs. Not to break the silence, Brunetti got to his feet, slid Griffoni's table back into the closet to give her greater space – however laughable – in her office, and let himself out.

Inside his own office, he closed the door and went over to his desk. He would have liked a coffee, but he pulled out his chair and sat. There was a new folder on his desk, from Officer Alvise, who, because he lived nearest to them, had been asked to see what he could find out about Orlando and his family.

Thus, here, two days later, lay a four-page report.

At the Ufficio Anagrafe, Alvise – wearing his uniform – had learned that Anna Maria Vitucci was thirty-one, unmarried, and had one child, a son, Orlando, fifteen, whose father was Dario Monforte. Four years before, she had cancelled her residence and written only that she was leaving the country.

Although the least brilliant of the squad, Alvise inspired trust in the people he spoke to because of his amiable manner and patent simplicity. At the suggestion of Signorina Elettra, he had shed his uniform and gone to the bar near Salizada San Francesco to see what he could learn about Anna Maria and her family. After he'd drunk several glasses of white wine and a coffee, the woman behind the bar spoke of Signorina Vitucci's son as a good boy and said that his father took good care of him.

A second paragraph declared that Signorina Vitucci had, some years ago, told some of her neighbours (names and addresses were given) that she had found another companion and was leaving Venice to go with him to Spain, where he worked as a silversmith. She was also taking with her a small annuity left to her by her grandmother, who had died when Anna Maria was twenty. Two of the women Alvise spoke to said she'd made a wise decision but should have taken her son with her.

Even Alvise noticed the difference between the female evaluation of Monforte and the admiration that many of his male neighbours expressed for him. *Proprio bravo. Forte. Un vero uomo.* As he read this part, Brunetti could not stop himself from muttering, 'A real man.' So easy to say, so hard to define.

Alvise found it noteworthy that most of the people he spoke to paused to consider their answers before speaking about Monforte. Although he received no negative comments about the man, Alvise registered the expressions of suspicion and unease on some faces – almost all female – when Monforte's name was mentioned. Alvise also learned that Monforte made a modest living with the installation and maintenance of safety systems for homes and offices.

The boy, Orlando, did well at school but was not among the most popular boys in the neighbourhood.

Brunetti finished reading the report, amazed that Alvise, of all people, could have written so clearly. Even if it had actually been written by his companion, Cristiano, the observations and perceptions were all made by Alvise.

Brunetti recalled other times when the officer had been, perhaps by dint of his own obvious curiosity in the lives and welfare of the people he spoke to, an auditor to tales of human peculiarity. It was Alvise who got the odd ones. There was the old woman who lived near Santa Fosca, who had insisted on leaving food for the stray cats she remembered from her youth: she ended up feeding the rats. It was Alvise who thought of giving her a stuffed toy cat, telling her that it was a special kind of cat and could not be fed, only petted and loved. The feedings stopped. When he told his colleagues about her, they immediately added her to the list of 'Alvise's strays'.

Although there were still hours left of his work day, Brunetti decided that he had had enough and gave in to his desire to go home and lie on the sofa and read, uninterrupted by the arrival or presence of another person.

Paola had recently found, misplaced among her own books, Brunetti's copy of the letters of the Marquis de Custine, a French nobleman who had travelled in Russia in the nineteenth century. She had returned it to her husband, saying it looked interesting, but she was reading *Washington Square* at the moment, and that provided her with more than sufficient misery.

Brunetti discovered his bookmark still in place and decided to continue from there: the Marquis had so far reached only St Petersburg. Lying on the sofa in Paola's study, Brunetti flipped through the book to see if he had underlined or drawn attention to any passages. He remembered that the Marquis's judgement had been overwhelmingly negative, and now, returning to the lines he had underscored in the text, he marvelled at what the Marquis noticed and noted. Not a happy place, Russia: 'the most desolate country on earth'. The Marquis judged the mildness of the people worthless, since it was the 'habit of submission'.

Custine and Brunetti had started out in early July of 1839, and by August, Custine had seen precious little that pleased him: not the people, not the aristocracy, not the buildings or the cities. 'The Russian nobility swivel like sunflowers: they speak to you without any interest in what they are saying, their gaze riveted on the sunshine of imperial favour.'

Perhaps the absence of even the possibility of imperial favour was what made the aristocracy of Venice so different, for they were always interested in what they were saying.

# 11

On Monday morning, Brunetti arrived late at the Questura to find on his desk some papers, neatly stapled together, a hand-written note clipped to them declaring that Signorina Elettra had obtained most of them from city and government records and admitting that friends had supplied others.

The papers regarded Dario Monforte, whose life had been eventful and had left behind a broad paper trail. He had been born fifty-four years before in Mestre, his father a driver and delivery man for one of the largest wholesale producers of milk and dairy products in the north-east. His mother was a cleaner in the local elementary school. There were four other children, two boys and two girls, Dario the youngest.

His school records showed that he was an average student in terms of his grades, but by the time he was twelve, he had been involved in two or three 'incidents' – Brunetti was sufficiently fluent in bureaucratese to recognize 'fights' when he read it. The boy always insisted that he had been provoked into defending himself against words or blows. At the same time, he was popular among the students, both boys and girls. He was quick-witted, made fun of the teachers and the principal, even of the priest who came twice a week for classes in religion.

By the time he reached the age to begin the *liceo*, his temperament appeared to have improved and he was accepted to the Morosini in Venice, which he finished with a good record, and then surprised his teachers by deciding not to continue to university but to join the Carabinieri. All of this information came from official school records as well as the memory of Nino Pedrini, who had been in the same class as him for years and now worked as the digital archivist at the Questura.

With his school record, Monforte was admitted to the corps and rose patiently through the ranks until, when he was only twenty-eight, he was promoted to the rank of maresciallo capo.

Because he was bright and eager to succeed, after only a few years he was promoted to quartermaster, assigned to the Gruppo Intervento Speciale, and sent to Iraq to help with peacekeeping in the area of Nasiriyah, a few hours from Baghdad. There, he was charged with seeing that supplies of every sort, from food to underwear, were available in sufficient quantities for the more than three thousand Italian soldiers reported to have been sent on this mission.

Brunetti paused here and looked at the heading of the next page. 'Operation Ancient Babylon', the name for the Italian intervention in Iraq. This was followed by 'Secret/Restricted/ Available to Service Personnel of the Rank of Colonel or Above'. And below, in red letters: 'Not to be passed to Iraqi forces'.

'*Maria Santissima*,' Brunetti said – as had his mother in moments of great surprise – then noticed that his hand held the paper in a death grip. Slowly, consciously willing it, he loosened his fingers, took the paper with his left hand, and placed it flat on his desk in front of him. He stroked it back towards smoothness, looking at the wrinkled corner and devoting all his attention to that.

Not for the first time, he asked himself how Signorina Elettra could do this so quickly and efficiently, and if she could, then did anyone else have this skill, and for what purpose did they use it?

Not for the first time, no answer came.

He continued, knowing what was coming. The twelfth of November, 2003.

In July of the same year, the report continued, there were incidents. An Italian military transport plane ran off the runway when landing at the air force base in Brindisi. Three returning soldiers were injured, but not seriously. In the cargo hold, what was first described as 'a wooden crate' was discovered to contain, although packed separately, four carved marble panels, each the size of 'a laptop computer', and a velvet jeweller's case containing thirty-seven golden Assyrian seals, both flat and cylindrical, all bearing a portrait of King Ashurnasirpal II, some showing him in his hunting chariot, killing animals. Another padded box contained seven metal cups of different sizes. Also found were two larger tablets, both depicting scenes of mass slaughter, this time human. What the accompanying papers called a 'wooden crate' was in reality one of the coffins used for the repatriation of the bodies of Italian soldiers killed while on a mission. The wooden box was free of all identification: no list of contents, no sender's name, no unit that should retrieve it.

A handwritten marginal note on the paper Brunetti was reading reported that the crate had been moved to the ammunition warehouse, but seemed to have disappeared after two days.

Its disappearance, rather than its arrival, prompted hurried communication between the command centre in Rome and the men in charge of the troops in Nasiriyah. To no apparent avail.

In August of the same year, a backpack of the kind carried by ground troops was left behind on a flight bringing thirty-five Carabinieri back from Nasiriyah to Aviano. When found by the cleaning crew, it was discovered to contain three copies of the holy Koran: 1367 Cordoba, 1573 Cairo, 1593 Isfahan. Each volume bore the seal of the Baghdad Library. No one came to claim them, and the volumes passed invisibly into the hands of private collectors to await the return of peace and security to Iraq, when they would be given back. They are still held in those protective hands, awaiting that event.

And in November came the suicide attack that most Italians remembered as the Massacre of Nasiriyah, where the Carabinieri had their headquarters. A fuel truck, two drivers, both shot and killed before the truck could crash its way into the centre of the base. But still, but still, but still it exploded at the entrance to the courtyard and instantly blew away the lives of – he remembered – eighteen Italian soldiers and one civilian, not to speak of the deaths it caused outside the entrance to the base or the seared, but spared, victims of its liquid contents.

Brunetti closed his eyes at the thought of the survivors. A fuel truck. An old memory of a photograph from about the time of the explosion, though later, tried to enter his mind, but he pushed it away.

To keep it far off, Brunetti returned his attention to the report, his eyes eager to see Monforte's name again.

The next page, however, listed only the names, ranks, and ages of the Carabinieri killed in the explosion. Brunetti could not bear to read it.

Monforte's name appeared again at the top of the next page: he was one of many Carabinieri medevacked to Italy and to diverse European burn centres. Two years later, he was allowed to retire from the Carabinieri, with a guarantee of a lifetime's access to military medical services.

Someone knocked on his door and Brunetti said, '*Avanti.*'

It was, as he thought it would be, Griffoni, with her copy of the report in her hand. She came across the room and sat opposite him. 'My God, Nasiriyah,' was all she could say. 'Someone I was at school with . . .'

She let the idea go free and sat a long time, shaking her head and keeping her eyes on the papers in her lap.

'The men in Nasiriyah didn't deserve this,' she finally said.

Brunetti thought it best not to mention that they were part of the foreign force who had invaded and occupied the country and said only, 'Maybe the men in that truck had other grievances.'

Griffoni said nothing.

'A Koran sold at Christie's last month for seven million pounds,' he told her. He thought she'd say something, but she didn't. 'And I've read that the library in Baghdad had tens of thousands of books and manuscripts.'

'It doesn't matter what they cost,' she surprised him by saying. 'It's their history . . . whoosh, all up in flames.'

He picked up the papers Signorina Elettra had left for him and waited until Griffoni looked at him. When she did, Brunetti said, 'I have a friend who works for Interpol. Art police.'

'Where?' she asked, as if that would make some sort of difference.

'Rome.'

'Doing what?' Griffoni asked, and before Brunetti could answer 'This and that,' she smiled and said, 'If you answer "This and that" or you say he's interested in a lot of things, I'm leaving.'

Brunetti nodded that he understood, but did it in a way that stopped Griffoni from asking more questions. He picked up his phone and dialled a number; after six rings, a man answered.

'Ah, how nice of you to call. It's been some time.'

Yet still he remembered the number, Brunetti thought uneasily. Or was it permanently registered in his memory?

'I don't like to bother people unless it's important,' Brunetti said.

'I wish you'd preach that in the streets,' the other man gave back.

In the background, Brunetti heard nearby voices and, at some distance, a broadcast voice giving a series of short announcements. Observing the unwritten ban on unimportant questions that prevailed in calls like this, he continued, 'Do you know if old things are coming out of Iraq at the moment? Not necessarily arriving from there, but had their origin there.' After a pause, he added, 'For the European market.'

'The really old things?' the man asked.

'Yes.'

'Small, medium, or large?' When Brunetti failed to answer, the man said, 'Are you asking about the head of Nefertiti, a full-sized god or goddess, or the Elgin Marbles?'

It took Brunetti a moment to answer. 'I think Nefertiti's head, and copies of the Koran.' In response to the grunt he heard, Brunetti said, 'I'll call in twenty minutes,' and broke the connection.

As soon as he'd done that, Griffoni leaned forward, saying, 'I think I know about someone who was there.'

'Where?' Brunetti asked.

'Nasiriyah.'

'Who?'

'I don't know, really. My landlord has a cousin – I think his name is Lino – who was there. I know because he always goes to visit him on the twelfth of November.'

Before Brunetti could say anything, she suggested, 'I could ask my landlord to find out if it's possible for us to go and talk to him.'

Brunetti nodded, but it was clear to her he wasn't much interested in doing this.

She got to her feet, raised the papers in a sign of agreement, and left his office, closing the door behind her.

When he'd waited twenty minutes, Brunetti called his colleague, who told him that, as he'd feared to say without checking, artifacts looted from Iraq had become common fodder for the international antiques market, a surprising amount of which took place, as it were, in the open. Photos and prices were available on a number of online sites: small bronze statues, small ceramic pots that could have come from anywhere and could have been made yesterday as easily as in Babylon two thousand years ago, countless cuneiform tiles, signature seals, single pages from what could, for all he knew, be the Holy Koran or a text about agricultural processes. All of this was a mere click away, and many quite ordinary people bought something to hang on the wall.

'Some of the best things, though, are hidden, and trade in them is so secret there's no way we can stop it.' Brunetti could almost hear him turning the pages in his memory. 'I've heard that there are a few what you might call specialist dealers who are bringing out the really good things only now. We manage to claw some of it back, but if you figure that fifteen thousand pieces were looted from the museum, it's not as if we're making grand progress.' He paused and waited for Brunetti to comment. When he did not, the other man said, 'That's all I have at the moment.'

'Fifteen thousand?' Brunetti asked, trying not to consider what it would be were the Accademia, or even San Marco, to be looted. In the aftermath of that thought, it came to him to ask, 'What in God's name does some office worker in Milano want with a ceramic cup that's two thousand years old?'

'I've often wondered. I've arrested some of them – we try to make examples to discourage people – and I've asked a number of them why they wanted whatever it was they bought.'

'What do they say?' Brunetti asked.

'Most of them, that other people will think they're interesting if they own something that's two thousand years old.'

Brunetti closed his eyes and rubbed at them. 'Jesus, help us,' he said.

The other man laughed. 'I've arrested people who have just sold pieces of the True Cross,' he said, 'so I suppose he doesn't help. *Ciao*, Guido.'

'*Ciao*, Francesco,' Brunetti answered, and broke the connection.

# 12

From habit, Brunetti went directly to Signorina Elettra's office, where she greeted him with what seemed to him to be unusual enthusiasm. 'What a pleasant interruption, or perhaps it's a reward for my having finished the Vice-Questore's performance analyses,' she said, using the English words.

'What are those?' Brunetti asked, knowing how enchanted Patta was with foreign jargon.

'When I was in elementary school, we called them report cards,' she said. Seeing his curiosity, she continued. 'Some years ago, he decided to write paragraphs encapsulating each officer's professional performance that year and keep them on hand in case his superiors ask for them.'

'He writes them?' asked a befuddled Brunetti.

'No, no, no,' she said. 'He dictated them to me, three years ago, and I . . . well, I suppose you could say I update them.'

Brunetti froze, curious but unwilling to ask.

When it was evident that he was not going to speak even in the most oblique way, she said, 'It's very simple, really, and saves a great deal of time.'

'How?'

'When he first got the idea, I took notes on what he had to say about each person, then I wrote a macro that allocates the texts randomly to a different person each year. It was really quite simple, and since the Vice-Questore doesn't bother to read them, and there's nothing negative in them, the reports lie forgotten in the file, only to be resurrected the following year, but never to anyone's disadvantage.'

Brunetti closed his eyes and said, aiming his comments at the ceiling, 'I know I'll wake up soon, and all of this will seem perfectly normal to me.'

Ignoring him, Signorina Elettra replaced the cap on her pen and shoved the papers to the side. She looked up then and smiled, changed her face and voice back to what he was more familiar with, and asked, 'What may I do for you, Signore?'

'Nothing at the moment, I only wanted to thank you for your report. I never realized that the archives and Caltanissetta could be such rich . . .' Brunetti began, but had no idea how to continue the sentence.

Signorina Elettra smiled: any database protection was a garden in which she delighted to play.

Brunetti started for the door.

'Commissario, I'm sorry, but I forgot to tell you. Bocchese has been looking for you.'

'Bocchese?' Brunetti made no effort to hide his surprise. 'Did he say what he wanted?' he asked, wondering if he or Griffoni had sent something to the lab and forgotten about it, or perhaps Bocchese had a correction to make on some sample his technicians had tested, or needed to correct the calibre of a pistol on his report, or tell him the pathologist had called to say that the person in the morgue had indeed died of a heart attack.

'No,' she replied. 'Just said he wanted to talk to you when you got here.'

'Thank you,' Brunetti said, completely bemused. Bocchese? The most sibylline person at the Questura, actually asking to speak to Brunetti? He went up to his office and dialled the lab director's number, but the call went unanswered. He looked through the list of names and mobile numbers in his *telefonino* but none was listed for Bocchese, only the chief technician's home number.

There was no other choice for it but to go down and ask Bocchese what he wanted. The door to the lab was open. Two white-jacketed officers stood at a work table in the back. Between them, on the surface of the table, he saw what looked like a piece of clothing, perhaps a denim jacket, blue, large. One of them was holding it taut while the other ran what looked like a miniature vacuum cleaner over it, back and forth, back and forth.

From the threshold, Brunetti called over to them: 'Where's the boss?'

The youngest assistant, Rodella, called back, 'Isn't he in his office, Signore?'

Brunetti walked over, looked inside, and indeed, Bocchese was there, standing in front of a far smaller work table, just then taping bubble wrap around what appeared to be a box of salt. There was an empty manila envelope large enough to contain it on the other side of his desk. While Brunetti watched, Bocchese slipped the package inside the envelope and then folded the flap and sealed it. As Brunetti stood silently behind him, Bocchese signed his name on a piece of paper as large as a visiting card and taped it across the already sealed flap.

Only in that moment did he turn and nod to acknowledge Brunetti's presence.

'You wanted to talk to me?' Brunetti asked, making sure to sound delighted to be able to ask the question. He usually got on well with the taciturn Bocchese, but he had spent a lot of time – years – creating the circumstances where that was possible. Recently, though, he had realized, Bocchese had been less communicative and decidedly less friendly.

'Yes.'

So it was going to be one of *those* conversations, Brunetti told himself. All right, prepare yourself for the long haul. 'You mind if I sit down? I've been running around all day.' He sat in the visitor's chair and allowed his grumbling self to take over, adding, 'Didn't even get to have lunch.'

'Disaster for you, isn't it?' Bocchese asked without irony, without sympathy, without any suggestion of mood. The technician walked around his desk and sat opposite Brunetti.

It was only then that Brunetti looked closely at Bocchese and had to stop himself from asking the technician if he was all right. Smaller and shorter than Brunetti, stooped over, Bocchese could have been his father today, so much did he appear to have decreased – the only word that was correct for what Brunetti saw. His hair, never abundant, seemed thinner, or perhaps that was because it had not been washed for some time and stuck to his head in oily patches that reflected the light in a strange way. Bocchese's face was pale and drawn, his eyes weary: he looked so bad and so exhausted that Brunetti was at a loss for what to say.

'Anything in particular?' Brunetti asked. When Bocchese didn't answer, Brunetti flailed around for a neutral topic and lighted on Bocchese's love of beauty, especially as manifested in small bronze statues of the fifteenth and sixteenth centuries, some of which he had shown to Brunetti in the past and of which he was inordinately proud. They were the few things he always treated with affection.

With patently false enthusiasm, Brunetti asked, 'Any new statues?'

Had Brunetti used a cattle prod on the other man, Bocchese could have been no more shocked. He pushed himself back in his chair and grabbed at the arms so fiercely that his knuckles grew white, and Brunetti thought he heard some of them snap from the pressure.

'Why did you say that?' Bocchese demanded, in a voice as strained as his knuckles had been.

'No reason,' Brunetti said brightly, or as brightly as he could manage, with Bocchese sitting two metres from him, chilled with suspicion. 'I like to see the new pieces you find. They're always so beautiful.'

Bocchese stared at him, eyes opened wide, lips pressed together. 'Are you playing with me, Guido?' he asked fiercely.

Bocchese's voice frightened Brunetti. It flashed through his mind that the other man was having a breakdown of some sort, not that Brunetti had any idea what that would look like. Certainly, his face was flushed and his body rigid.

For a moment, Brunetti thought of trying to joke his way – their way – out of this, but couldn't think of how to do that. Instead, he leaned forward, laying his palm flat on the surface of the desk in lieu of placing it on Bocchese's forearm, and said, 'Enzo, listen. You're one of my few friends here. You, Vianello, Signorina Elettra, Griffoni, Pucetti, and even Alvise – I'd trust any one of you with my life.' He paused until it was clear that Bocchese had heard him. Brunetti hoped he had also understood him.

'No, I'm not playing with you,' he went on. 'I don't know what you mean by that. If anything, I respect you and am grateful to know you.'

'What about the statues?'

'What statues?' Brunetti said, too upset to remember exactly what he'd said about them, though he did recall Bocchese's strong reaction.

'You asked me if I had any new statues.' From the tightness of Bocchese's voice, it sounded like an accusation.

Easily, softly, smiling, Brunetti said, 'I've been asking you that for the last ten years. Ever since you showed me the first one and I told you I thought it was beautiful.'

Suddenly Bocchese propped his elbows on the table and lowered his face into his hands. Brunetti could hear his breathing grow slower, and then the technician took a deep breath and uncovered his eyes. He looked across at Brunetti and said, 'If you loved it so much, can you tell me what it was?'

Oh, where was Paola with her perfect memory? Brunetti looked up at the window behind Bocchese and started to reconstruct that scene. 'Your desk was over there,' he said, pointing to the right, 'and I saw the statue on your desk, but from the side, and I remember asking you what it was, and you said that was the wrong question, and I should be asking who it was. Venus, you said, and you made her sound like your wife, you were so familiar with her.' As Brunetti spoke, Bocchese's face loosened, as though he'd decided he did want to breathe the air around him.

'She was wearing a long gown of some sort. It covered her left foot, and I remember asking you how they managed to get the folds to look so perfect. And you explained it to me, although I've forgotten what you told me.'

He stopped and looked over at Bocchese, who had somehow returned to looking more like himself. The technician heaved himself into a more upright position. 'Yes,' he said. 'I remember the Venus. I still have her. Florentine. Fifteenth century, early.'

After that, Bocchese stopped moving and looked steadily towards the end of the room, where the two members of his staff were still working on the jacket, doing whatever it was they were meant to be doing. Brunetti watched them. The one holding the jacket spread it open, and the one with the vacuum cleaner started moving the nozzle back and forth on the inside of it.

'What are they doing?' Brunetti asked, thinking it might be wise to return the mood in the room to normal.

'They're taking DNA samples from the jacket of a suspect who was caught trying to sell a stolen watch.'

'Why?'

'It's what he does for a living: hits a tourist on the vaporetto with the backpack he's wearing. Knocks him into another person, then grabs him to stop him falling, which is when he also grabs the watch and passes it to another person with him. Does it just as the boat is mooring, so they're the first persons off, long gone before the victim realizes his watch is gone too. This one's been arrested at least ten times – insists he doesn't know what we're talking about. So they're checking his clothing for the DNA of the man who was robbed. If they find it on the jacket, it means he had contact with him.'

Brunetti looked back at the men and noticed only now that they wore plastic gloves and handled the jacket delicately. He smiled at Bocchese in what he tried to make a complicit way and said, 'The machines are going to make us all obsolete.'

Bocchese did not comment. Brunetti decided he should not speak again but leave it to the other man to resume the conversation.

Before that could happen, one of the two officers came over and tapped at the frame of the door to Bocchese's office. 'We'll send it to the lab.'

'The jacket?' Bocchese asked in surprise.

'No, sir, the vacuum bag. We've already got it sealed and the request filled out.'

'Good. Yes,' Bocchese said absently and waved a hand to send the man back to his workplace.

Apparently having already forgotten the officer's remarks, Bocchese made some strange, semi-snorting noises and finally said, 'There's something I've been wanting to tell you for some time, but I never found the . . .' The sentence drifted away. 'That is,' Bocchese tried again, 'I never found the right opportunity.'

'I hope you've found it now, Enzo,' Brunetti said, speaking short and speaking true.

'It's about my neighbours,' the technician said.

'At your house? Those neighbours?' Brunetti asked to disguise his confusion. What other sort of neighbours could there be?

'Yes, those neighbours.'

'What is it they're doing?'

'They're not doing anything. I suppose that's what's wrong,' Bocchese said, then went silent while he considered what he had just said. 'Maybe they're afraid, too. God knows I am.'

Brunetti kept his body almost motionless, tried to give the appearance of being part of the chair.

'What are you afraid of, Enzo?' Brunetti finally asked, wondering what would cause a person to be afraid of his neighbours: an argument about a door always left open, stairs unswept, late-night noise, garbage bags blocking the door?

'Their son,' Bocchese said, sounding relieved to be able to say it.

'Does he live there? In your building?'

'Yes.'

'How old is he?'

'I don't know. Sixteen, perhaps.'

'What sort of boy is he?'

Hearing himself say that, Brunetti asked himself how he'd answer the same question about his own son. How would any parent?

'He's bad,' Bocchese said in a soft voice, the kind of voice one would use when the person under discussion was listening at the door.

'Bad how?'

'He hits them.'

'Who? His parents?'

Bocchese pulled a handkerchief from his pocket and wiped at his face, and Brunetti saw that it came away wet. The technician refolded the handkerchief into a small square, but then his hand fell limply on his lap and he seemed to forget he was holding it.

'And his brother and sister, too,' Bocchese said, answering both questions in one.

'For any reason?'

'It's because he's bad, Guido. Simply that. He's tall and built like a bull and likes to hurt people.'

'Has he actually done anything to you, Enzo?' Brunetti asked.

'Not yet.' Bocchese looked at Brunetti, confused to find himself in this conversation. 'He's tried to trip me on the steps a few times.'

'How?'

'By getting his feet between mine or running up the steps at full speed when I'm carrying something and bumping into me.'

'For any reason? Have you ever had an argument with him or with anyone in his family?'

'No. I told you – he's just bad, or maybe he doesn't like it that I'm a policeman.'

Had he had a magic talisman – or his mother's rosary – Brunetti would have put his hand into his pocket and caressed it. Oh, praise the Lord for his decent neighbours. Eight families in one building, using one staircase, and never yet a raised voice or a slammed door.

'He hasn't actually done anything?'

'No.' Then, when Bocchese had allowed enough time to pass to allow him to lay heavy emphasis on his next words, he said, 'Not yet.' It sounded cranky and overblown to Brunetti, but there was no denying Bocchese's fear.

'Do you know if he's ever had trouble with us?' Brunetti asked.

'Not that I know of, no,' Bocchese said, and Brunetti was relieved to see that he had relaxed a great deal.

'Have you told anyone about this?'

Bocchese shook his head, as if admitting to cowardice could

be done only without words. He sat up a bit straighter in his chair and said, 'You've known me for years, Guido, and you know I'm not a particularly brave man, nor a very strong man, not at my age. But I've been in the corridors of this place when killers have been brought in, the blood still all over them, and it hasn't frightened me to have them walk past, but this boy frightens me.'

'Has he threatened you?'

'No, but he's threatened my statues. Twice, on the stairs, he's said something about my collection.' Before Brunetti could ask, Bocchese said, 'Twice.'

'What did he say?'

'That I must be proud of having so many beautiful things. And how I must worry about them.'

He raised both arms and slapped his hands flat on the table. 'How does he dare?'

Brunetti had no idea, nor had he any practical suggestion to make. The boy had committed no crime; it could be all talk. But surely Bocchese saw it as far more than that.

Bocchese looked at the top of his desk and said, 'I think he can get into my apartment. And I think he does.'

'How?'

'I don't know. The doors are old, and the locks aren't very good. But this is Venice, for God's sake: we don't have to be afraid in our own homes.'

'What, specifically, have you seen that makes you think he goes in?' Even as he spoke, Brunetti realized how much he sounded as though he were questioning a suspect. He knew he was in for a long wait with this one.

Rodella appeared at the door, unseen by Bocchese, who had turned away from it. He raised his hands in an interrogative gesture, and Brunetti, seeing that Bocchese was busy clinging to his handkerchief, shook his head and waved him away.

Brunetti sat silent for a long time, considering what Bocchese had told him. If the boy was like this at sixteen, what would he be at twenty? All he could say was 'You're a police officer, Enzo, with a rank equivalent to lieutenant. I don't think he'd try anything with you. That doesn't make sense.'

'Trying to trip me down the steps doesn't make sense, either, Guido.' After a moment's reflection, Bocchese said, 'Your silence sounds like there's nothing I can do.' He gave Brunetti a dejected look, turned away from him and said, 'To answer your question about how I know, someone has moved the statues around while I wasn't there.'

'How do you know that?' Brunetti asked the back of Bocchese's head.

'They each have their place. They always stand in the same place, all of them. But sometimes I come home and find them moved, or in the wrong place.' Before Brunetti could speak, and in a very sharp voice, Bocchese said, 'Don't tell me I'm imagining this, Guido. He's been in there, and he wants me to know it.'

'Try to stay away from him,' Brunetti suggested, embarrassed by saying it.

'And what about his friends?'

'Excuse me. What friends?'

'The ones in his gang. They come by sometimes at night and call up to him, ringing all the doorbells in the house to announce their arrival.'

'And then what?' Brunetti asked, growing more concerned with the mention of the 'gang'.

'Then he goes downstairs and they run out into the *campo*, and that's the last I hear of them until he comes back.' Bocchese's face contorted into a mask of contempt. 'He rings all the doorbells then, too.'

Brunetti sank a bit lower in his chair, then suddenly pushed himself to his feet, feeling defeated and useless, as he probably should.

'I'm sorry I can't help you, Enzo, more than to assure you that there is little chance this boy will bother you.'

'He already bothers me,' Bocchese snapped back.

'All right . . . hurt you, then.' He spoke from irritation, without thinking that this was one of his oldest comrades and Bocchese deserved far more than Brunetti had been able to give him. He leaned over and put his hand on Bocchese's shoulder. 'I'm sorry, Enzo; I shouldn't have said that.'

Bocchese stood but moved no closer to Brunetti, nor did he attempt to shake his hand or put a hand on his shoulder. 'We live in crazy times, Guido, and there's very little we can do to change that.' Then, in an entirely different voice, he said, 'Can I ask you a favour, Guido?'

'Of course.'

'It's stupid, but you're the only person I know well enough to ask.'

'If it's stupid, you've found the right person,' Brunetti said, and Bocchese gave his puppy-bark laugh, not heard for some time.

'It's about the statues,' Bocchese said, sounding almost embarrassed.

'What about them?'

'I'm getting rid of them, all but a few.'

'What does that mean?'

'Just what I said. I'm getting rid of most of them.'

'Melting them down? Selling them? Putting them out with the garbage?'

Before Brunetti could ask more questions, Bocchese said, 'Stai zitto, Guido. I've found a buyer for them, but we've agreed I can keep three. They're my emotional annuity, I suppose.'

'A buyer?' Brunetti asked.

Removing the question mark, Bocchese repeated, 'A buyer.' His tone was a warning that this was not a subject to be pursued. 'And, yes, I'm selling them so they'll be safe. Because they're not safe here any longer.'

In the face of such determination, Brunetti could only ask, 'And what's the stupid thing you want me to do?'

'I'd like you to help me decide.'

'Haven't you done that already?' Brunetti asked, surprised by his friend's decision after his years of devotion to these objects.

'I haven't selected them yet. I'd like you to come and give an opinion.'

'Are you joking?' Brunetti asked, unable to disguise his astonishment.

'There's no one else.'

Wanting to forestall an explanation of that and thinking this would be a way to make up for some of the things he'd said, Brunetti answered, 'All right.' Then, as practicalities presented themselves, he asked, 'But where?'

'My house, of course,' Bocchese said. 'You might even be lucky enough to meet my nemesis.'

'When would you like to do this?' Brunetti asked, not sure what ritual was proper for giving up a life's true love.

'It has to be tonight. The buyer's leaving for London the day after tomorrow and wants to get them insured tomorrow. I promised I'd meet him at my bank in the afternoon and give them to him.' Having said that, Bocchese turned to Brunetti and gave a very small smile. 'Besides, if I wait too long, I might change my mind.'

'But—' Brunetti started to say.

Bocchese cut him off. 'Please, Guido. This will be the last of it.' Then, boldly, 'You can help me say goodbye to them.'

Brunetti's decision was a fine calculation that took in the

person who asked, the subject of the request, the time it would take to walk there and back home, and Paola's probable reaction. Thus it was some time before Brunetti said, 'I could come at nine-thirty.'

Bocchese agreed and smiled, and they shook hands on the deal. Bocchese gave him his address, then explained how to get there; knowing the *sestiere* number would be of little help. Brunetti turned and started towards the door.

Bocchese looked down and saw his handkerchief on the floor, put his hand on his desk to brace himself and bent to pick it up. When he stood, Brunetti was already at the other end of the laboratory. Bocchese watched him disappear.

# 13

Brunetti timed it perfectly: he told Paola he had to meet someone after dinner just as she was placing a large bowl of fusilli with scampi and the season's first asparagus – Spanish but perfectly fine – on the table and had turned to get the bowl of grated *parmigiano* from the counter. Distracted by a question from Raffi, she nodded when Brunetti told her and concentrated her attention on feeding her family.

After the *torta di ricotta e limone*, given to Paola by an English friend who had grown up in Venice, he went into the living room with her, explaining only that he had to go and meet a member of the force who said he wanted to talk to him informally. But first he wanted to drink a coffee in the peace and comfort of his own home.

'Talk about what?' Paola asked, curious that he would agree to go out to meet someone after dinner.

Brunetti smiled and said, 'I won't know that until he tells me, will I?'

'Is he a drinker, or could it be drugs?' she asked, showing a certain lack of imagination in what a man might want to talk about with another man. 'How old is he?' she finally thought to ask.

'In his sixties, I'd say, but not far into them. I think he doesn't come into much contact with criminals.'

'Most of us don't, thank God,' Paola said, and then, 'Strange, though, if he works in the Questura.'

Brunetti began to say something and then looked off at the rooftops visible from the sofa. 'I never thought of that before. He's surrounded by the physical evidence of crime every day: he measures the knives, tests for the presence of poison, and determines the gun the bullets came from.' Reminded of another job Bocchese took care of, he added, 'He's also our armourer.'

'Which means?' she asked, looking up from that day's *Gazzettino*, which she had saved for dessert.

'He checks our guns for us and keeps them working.'

'You make it sound like Dodge City, Guido,' she said, shaking the pages of the newspaper to voice her displeasure with the idea of guns. 'How many times have you ever fired yours?'

'Do you mean the total number of bullets I've used or the times I've gone to the shooting range?' he asked, seeking clarification in what he knew was one of the subjects on which they held similar views.

When she didn't say anything, he decided to answer both questions and have done with it. 'I've been to the firing range ten times, perhaps, in all these years. Maybe fifteen.'

'And the bullets?'

'I never counted. Sometimes, if there were a lot of people waiting, I left without bothering to shoot, so I imagine the number is lower than the average. Whatever that is.'

'What would you do if someone pointed a gun at you?' she asked, but the way she said it made it seem impossible, like asking a person what animal he'd like to be if he could be any animal he wanted.

'Try not to move so they aren't frightened into shooting,' Brunetti answered.

After some time, Paola responded. 'The American police prove that's a useless tactic.'

'Oh, Americans,' he said with a dismissive wave of his hand. 'Their police shoot at anything that moves. Especially if it's lying on the ground.'

He decided this subject would lead them nowhere, so, after glancing at his watch, he stood and said he would be back before midnight.

He crossed the Rialto and cut towards San Marco so that he could walk alongside the water and, if he walked quickly enough, see whether the moon had risen from behind the Lido. Nature did not disappoint, and the last part of his walk was so bright – there was a bit of help from the artificial lights along the way – that he could easily have read, had he so pleased. Surprisingly, there were few people; perhaps the tourists were still at dinner.

He turned into the first *calle* after Ponte del Sepolcro and was soon in Campo de la Bragora. They had been taken here as students to see the book that recorded Vivaldi's baptism in the church of San Giovanni, not that any of them knew what or who Vivaldi was, or cared. It was only another drop in the depthless sea of culture in which this group of fifteen-year-old plankton was destined to float for the rest of their school years. He remembered how the names used to overwhelm him: Doge this and Doge that, Admiral up and Admiral down, the Battle of Lepanto and the Battle of Zara, and the endless triumphant buildings: basilica, church, *palazzo*, docks, warehouses; even the boats had noble names.

He'd gone along with it all, sort of paying attention, looking around, sometimes not, occasionally struck by majesty or splendour, even glory, until one day, alone in front of the Frari, he'd suddenly understood how gracefully the gigantic church rested on its foundations and how the empty *campo* in front and at its side only increased the beauty. And he was part of it. And it was part of him.

So distracted was he by his memory of past glory that he had already taken a few steps into Calle della Morte before he realized he had gone too far and turned back into Bragora. He paused after two steps to look around the *campo*. There was the Vivaldi church, there were the stores selling souvenirs, the coffee store, off to the left, an enormous hotel that looked like a monastery, and might well once have been one. A few centuries ago. There were benches under the trees, emptied by the growing chill in the air. He was suddenly amazed by how, under the glow of stronger night lighting in the streets, he could see the waving surface of the pavement, the roots of the trees pushing ever upward.

Satisfied that his memory held the proper image of this *campo*, Brunetti turned into Calle Terazzera and walked down to the canal at the end. Some light reached him from a street lamp on the other side of the canal; he found Bocchese's name on the wall of the last house and rang the top of the three bells; thought he heard it sounding from above. He waited for some time and pressed the bell again, this time for much longer, and heard the sound once again.

He went and stood with his back against the house on the other side of the *calle* and looked up at the third floor. Lights were on, but dimly, as though the lamps were located at the back of the room or rooms. He thought of calling up to Bocchese, but the windows were closed and, given the distance, it was unlikely Bocchese would hear him anyway.

Bocchese could have gone out to dinner, Brunetti thought, or been delayed, or he could be at the rear of the house and not have heard the bell. Brunetti walked down to the water to see if the lights at the back were on. To be at the proper distance to check them, he would have to climb down the stairs leading to the water and look back, but the algae-covered steps warned him not to try it. He rang the doorbell again. Hearing only some faint noise, he turned and walked back across Campo de la Bragora, following the curve to the right until he was again on Riva degli Schiavoni. He headed towards San Marco, stopped to look up and down the *riva*, resumed walking and turned again into Calle del Dose, then back to the *campo*, and stood once more under Bocchese's windows. Futilely, he rang the bell again. Same same: bell ringing and no response. But if Bocchese said nine-thirty, then he would be home at nine-thirty.

Brunetti tried the door. It was closed. Then he did what he told recruits they should never so much as think of doing: he took his wallet from his pocket and pulled out his boat pass, which gave access to the entire transport system of the city. Thin, resilient, tough. 'Rather like me,' he muttered under his breath as he bent forward to insert the card to the right of the keyhole. It slipped effortlessly into the space, creating that easily recognizable muffled click that locks so enjoy making, and the door snapped open.

Standing in the entrance hallway, feeling a fool for not having thought simply to try to call Bocchese, Brunetti pulled out his phone, found Bocchese's number and punched it in, embarrassed that he had left this simple solution so late. He heard the first buzz, then, after eight rings, a male voice answered very softly, 'Yes?'

'It's me, Enzo. Guido.'

'Come up.' It was Bocchese's voice, tight and, yes, nervous.

The door behind him clicked again, but he was already inside. Brunetti pushed it shut. 'Coming,' he said, for some reason speaking as softly as Bocchese. He started up the steps. A filthy cloth lay in the corner of the first landing. He ignored it.

There was enough moonlight to illuminate the staircase and

on the wall was the tiny, ever-lit switch that would turn on the light.

Because the stairway was near the front of the house, Brunetti could hear random noises from outside. From time to time, one of the boats moored in the canal hammered against the wall. He continued up and saw the name 'Porpora' beside the door from behind which issued the steady thud of some sort of angry music. The other door on that landing was decorated with a bouquet of blue balloons celebrating the birth of a baby boy. He started up the remaining flight.

Laughter rose from the floor below, the kind of laughter machines produced for television. He tried to hear if the laughter covered any other noise, but it did not. At the top, directly in front of him, was a door, beside it a small plate with 'Bocchese' incised into the metal.

He moved towards the door and, because of the way Bocchese had spoken, tapped lightly and said very softly, 'It's me, Enzo. Guido.' He heard some sort of shushing noise from behind the door, then the voice said, 'Stand back, please.'

Without hesitation, Brunetti stepped back and stood still, wiping all expression from his face.

The door opened a hand's breadth, stopped by the chain lock. Fingers appeared in the crack, the door opened more, and he finally saw Bocchese, peering out at him from a darkened room. The door closed to allow him to remove the chain, and then Bocchese pulled it fully open. A pistol hung heavily from his hand, pointing at the floor.

Brunetti waited, immobile, to be told what to do, well aware of how situations like this could become deadly in the passing of an order or the motion of a hand.

Using his normal voice, he said, 'I don't have a gun, Enzo, so maybe you could put yours away.'

Bocchese looked down at his hand, and Brunetti saw him jolt

in surprise when he saw the pistol there. Bocchese stepped back from the door to let Brunetti into the apartment. 'My God, I'm sorry, Guido,' he said and set the gun on a small table near the door. 'It's not loaded. They never gave me any bullets.'

Bocchese closed and locked the door before turning back to Brunetti. It was only then, in the brighter light of the apartment, that Brunetti saw the dark stains on the front of the grey jacket Bocchese wore. Now that he was closer to him, Brunetti noticed that Bocchese's nose was swollen, and had faint traces of blood below it.

'The bastard tripped me,' Bocchese said without introduction, in a savage voice Brunetti had never heard him use.

'The kid downstairs?'

Bocchese nodded. 'After I came in and started up the stairs, I saw him above me, coming down. We ignored each other, the way we always do, but when I went past him, he banged into me and I lost my balance and knocked my nose against the railing.' He reached out and wrapped his fingers around Brunetti's upper arm. 'It's nothing, Guido. It must look bad, but it's really nothing. I didn't even fall, just banged my nose.' Then, smiling, he added, 'I've had far worse things happen in fights, believe me.'

Seeing that smile, Brunetti believed him. Bocchese had grown up on the Giudecca, after all.

'Lots of blood on my jacket. But nothing's broken, not even my nose. Hurts like hell, though.'

'Did anyone hear it?'

'With that music blaring?'

'Where else are you hurt?'

'My pride,' Bocchese said, trying to laugh it off.

Neither of them spoke for some time, until a reflective Bocchese said, 'This damned kid knows he's pretty much untouchable until he's eighteen.'

'Most of them know it now,' Brunetti agreed, and asked, 'Are you going to report it?'

Bocchese laughed at the idea, the real laughter of a cynic proven right. 'He's a minor. Nothing will come of it.'

'At least it will be put in his file,' Brunetti said.

Bocchese's laugh grew louder. 'Which no one is allowed to see.' He threw up his hands and said, 'But you know this already, for God's sake.'

Then, as though he'd recalled the proper behaviour with a guest, Bocchese asked, 'Can I offer you something to drink, Guido?'

'No. Thanks, Enzo. If I drank anything now, I'd be awake all night.' Always best to begin a conversation with a lie, Brunetti said to himself. He went over and sat on the sofa.

Bocchese crossed the room and brought back a chair. He sat and looked at Brunetti, then said, 'You're the first person from the Questura to come here.'

'I'm honoured, then, Enzo,' Brunetti said, using what he hoped sounded like a cheerful voice. He'd spent his time since entering to look at a house that might have passed directly to Bocchese from Brunetti's parents: there was the same cheap parquet, single-glazed windows, plump green velvet upholstery on the sofa and chairs. Before the silence could grow again, Brunetti continued, looking interested, not impatient. 'You said the buyer will let you keep any three you want,' he began. 'Must be a difficult choice.'

'Yes,' Bocchese said, his hands running to one another for support. 'And it's not even necessary any more that we do this today. His flight was cancelled, so he's got two more days here. We could wait another day before going to the bank.'

'Why don't we do it now, anyway? After all, I'm already here.' Brunetti looked at his watch. 'It's after ten, Enzo. Let's begin it, and then it will be done.'

Bocchese cleared his throat but then found it impossible to

speak. He stood and started towards the back of the apartment, waving his hand in an invitation for Brunetti to follow him.

Brunetti got to his feet and trailed the other man down a corridor that led, he thought, towards the canal. Bocchese paused outside the second door on the right, turned to see that Brunetti was with him, opened the door, reached inside and patted around until a light came on.

Brunetti followed him in and saw that the room was large: perhaps a wall had been removed sometime in the past to make one room out of two. There was only one long wooden table, its surface covered with a herd, a flock, a gaggle of bronze statues. At first, Brunetti noticed the humans: gods and goddesses sitting and standing; a muscle-bound man on one knee, squeezing the Nemean lion to death; a very silly but very pretty Apollo with a gold cape thrown over one arm; but then he noticed a goat that looked like he was up to no good, a very stout war horse, and a sleeping lion. There could have been twenty, perhaps twenty-five.

In the very last row, a little apart from the others, Brunetti recognized the Venus he could not stop himself from thinking of as 'his', not in the sense that he had some claim to it but because it was the first statue to which he had felt an emotional response. She remained as she was the first time he saw her: ultimately unattainable, beautiful as a woman could be, but always as remote and private as the goddess she really was.

'They're all sold?' he asked Bocchese.

'Yes – that is, agreed to be sold – except for my three. Unless you can convince me to change my mind.' Bocchese avoided temptation and kept his eyes on Brunetti. 'Can you guess which ones they are?'

'Let me look again.'

'See if we'd save the same ones,' Bocchese said, and for the first time that evening, his face relaxed.

Brunetti moved closer to the table and began to walk down one side, looking at the human figures. 'May I touch them?' he asked Bocchese.

'Of course.'

Brunetti reached out, then down and up, in the manner of a crane, and lifted the statue of what looked like a woman wearing a helmet and armour. 'I'd save her,' Brunetti told him. 'And of course my old friend, Venus,' he said, taking her from her place and putting her down next to the Athena.

'And the third?' Bocchese asked.

'Probably the Hercules,' Brunetti said as he took the statue from its place in the penultimate row and looked more closely at it. 'The muscles are on the edge of vulgarity, aren't they?' he asked, holding out the god towards Bocchese.

Bocchese gave something that sounded like a laugh, took the statue, and set it down on the other side of Venus. 'We match with Venus and Athena, but my third is definitely this,' he said, reaching to the statue of a dog who seemed to be yapping at the herd of humans lined up ahead of him. 'I've never seen anything like this before. It could have been made yesterday.'

Brunetti was about to suggest that it might well have been, but the goddess of good sense intervened, and he remained silent. 'He's certainly beautiful.'

He lowered himself to be level with the top of the table and looked at the four statues now standing near the edge. He turned the dog a bit to the side and liked him more. Even with the extra muscles, the Hercules was still beautiful, and the Athena was wondrous. But it was still Venus who won a place in his heart, as she had from the beginning.

He put his hand on the table, pushing himself to his feet, and was surprised to hear himself ask, 'You're really going to sell them?'

'Yes.'

Brunetti realized that to ask Bocchese why he was doing this would be invasive and would force him to confront his own cowardice, but the thought that his friend was being frightened into losing what he loved most both angered and worried Brunetti.

Before he could speak, Bocchese said, 'I suppose it's what parents feel when their daughter is getting married. She's going off to a new home, and she'll never be theirs any more. The waiting is painful.'

Saying nothing, Brunetti took a few steps towards the door and finally said, 'Thanks for giving me a chance to see them all.' Then, risking it, he added, 'I think you shouldn't sell them, Enzo.'

Bocchese held up his hand and stopped him halfway between the table and the door. Pointing back to the statues and apparently having decided to ignore Brunetti's remark, he asked, 'Do you notice anything about the way they're lined up?'

Brunetti turned and studied the objects on the table until he noticed one thing and said, 'You put most of the best ones at the back.'

A smile took over Bocchese's face. He put his hand on Brunetti's arm and said, 'Thank you, Guido. Thank you.'

Honestly confused, Brunetti asked, 'For what?'

'For noticing.'

'Noticing what?'

'That the best ones are at the back.'

'I don't understand, Enzo.'

'I put them in chronological order.' Then he quickly added, 'Except for Venus. She was one of the first.'

Brunetti raised his chin to ask for greater clarification.

'The ones in front are the ones I bought first, and after that they're lined up according to the year I bought them, the most recent at the back.'

After what seemed a very long time, Brunetti gave a very small 'Ah,' and then said, 'It's a kind of history of your taste, then?' he asked. 'As it gets better.'

Bocchese looked away, still smiling, then stuck his hands in his pockets and walked over to the table. He stopped, looking at the collected statues. His family? His past? His beloved? His folly? Brunetti had no idea.

Bocchese pointed to the figures that covered so much of the table, 'I didn't realize that until tonight,' he said.

Suddenly no longer willing to prolong this conversation, Brunetti said, 'Everything has an end, Enzo,' wished him good night, shook his hand with real affection, and started back home.

Paola was asleep with a book lying open on her stomach. He removed her glasses and folded them closed, put them on the nightstand, and switched off her reading light. He got into bed, rolled onto his back, and closed his eyes. Ten minutes later, he moved to his right side, but he still saw Bocchese in his bloody jacket, looking at his collection.

When the nearest bell sounded twice, Brunetti switched on his light and drew the Marquis de Custine into bed between himself and his comatose wife. After a few pages, he realized that it was an act of grace and charity from above that Paola Falier, daughter of a count, whose ancestor had been doge almost a thousand years ago, had been spared hearing her husband, had he chosen to, read aloud Custine's question: 'What explosion of revenge against autocracy is being prepared by a cowardly aristocracy's abdication of its responsibilities?'

# 14

The next morning, Brunetti got to the Questura well before nine so as to have time to go and speak to Bocchese and see how his spirits were. Brunetti himself felt the emotional weight of their meeting; heaven alone knew how a person as restrained as Bocchese would have reacted to their time together and its exposure of deep feelings. When Brunetti got to the laboratory, Bocchese was not at his desk. The technicians had no idea where he could be: he was always on time. No, he hadn't called, had not sent a message to any of them.

Very casually, Brunetti said he'd gone over to see him at home the previous evening because the technician had asked him to stop by to discuss something. And he'd seemed fine. The other technicians failed to disguise their surprise at this invitation from the notoriously solitary Bocchese.

'Ask him to call me when he comes in, would you?'

'Yes, sir.'

By eleven, word of Bocchese's absence had spread through the Questura. With no one giving them orders, the technicians decided among themselves to do an inventory – if that was the right word – of the instruments, tools and implements in the lab while at the same time drawing up a list of the things that needed to be replaced or discarded, adjusted or sharpened.

In the meantime, Brunetti had in vain tried Bocchese's home number. There was no answer.

Finally, having picked up the general nervousness, he went down to Signorina Elettra's office to see if she perhaps had some other phone number listed for Bocchese. As it happened, Patta arrived at his office just as she was explaining that she had nothing more than Bocchese's landline. Hearing the name, Patta asked why they wanted the number of the chief technician, surprising them both that he should know even this much about Bocchese.

He surprised them again by adding, 'He's always here, isn't he?'

'It seems today he's not,' Signorina Elettra answered. 'I've called his private number a few times, but there's no answer.'

The Vice-Questore remained silent for some time, then said, 'He fixed my watch for me, some years ago.' Then, as Brunetti knew he would, Patta added, 'It's an IWC. I wouldn't let anyone in this city even open it to look.' Brunetti heard the peculiar emphasis Patta put on the words 'this city', as though he'd found himself in a village in the Amazon.

Signorina Elettra smiled and said, 'Yes, he's very clever.'

'Sick?' Patta asked.

'No, never, that I know of.'

'Then someone should go and check on him,' the Vice-Questore said. Brunetti saw Patta's fingers make the sign of the horns to ward off bad luck and joined him in the wish.

'I'll ask Foa to go,' she said. 'He can get there in no time.'

'Good,' Patta said, pleased to have responded like a determined leader. Then, as an afterthought: 'Why don't you go along with him, Brunetti? I'd like him to know how concerned we all are for his well-being.'

Brunetti studied Patta's face for a moment, then studied his words and found himself believing that Patta was honestly pre-occupied with the well-being of one of his officers. 'How very kind of you, Dottore,' he said, trying to disguise his surprise that, after all these years, he could finally say this to him and mean it.

Soon after, he and Foa stepped on board one of the police launches and headed towards Bocchese's home, even though both of them knew they could walk there in the same time. The morning was warm and bright and filled with the promise of good things: sun, warmth, flowers sneaking back where they belonged. Foa did not hurry, and Brunetti stood on deck, his nose raised to gather all the scents he could, his eyes open to colours that winter had kept from him for months.

Foa pulled up in Rio della Pietà, slowed, and stopped the boat. Without being asked, Brunetti grabbed the rope, jumped onto the *riva*, and tethered the boat to the metal ring in the pavement. Before Foa could ask, Brunetti said, 'It's this house on the right.'

Foa turned off the engine and locked the doors to the passenger cabin. That done, he joined Brunetti on the *fondamenta*.

Standing where he had been not many hours before, Brunetti pushed the bell and listened for any sound that came down towards them. Only a far-off chiming reached them. Brunetti rang the bell again, leaving his finger for a long time, with the same semi-result of a far-off noise.

'What do we do, Commissario?' Foa asked.

'We follow the Vice-Questore's orders,' Brunetti answered without hesitation, and pulled his boat pass from his pocket.

Arriving at the door to Bocchese's apartment, Brunetti knocked with all the authority and confidence of a police officer doing his job, then called Bocchese's name twice. Neither had any effect. He tried the handle, and the door opened with no resistance.

He hadn't noticed, the night before, that the corridor had no access to light from outside, at least not if the doors to the rooms on both sides were closed, as they were now. Blind in the new darkness, Brunetti tapped along the wall to the right until he found a switch and pressed it, causing two tired bulbs to do their best to illuminate the corridor in front of them.

'What's this?' Foa asked, casting his eye down the right side of the corridor and back on the left, where there were eight white platforms nailed to the walls. Brunetti had not noticed them the night before.

'I suppose they're places where he puts some of the things he likes the best.'

'What sort of things?'

'Small bronze statues, the things he sometimes brings to work on in the lab.'

'How do you know that, Commissario?'

'He talks about them sometimes, describes them.'

'What sort of things does he say about them?'

Brunetti was at a loss to understand where this was leading. Had Foa never felt the attraction of a beautiful object? 'He's talked to me about how lifelike they are. The way they're posed, the way their clothing seems real, how attractive their faces are.'

'Even though they're so small they fit on those shelves on the walls?' Foa asked, waving vaguely towards the empty platforms.

'Yes.'

The pilot nodded. 'Small things can be beautiful, too? Is that it?'

Brunetti smiled and said, 'Babies are, aren't they?'

After a moment's confusion, Foa got it and laughed out loud. 'Oh, that's very clever, Commissario. Babies and statues. I hope I can remember it to tell my wife when I get home.'

Enjoyable as it might be to discover a new side to Foa, they still had to find Bocchese, or discover where he had gone.

'Let's have a look around,' Brunetti said and started down the corridor, opening the doors and glancing inside as he went.

There was order in the kitchen: no food left out, no plates in the drying space above the sink. The table had a grey linoleum top; in the centre was a tin tray holding salt, *peperoncino*, olive oil, and toothpicks, all covered with a light layer of dust.

As they walked through the rooms, it became more and more difficult to view it as a normal police visit, when really it was an invasion of a friend's privacy.

That view shattered, however, when they entered what must be Bocchese's bedroom. Lying on the floor – in what crime novels often refer to as a 'pool of blood' – was Bocchese. He was fully dressed, wearing the bloodied jacket he'd had on the night before, and lay on his back like a man doing the backstroke, his left arm stretched out to its full extent behind his head, which was turned sharply to the right, obscuring that side of his head and face.

Bocchese's right arm lay close beside his right leg, palm downward, as though he were about to push it up into the air, only to straighten it out and slap it down in the water to help pull his body forward, away from where it was.

The front of his beige pants was darkened by urine. It smelled.

The blood, Brunetti saw, was no longer wet but had solidified into a disgusting paste to the right of his head, a lopsided halo that had slipped down and under his right shoulder. There was no sign of blood anywhere else in the room, and the circle beneath his head was only the size of a dinner plate.

When he glanced aside at Foa, Brunetti saw him doubled over, making a low, guttural noise, as though he'd been punched in the stomach, and then a rasp of deep breathing that failed to be deep enough.

'*Oddio, oddio,*' muttered Foa.

Brunetti made no attempt to summon the deity, but instead remembered the drill they'd been trained to use when they found a scene like this. He knelt and picked up Bocchese's hand, searching for his pulse with nervous fingers. He hoped for any trace of motion, even something that would come next in line before nothing.

Brunetti was swept with remorse: he had not said good night properly when he left, had spoken coolly to Bocchese, telling him – how horrible it sounded now, in memory – that everything has an end. Even as he remembered this, he felt that the hand he was holding was warm, not the cold flesh of the dead. He closed his eyes and got to his feet, feeling wobbly. Pulling out his phone, he put in the number of the ambulance service at the hospital, gave his name and said that a police officer had been attacked and they were to send an ambulance immediately. He gave them directions and told them they'd see the police launch and could dock behind it.

He heard a noise from the other end of the line as the person who took the call used another phone to ring the ambulance driver and report the call, repeating what Brunetti had said about the victim being a police officer.

The voice came back to him and said the ambulance would leave in a matter of minutes and shouldn't take more than ten minutes to get to Bragora.

That done, Brunetti dialled the emergency number of the Questura and reported that Bocchese was being taken to the hospital: it looked like he had been attacked at home. No, he knew nothing, only that. And then he asked that the crime squad be sent to Bocchese's apartment. That broke him, asking for the squad that was usually headed by Bocchese, who came along to point out the overlooked and to patiently instruct his men in the nuances of violence and death.

Brunetti told the officer to hold on a moment, then slipped the phone into the pocket of his jacket and used the sleeves to wipe his face. When he was calmer, he took the phone, repeated the address, and asked the dispatcher to page Dottor Rizzardi, who was surely in the hospital, and ask him to be on the dock when the ambulance arrived. That done, he called Rizzardi's number but found, as he feared he would, that no one was answering. He left a voice message and sent an SMS asking Rizzardi to speak to the doctor in charge of Bocchese and request that he keep a special eye on him.

He went back to the bedroom and pulled the blanket from the bed, brought it out and placed it over Bocchese, pulling it up to his chin. Foa stood in front of one of the windows, staring at the house across the *calle*, apparently still incapable of speech.

'Foa, get some water from the kitchen.' As though Brunetti had spoken the magic formula, the pilot left the room and came back almost immediately with a glass.

Brunetti took it from him and walked over to Bocchese. He knelt down, pulled out his handkerchief and soaked one of the corners in the water, then used it to wipe at Bocchese's lips. He tried to remember all the things he'd been taught about emergencies and wounds and what to do when disaster struck, but he could remember nothing.

He dipped the handkerchief in the water again and set the glass aside. Carefully, he twisted the wet corner until some drops of water fell onto Bocchese's lips. Time passed, Foa had disappeared, but then he forgot about Foa and listened to the faint noises Bocchese made when breathing.

He heard the siren and moved closer to the window to listen to the sounds: the dying siren, the engine stopping, the feet and muffled voices, the footsteps as the men walked towards the house. Then on the stairs and then at the door, and then they were in the room with him.

A young doctor came in and knelt, as Brunetti had, next to Bocchese. He felt his pulse, then opened Bocchese's jacket and shirt and placed the stethoscope on his heart. He opened Bocchese's eyes one after the other and shone a light into them.

Brunetti rejoiced to see Bocchese shut one and then the other. While the doctor was doing this, two white-jacketed attendants came into the room and set a stretcher on the floor.

The doctor peered down at Bocchese and lowered his head until he was only a few centimetres from Bocchese's face. Speaking slowly and softly, he said, 'Your heart sounds all right, Signore. But we have to get you to the hospital to have a better look at you. It might hurt when they pick you up. If you understand me, make a noise or open your eyes.'

The two men were unfolding the stretcher, and the doctor waved a hand to halt them. They stopped. A low noise that was probably a groan came from somewhere in Bocchese's body.

The doctor waved his hand again, and they quickly slid it nearer the injured man.

'You can make as much noise as you want, Signore. I'm sorry – no painkiller until they take an X-ray of your head.'

He stood and the two orderlies lifted Bocchese, groaning louder this time, onto the stretcher and carried it over to the door.

At a nod from the doctor, they went through the door and, keeping the stretcher as level as possible, started down the stairs. Brunetti heard another deep moan: his heart lifted at the sound. The doctor came over to Brunetti and said, 'He's got a jagged cut on the side of his head. That's why there's so much blood. I need a scan to tell me if there's more damage. But his pulse is strong, and his eyes focus correctly.'

Brunetti was touched by the doctor's kindness in telling him, but he was a young man and would learn, with time, not to raise the hopes of anyone who knew a victim.

He had been too distracted to hear the other boat arrive, but very soon after the ambulance left, siren blaring, the crime squad arrived and set themselves to work.

# 15

Brunetti was always to remember the silence with which the crime-scene crew went to work. There was no idle talk, no unnecessary conversation. Genesin was in charge, but he spoke seldom and only to direct men to a different room or remind them of something they might have forgotten to do. They started in the kitchen, moved to the bedroom and bathroom, and paused only when Genesin asked them a question or told them what to do next.

The first thing that caught Genesin's eye was a bronze statue that lay in a corner about a metre from the edge of the ring of blood. Brunetti saw him stop, motionless, for a second and then get down on his knees. As Brunetti watched, the technician bent over the statue and studied it before moving in a complete circle around it, taking a photograph each time he moved to a new point. He pocketed his *telefonino* and pulled a roll of plastic Ziploc bags from one of the pockets on his chem suit, ripped one off and slid the statue inside with the tip of his pen. He sealed it and wrote something on the outside label.

'Rodella,' he called, and handed the bag to him when he came.

When Genesin got to his feet, Brunetti asked, 'What was that?'

'One of the statues. Looks like a woman wearing a pointed hat, or maybe a helmet. Whatever it is, it's got blood on it.'

For anyone not taking part in the search, time passed slowly. Brunetti was standing in the corridor, talking with one of the men, when Rodella stuck his head out of the door to the room where Bocchese had shown Brunetti his collection. 'Could you come here, Commissario?' he asked shakily. Brunetti and the two men with him turned and started towards the room, lured by the fear in Rodella's voice.

When he entered the room, Brunetti was stunned. There was no need for fear, only shock, even horror, for the statues no longer covered part of the table. Instead, they were strewn around the room, some intact, some missing arms or legs or even their heads, ripped from their bodies. Some of them had been rubbed together, leaving long scratches on the patina of centuries; some had been thrown on the floor and stomped on, driving their faces into the parquet.

'Don't touch anything,' Genesin said unnecessarily. Though the technicians did not know the names of the victims of the massacre, some of them remembered seeing them in the lab, Bocchese's guests, come to have a shine or a polishing or perhaps even a foot set right. Thus they viewed the treatment the statues had received as an outrage and yearned to be of help to them, if only they knew how.

Because it had to be done, the search and dusting of Bocchese's apartment continued. Brunetti decided to remain, aware that nervousness and surprise had prevented him from registering much the night before except that the apartment was ugly. It confused Brunetti to think that the same sensibility that had brought the occasional beautiful Renaissance bronze piece into the lab to polish or repair or simply to show him could live in these rooms.

Genesin approached and placed a hand on Brunetti's arm. 'Commissario,' he said, 'we found something else. Could you come and have a look?' Without waiting for an answer, the man turned and went towards the kitchen. The refrigerator door had been left open – carelessness that Bocchese would not have tolerated. Brunetti saw that it held a bottle of white wine and two oranges.

The technician walked towards the open door to the closet at the back of the room and stopped, still outside. Brunetti followed and stopped as well, next to him. He glanced into the closet and saw a room he'd seen scores of times in his life. Grandmother's legacy: the Orderly Closet, with pasta and grains on the top shelf, unopened packages with faded lettering to the left, opened packages – all neatly held closed by clothes pegs – to their right. At least the packages were not in alphabetical order. He wondered if Bocchese had ever handled anything in the closet.

Below them were cans, mostly *pelati* or beans, two jars of olives, one of black and one of green, and on a lower shelf sweet things: honey, sugar, four sorts of sweet biscuits. Brunetti pulled out the unopened kilo box of rice and saw that it had expired six years before. The next shelf held small jars with the names carefully printed on them: rosemary, tarragon, mint, oregano, the labels peeling off, the leaves desiccated. The red peppers had no label. Lastly, on the bottom shelf, a few packages of herbal teas and coffee.

'What is it?' he asked Genesin, keeping to himself the thought that the last person to use anything in this closet had probably been Bocchese's mother.

'Not the shelves, Commissario. In those bags.' So saying, he pulled Brunetti inside and pointed to three shopping bags hanging on three nails on the back of the door, invisible to anyone who merely looked inside. They were bags that any Venetian would recognize: La Casa del Parmigiano, Mascari, La Baita, which clustered together at the Rialto market in almost the same propinquity as did these bags, hanging side by side in peaceful invisibility. Three bags in a row and then a fourth nail holding a neatly ironed kitchen towel. It made Brunetti think of the opening of Beethoven's Fifth: 'da da da DUM', another idea he chose to keep to himself.

Mistaking the reason for Brunetti's silence, the officer said, 'Everything's been checked, sir. You can touch them.'

Nodding his thanks, Brunetti reached for the first bag, remembering the mascarpone-covered gorgonzola they sometimes sold at Christmas, and was amazed by its weight as he took it from the hook. His surprise slowed his reaction, and the bag banged against his thigh before he yanked it to a stop just below his knees. Turning to Genesin, he said, 'Dio buono, what's in here?'

'Take a look, Commissario,' the officer answered, and stepped away from a waist-high shelf where Brunetti put the bag.

Brunetti pulled it open and saw nothing but crushed plastic wrap. Peeling that aside, he saw a shoulder he recognized and drew out the statue of the sleeping lion. He set the bag down quickly and wiped his hands on his trousers.

Again, Genesin assured him. 'It's all right, sir. You can touch everything in there. We dusted for prints and photographed them.'

'You found these here?'

'Yes, sir,' he said, taking down the second bag and handing it to him.

Inside was the statue of Apollo, and in the third, as Brunetti knew – because he'd felt it from the outside before he looked – was the dog, seeming too tiny and inoffensive to be put by himself in such a large bag.

Genesin took them from Brunetti and put them back where they had been found, on the back of the door. 'They told me they'd searched the kitchen, but I know these guys, so I decided

to take another look.' His voice softened and he said, in mitiga-
tion of his team, 'The bags were on the back of the door, so they
weren't visible when they came in here.'

'And you found them,' Brunetti said, calmly, gesturing towards
the three bags.

'Yes, sir. And the minute I took a look in the first one and saw
how old it looked, I knew it was important.' There was, strangely
enough, no self-praise in the way Genesin spoke: he had simply
been doing his job.

'Good work.'

'Thank you, sir.'

'Do you have any idea how long ...' Brunetti began, but
stopped when he realized that the lab was no longer in the
hands of Bocchese.

Genesin's face tightened and he said, 'We don't know anything, sir.'

'You've been working in the lab a long time, haven't you?'
Brunetti said, not really asking a question.

'Yes,' he said. 'More than twenty years. He's been very good
to us, you know.'

'Yes, I do know,' Brunetti said. 'To me, too.'

Genesin pulled his lips together, and Brunetti wondered if it
was to prevent himself from saying something wrong. 'He
always liked it when you came to visit. Said you were the only
person who understood how beautiful things could be.'

'His eye is much better,' Brunetti said instantly, stating the truth.

'I never understood it, not really.'

'What?'

'Why some things could be more beautiful than others.'

Brunetti was at first flattered that Genesin would entrust him
with a confession like this, until he realized that, for Genesin,
this was the way things were for most people, and there was

nothing at all unusual about it, surely nothing that had to be 'confessed'.

Brunetti asked when he thought the team would finish, and the technician said they were almost done: fifteen minutes, not more.

A quarter of an hour later, Brunetti paused outside the door to Bocchese's house to check his calls but found nothing he had to answer immediately, not even the two from Patta. Genesin came out and seeing Brunetti there, paused, then asked, 'Are you going back, Commissario?'

'Yes,' Brunetti answered, feeling the need to walk, even though it was a short distance. They started off and passed through Bragora, still silent. At the sight of the Pasticceria Alla Bragora, Brunetti asked, 'Coffee?'

'You know this place, too?' the officer asked, turning automatically into the *pasticceria*.

'We used to live down here. When I was a kid,' Brunetti said. 'Our big treat every Sunday was to come here and order any pastry we wanted.'

'Who?'

'My brother and I.'

'He a cop, too?'

Before answering, Brunetti asked for two coffees. Even though he was hungry, the thought of eating was not pleasant.

The coffees came. He stirred in some sugar and took a sip, then nodded. 'No, he's a technician. In charge of the radiology lab at the hospital in Mestre.'

It was the reference to a lab that turned them both to thinking about the laboratory at the Questura. 'Who'll take over while he's in the hospital?' Brunetti asked.

Genesin finished his coffee and, setting the cup back on the saucer, said, 'I've been there longest, and I usually take over when he's on vacation.'

'That's as evasive an answer as I've heard in some time,' Brunetti said.

Genesin laughed and turned towards the door. When they were walking again, he said, 'I suppose it depends on how long the substitution will be and what the Vice-Questore decides.'

'Does he know who you are?' Brunetti asked.

'Perhaps. If he ever asked about the lab or showed interest in how it runs or had much interest in what we do, then he would.'

'You don't sound very hopeful about those things.'

The officer turned his head and looked at Brunetti, then looked in front of them again. 'I'm not,' he said, and it was clear to Brunetti that the subject had best be abandoned.

They continued walking, and Brunetti was conscious of a certain nervousness in Genesin, if only in the determination with which he placed every step. The officer stopped as they reached the always closed church of Sant'Antonin and walked around to the front door. He waited until Brunetti was standing beside him, then said, slipping into Veneziano, 'I'll never get the job, anyway. I argued with Scarpa.'

'About what?'

'How he treated one of the translators.'

'A man or a woman?' Brunetti asked, also now speaking in dialect and knowing what the answer would be.

Genesin turned to face Brunetti and said, 'A woman.'

'If that's the case,' Brunetti said, 'you're right.'

Genesin closed his eyes and gave a shrug he tried to make look casual. He stood like that for some time, then looked at Brunetti again and said, 'Can I talk to you as a colleague?'

'Of course,' Brunetti said in return, meaning it.

Genesin took some time considering this, and when he did, he answered with a question. 'You know what I want to say is about Enzo, don't you?'

Brunetti nodded.

The officer paused again before he continued. 'I don't know anything for sure, but he's been nervous for some time. And short-tempered.'

He read Brunetti's lack of surprise and said, 'I know he's not the most cheerful person in the place, but he was always fair and willing to listen if someone explained a mistake or why a test failed.' He stopped, looked at Brunetti, then immediately resumed walking.

'How long has he been like this?'

'A month,' Genesin said. 'Two?'

'Is it related to the lab or someone who works there?'

'No, I don't think so. In fact, he seems relieved when there's a complicated problem or someone calls in sick and he has to do their work for them that day.' Genesin struggled to find the correct words. 'He's grumpy all the time. There's no other way to say it.'

'Has anything happened recently to cause him trouble?' Brunetti asked.

'He never has trouble.'

'He's in the hospital, isn't he?' Brunetti asked.

'Maybe he fell.' Genesin had to look away from Brunetti when he said this.

'If he left a window open, he could have been hit by lightning,' Brunetti snapped back.

Genesin put his hand to his mouth, like a person caught telling a lie. He started to speak, but his voice was suddenly drowned out by the motor of a transport boat from beyond the church, coming in from the *bacino* and heading towards them. They could have used this as an excuse to stop talking and continue towards the Questura, but neither of them moved. They waited. The boat passed under the bridge and drew up in front of a wine store on the right, just beyond the bridge. After a final growl, the engine stopped, and the man in the middle of the boat jumped up to the *riva* and secured the boat to the stanchion.

Both of them watched as he leaned down and pulled his wheeled cart from the boat and set it on the embankment. The pilot walked to the middle of the boat and started to toss cases of wine up to the other man as though they were empty boxes. When there were eight of them on the cart, the pilot sat down on another pile of boxes and lit a cigarette.

He smoked peacefully until his colleague returned, when he threw his cigarette into the water and tossed up eight more cases.

Brunetti wondered if watching this, for Venetians, was a form of meditation, like monks when they watched bees extract pollen from a flower.

Then the first man came out of the shop, lowered his dolly into the boat and jumped aboard. The motor roared, and the boat continued, its noise diminishing as it moved deeper into Castello.

Either he or Genesin, Brunetti thought, must now break the silence created by the disappearance of the boat. He thought it wiser to let Genesin be the one. After more than a minute, the officer had still said nothing, and Brunetti decided to leave it like that. They continued back to the Questura in friendly silence.

They separated once they were inside the building, Genesin back to the lab and Brunetti to his office. He phoned Vianello, newly returned from vacation, and started to explain what had happened, only to hear the Inspector say the word had already spread through the Questura, and Patta had asked if it might be possible that Brunetti come in to speak to him sometime that day. 'His words, not mine,' Vianello added.

'I'm on my way,' Brunetti said.

# 16

Brunetti went directly to Patta's office and was surprised that
Signorina Elettra was not at her desk, surprised until he remembered that it was Tuesday and thus the day she went to the Rialto
market to get fresh flowers. He thought it foolish to call Patta
when he was standing just outside his door, so he went over and
gave three quick raps.

'*Avanti*,' came the well-known voice, brusque as ever. When
he entered, Patta said, in a more civil tone, 'Ah, what news do
you have?' quite as if he believed that something could have
happened in the time it took Brunetti to walk to the Questura
from Bocchese's apartment.

'The doctor who came with the ambulance ...' Brunetti
began, and Patta waved him towards a seat. From it, Brunetti
continued: '... said his heart and visual reflexes seemed
unharmed. And he certainly was able to respond to the requests
the doctor made of him.' He paused and looked at Patta, who
sat at his desk with his fingers folded together as he listened.

'Anything else?' the Vice-Questore asked.

'There was blood on the floor from a wound on his head, but the doctor didn't seem worried about it.'

'Anything else?'

'Foa and I had looked in some of the rooms before we found him, Dottore, and nothing seems to have been disturbed except in the room at the back of the house, where he kept his collection.'

'The famous statues?' Patta asked, leaning forward.

'Yes. And whoever did this knew how much he valued them.'

'Why?'

'Because they destroyed some of them and damaged others, as if they knew that would hurt Bocchese even more than being attacked himself.' Before Patta could ask, Brunetti said, 'I don't have any idea what they're worth or what he paid for any of them, so I have no idea of what the monetary loss will be. But certainly some of them are ruined. In a way, they've been killed.'

'Do you honestly believe that, Brunetti?'

'No, sir. I don't believe it, but the statues don't belong to me, so I have to look at them the way Bocchese does, and that's the way he thinks about them.' Then, before Patta could comment or contradict him, Brunetti said, 'I could easily be wrong, of course.'

Patta nodded in agreement with that possibility and said, 'Does he have any idea who it was?'

'He wasn't in any condition to answer questions, Dottore,' Brunetti said and decided he'd say nothing about the son of the family who lived below Bocchese. In his current mood, Patta was entirely capable of sicking the dogs on the boy, even though there was no evidence yet and no way to know who had been in the apartment.

Silence descended upon them, hardly a friendly silence, but certainly not the combative mood that often filled the room when they held different views.

Brunetti got to his feet, and in the absence of any command

from Patta, said, 'I'll go back to my office, then, Signore. I'll keep
you posted on any information I get from the hospital.'

'Good,' Patta said, the word he always used in place of 'thank
you', as if the mere saying of those words would acknowledge
owing a favour.

There still being no sign of Signorina Elettra, Brunetti went
back to his own office and found that she had left a folder on
his desk.

Writing under the Vice-Questore's authority, Signorina Elettra
had sent a formal request to the Office of Human Resources for
information concerning the service in Iraq of a retired member
of the Carabinieri: Dario Monforte. This was followed by
Monforte's date and place of birth, his service number, and the
dates of his arrival in and departure from Iraq.

To Brunetti, it sounded like a routine request for information
to pass from one agency of the Interior Ministry to another.

The response, however, confused him, for it stated that the
Carabinieri could do no more than confirm that Dario Monforte
had retired from the Carabinieri for medical reasons. Given
the new rules concerning the privacy of medical information
regarding members of the order, whether serving or retired, this
request could not be granted. It was short and direct but made
reference to a rule that, to the best of Brunetti's knowledge, did
not exist.

Why wouldn't the Carabinieri provide a simple answer and
say that this man, who had been in the Carabinieri for many
years, and who had certainly been awarded medals for his
valour ... Brunetti paused there and said aloud, 'But was he?'
From there, the next question he spoke aloud was 'Who would
know?'

He turned to his computer and was suddenly excited by that
same jigsaw-puzzle rush that came when pieces began to fit
together. Surely to be awarded with a medal by your group,

even if it's only the Boy Scouts, would be an honour, not that Brunetti knew anything about them. Information about having won a medal for bravery in combat would be more important than public information like an address or place of employment: it ought to be information that people want others to know about, so it should be easy to find.

Then he began to wonder who would be interested in what sort of medal a person had won and for what activity he or she had won it. After a period of time, who is interested in information like this? Who cares? Who wants to know? Where could this information be found?

He'd left that day's issue of *Il Gazzettino* on his desk, and he began to page through it again, using it, as he often did, as a mantra that would so slow his mind as to free his memory to wander where it would. His first thought was the resemblance between his use of the *Gazzettino* and his mother's of the rosary. But nothing came.

He flipped through the local news, the sports, the financial information, and ended up looking at the obituaries and learned that Giovanni Soligon, 84, of Mira, would be buried on the coming Friday. A famous *pasticciere*, he had won the medal for the best panettone in 2002 and had twice been elected to the city council.

'Of course, of course,' he said and dialled from memory the number of a subeditor of *Il Gazzettino*. She, in her turn, gave the email address of the office of the Carabinieri in charge of overseeing the bestowal of medals and awards, and then, in a moment of excessive solidarity with a fellow researcher, provided the phone number of that office and confided that Signora Ducoli, the director, would sometimes answer both the phone and then the questions that followed.

Brunetti was suddenly nervous at the realization of how

many things he had achieved so quickly. Surely, this run of luck had to change.

But no, Signora Ducoli took down Monforte's details, appeared not to recognize his name, and reported after only a few minutes that Signor Monforte, who had retired from service almost twenty years before, had not been awarded any sort of medal, not for valour and not for length of service, and did Signor Brunetti have any other questions?

No, he did not and he was profuse in his thanks. Signora Ducoli was satisfied with his praise, wished him a busy and successful day, and replaced her phone.

Well, well, well, he thought. The Hero of Nasiriyah didn't get a medal. He got the first page of the press for some time, was mentioned in countless television news programmes, and had the covers of the magazines. Everyone had a piece of him, but Monforte himself was in the burn centre in Barcelona, where he remained while things quietened down. And he never got a medal, not even the most common ones, and surely not the better known, the Cross of Merit and the Medal of Valour.

Vox pop: his fame was given him by . . . ? Who had carried the news of his bravery back to Italy? Survivors talking to their families? The men who went to help the wounded after the fires had been extinguished? Those who went to find the dead? The two men he saved from the fires?

The Carabinieri wouldn't give basic information about the Hero of Nasiriyah. Monforte shook the hand of the President of the Republic, but he never received a medal for bravery. We all got a little tired of reading about him, but no one had the courage to say it. But then he disappeared, as if someone had finally listened to our grumbling and had taken his name and removed it, the way the Church finally got rid of all of those invented saints – how long ago was that, and who even remembers the names of the disappeared ones? Philomena, Christopher, Barbara, Nicholas, Ursula and her Virgins: demoted, stripped of their honours, named as frauds and inventions, and disposed of silently.

If it could be done with Christopher and no one noticed, how difficult could it be to dispose of a maresciallo capo? He was a hero? And what was Christopher, if not a hero?

# 17

Brunetti had been in his office for almost an hour when he heard a knock at the door and called, *'Avanti.'*

It was Salmasi, who had joined the force only a few years before. He stood in the doorway and said, 'The lawyer is here to see you, Commissario.'

'What lawyer?' Brunetti asked.

Salmasi stepped back and disappeared for a moment, then reappeared. 'Dottor Cresti. He says he has an appointment with you at four, Dottore.'

Although Brunetti could not remember any appointment, he thought it might be quicker to speak to the man and redirect him than send both of them back downstairs and have Salmasi try to find out whom the lawyer wanted to see. Brunetti nodded and made a waving gesture with his hand.

Having no further interest in the file he had been looking at, Brunetti pushed it aside but left it on his desk to serve as evidence that this lawyer, whoever he might be, was interrupting his work. Brunetti did not look up until Salmasi was again a few steps into the room, the lawyer obscured by his body. Salmasi said, 'Dottor Cresti,' saluted, and left.

His departure revealed none other than Beniamino Cresti, more commonly referred to as Beni Borsetta, this in homage to the battered leather briefcase – once beige, then a mottled brown, and now a dark mixture of brown spots and oily black – that was rumoured to have contained some legendary bribes he both paid and was paid in the days before the first of his temporary suspensions from the album of lawyers.

Ordinarily, Brunetti would not have got to his feet in the presence of this man, but he stood in the hope that politeness would be more effective in getting rid of him than the rudeness someone like Beni was surely familiar with. He was careful to remain behind his desk and to make no gesture that might suggest Beni should sit in the visitor's chair.

'You're looking very well, Commissario,' Beni began, adding a smile that was not in the least ingratiating. If anything, it was an aggressive smile, if such a thing were possible.

Beni had changed in the years since the two men had last met. His hair was thinner, but he disguised that – badly – by letting it grow long on one side and combing that over the top, bald, part of his head. His paunch was larger, and his shoulders were narrower, a combination of changes much too challenging for his jacket, which gaped where it should open, squeezed where it should be closed.

'I hope you're well, Avvocato Cresti,' Brunetti said with heavy neutrality.

'Thank you, Commissario,' Cresti said, and, uninvited, walked over and sat in the chair in front of Brunetti's desk. 'I've come on behalf of someone,' he said, setting his briefcase next to him on the floor, where it sat quietly, in the manner of a faithful dog.

'A client?' Brunetti asked with seeming innocence. He had no idea of Beni's current professional status, whether he had been readmitted to the order of lawyers, in which case he could speak of having a client, whereas if he were still disbarred, it was illegal for him to have a client at all.

Cresti smiled and crossed his legs, a manoeuvre that put further strain on the buttons of his jacket. 'Let us use an old and respectable term, shall we, Commissario?'

'That depends on the term, Dottor Cresti,' Brunetti responded with apparent respect.

'*Il mio assistito*, as those of us trained in the old school of law were wont to refer to the people we tried – in our small way – to assist.'

'And, I suspect, as those who are temporarily deprived of their licence to practise law refer to those they try – in their small way – to assist.'

Cresti laughed as though he really found Brunetti's remark funny. 'Oh, how I've missed the pleasure of exchanging remarks with you, Commissario Brunetti. Some of your colleagues, I'm sorry to have to say, don't even pretend to treat me politely, which I've always seen as an offence to our . . .' here he lowered his head in respect to what he was about to name '. . . mutual professions.'

'They no doubt are made uncomfortable by the lack of certainty as to whether they should or should not refer to you as "avvocato", your situation being so . . .' Brunetti began, his voice rich with sympathy for his own colleagues, and for Dottor Cresti as well, '. . . shall we say, "fluid", Dottore?'

Again, Cresti laughed with every sign of goodwill and amusement.

This appearance of a normal human response led Brunetti to say, 'Might we stop exchanging compliments, Dottor Cresti, and turn to whatever it is you've come here to discuss?'

'With great pleasure,' Cresti said and pulled his briefcase from beside him on the floor, set it on his lap, and opened it.

Brunetti heard the rustle of papers as Cresti hunted through the bag. Finally, he pulled out a simple transparent plastic folder, replaced the bag, extracted the papers and put them on his lap, and then began to page through them.

Brunetti made no attempt to hurry him.

After some time, Cresti took out a single sheet of paper. He set it on top of the others, glanced at Brunetti, and said, 'You have a colleague named . . .' He looked down at the paper and then at Brunetti. He had, unfortunately, failed to prepare a bland expression before meeting Brunetti's eyes – or his feelings were too strong to be overcome – and he let a flash of rigorous malice escape his eyes. At the realization of his error, Cresti closed his eyes, as if he'd decided this would somehow erase what he might have revealed to Brunetti.

'Claudia Griffoni, I believe,' he completed.

Brunetti's expression did not change in the least. He nodded.

'Her name recalls a bird of prey, doesn't it?' Cresti asked.

'I believe so.'

'How apt,' Cresti allowed himself to observe, confusing Brunetti entirely but not inducing him to question the remark.

'But let me get on with what I've come to ask you about, Commissario.'

'Please.'

'Is it true that on the seventh of this month, at about five-thirty in the morning, Dottoressa Griffoni left the police station at Piazza San Marco and began to accompany a young man –' Cresti picked up and examined the paper on his lap with a gesture so patently theatrical that Brunetti was sure he'd rehearsed it '– Orlando Monforte, to his home at . . .' Here, Cresti glanced at the paper again and read out, '. . . Castello 3165?'

'I've not read the complete report,' Brunetti said, 'so I'm not sure of the precise time nor of the young man's address, but the basic facts are true. As you already know, if that is a copy of our report that has somehow come into your possession.'

'I'd rather not respond to your insinuation, Commissario, but the facts are pretty much the same.' He graced Brunetti with a smile and continued. 'And is it also true that she and the boy arrived at and entered a bar near Salizada San Francesco at about seven in the morning, where the boy had a pizza? And they were seen by a number of men who are neighbours of the boy?' Having finished reading, Cresti turned the paper face down and looked across at Brunetti and smiled, as one would at the revelation of the Happy Ending in a story.

'I believe that is what the report states,' Brunetti said, wondering all the while what Beni Borsetta was up to, for it was impossible for Beni to involve himself in a legal matter, no matter how trivial, without being up to something that would eventually lead to his profit or benefit. This being, of course, at the cost of some other person.

'And is it also true that Commissario Griffoni told the men in the bar that she was the mathematics teacher of this boy? And did not, as is customary, identify herself as a member of the police?'

'I don't remember reading that in the report,' Brunetti said, forcing himself to speak calmly at the same time as a grotesque suspicion was growing in his imagination.

The lawyer resumed his reading. 'Four of the men who were in the bar when she and Orlando Monforte arrived remember clearly that she presented herself in this way.'

'Oh, really?' Brunetti asked and looked down at the file on his desk as though he were eager to return to it.

Cresti picked up his paper and studied it from top to bottom. 'Ah,' he said with well-managed surprise. 'I've forgotten your own involvement in this, Commissario.'

'Since I don't know what "this" is, Dottor Cresti, there is no way I can imagine what my involvement might be.'

'Did you not go to the same bar some days later to ask the boy questions?'

'Oh, that,' Brunetti said casually. 'My colleague had given him a scarf, and she wanted to get it back.'

'Not very generous, is it?' Cresti asked.

'Why should she be generous to a boy who had been taken into the police station for disturbing the public peace?' Brunetti asked, managing to stuff a lot of indignation into his tone.

Beni smiled and said didactically, '"Accused of", surely, Commissario.' His smile was one used to reprove careless students. 'It sounds to me like the police are abusing their powers here and paying attention to one innocent boy while, apparently, paying no attention to the other boys taken to the police station with him.'

Using a voice filled with reason and restraint, Brunetti said, 'Who, also, are only accused of these things.'

'Exactly,' Cresti said and picked up his bag, slipped the file inside, then closed it and set his folded hands on it. 'All right, Commissario, let me get to the real question.'

'Thank you,' Brunetti said curtly.

'The most important question that has not been raised, but which now has to be, is the matter of where they were after leaving the police station at San Marco.'

'As far as I know, they all went home with their parents,' Brunetti answered, deliberately misunderstanding Cresti's question.

'I'm not speaking about the other young men who were taken to the station.'

'Then who *are* you talking about? Surely not Commissario Griffoni and this young man?' Brunetti asked.

'Boy.'

'I beg your pardon,' Brunetti said, this time really confused. 'He's fifteen. So he's a boy.'

'Excuse me, Signore,' Brunetti said, 'I think I know what you're aiming for, so please save me time and make it clear.'

'Where were they in the time that elapsed from leaving the police station and getting to the bar in Castello? Where were they for those two hours?'

Mildly, Brunetti said, 'I believe the time between five-thirty and seven o'clock is usually considered to be one hour and a half.'

If he did not despise the man so thoroughly, Brunetti would have admired him for this boldfaced question, like something out of a cheap nineteenth-century novel. No accusation was made directly, but wickedness was exposed by every word. A woman – and what was worse, a woman with a job – who had no desire but to seduce and despoil the innocence of youth.

Brunetti stared across at him and watched Cresti put on the trappings and dress of outraged morality. There was surely more to come of this pottage of clichés: the debased police, the predatory woman, the innocent boy, stolen hours, moon shining on the water, coffee instead of champagne. And lust, savage lust, from the insatiable (and single, and perhaps divorced) BLONDE woman from the South.

Speaking softly, as though there were a baby in the room and loud voices would wake it, Brunetti leaned across his desk and prepared to tell Cresti to get out, but curiosity, to make no mention of caution, overcame him and, instead, he asked, 'What do you want?'

# 18

As though unable to free himself from the cheap melodrama of the role he was playing, the sometime lawyer slapped his palm to his chest and declared, 'I couldn't live with myself if I were to desire anything other than to help my cli— the person I am assisting with my advice and experience.'

To Brunetti, it was pure commedia dell'arte. Cresti had been assigned, or had chosen, the role of the hero's virtuous aunt, whose purpose was to sweep accusation out of his path and upset any plot to soil his reputation.

'*La calunnia è un venticello,*' Brunetti said.

The reference was beyond Beni Borsetta's scope, so the lawyer asked, 'What's that?'

'A comment on how gossip spreads,' Brunetti told him. 'It starts very small and grows and grows until it's unstoppable.'

Cresti gave a broad smile and said, 'That's more or less what I've come to talk about, Commissario.'

'Oh, really?' Brunetti responded. 'Could you tell me more?'

'What "really" happened that early morning is known only to Orlando Monforte and Dottoressa Claudia Griffoni. They were together somewhere, but the Dottoressa, for reasons we might discuss later, makes no mention in her report of where they were.' The lawyer seemed concerned by Griffoni's lack of detail, as if suspecting she and Orlando – a minor – had passed the morning in one of Dante's more lurid circles.

Brunetti, sounding unconcerned, said, 'Presumably, they were somewhere between Piazza San Marco and Salizada San Francesco. Either one of them could walk the distance between the two places in ten, fifteen minutes.'

'Exactly,' Cresti said.

His response confused Brunetti, who had yet to understand fully what the lawyer was talking about.

'You tell me where they were, Commissario, and I'll stop wondering what . . .' and here Beni's voice revisited his previous melodramatic tone '. . . the woman police officer might have led the boy to do in the time that is not accounted for.'

The idea was so wild to Brunetti that when he finally understood, he marvelled that this was the best idea Beni – or whoever had sent him – could come up with. Brunetti had first encountered these temptresses in the epics of Ariosto and Tasso, but he doubted that Beni had read either. Brunetti, however, had known them since his student days: Alcina and Armida, beautiful, powerful queens; amoral, insatiable consumers of warriors. Beni's villainesses, on the contrary, would be more like something from a Disney cartoon, or perhaps, with effort and imagination, might rise to the level of Lucrezia Borgia. He reached out with his left hand and pulled the folder closer.

'Someone must have seen them,' Beni offered when Brunetti remained silent. 'They'd remember seeing a woman and a boy at that time of day, I think.'

Beni had no patience. Brunetti recalled this fact when the lawyer went on: 'Your men could ask around – people running bars, the garbage men, the men on the first boats that go to Piazzale Roma.'

'And if no one saw them?' Brunetti asked.

Beni looked down at his briefcase, which nestled in his lap like an affectionate, overweight dog. The lawyer must somehow have read Brunetti's mind, for he began to stroke the bag, his hand running back and forth from mouth to tail.

'If you don't think it worthwhile, Commissario, to authorize a search like that, I could tell you that a barman in one of the cafés on Riva degli Schiavoni recalls a couple like that.' The smile he gave after saying this was as innocent and plump as a baby's. He continued in the same reasonable vein. 'And if no one else saw them, perhaps they stopped somewhere.'

That Cresti now referred to them as a 'couple' put an end to any interest Brunetti might have taken in Beni's performance. 'All right, Beni,' he said in his roughest voice, the one he used when arresting men who were bigger than he was, 'that's enough for now.'

The lawyer's eyes grew large and round as he said, 'But I'm just trying to think this thing through for you, Commissario.'

This was exactly what Brunetti was trying to do: think it through. The boy was involved in an event that was of interest to the police. What better way to deflect police interest than by redirecting public interest to the siren who had drawn the boy's attention to herself, who had spent a disputable amount of time alone with him, given him her scarf, and then returned to speak with him under the guise of having come to get that scarf. It was nonsense, but it was also the stuff of television drama and thus, to many people, entirely believable. Attention would be diverted to the possible. And just how was it that Beni knew about this?

Brunetti's thoughts returned to Beni's suit jacket. The material was cheap, the buttons plastic. It did not fit him well, but it suited him perfectly. So with an investigation of Griffoni's private life: it did not fit with the facts, but it suited Beni perfectly.

Having dealt with Beni a few times, Brunetti knew the limits of his intelligence and the weakness of his character. Believing in his own superior intelligence, in the face of all evidence to the contrary, Beni was prone to complicated situations as well as to complicating situations. His only unquestioned talent was his ability to spend an inordinate number of billable hours on even the simplest case.

As to his character, he was dishonest and a liar, but he had a feral cunning that easily earned him the sympathy, sometimes even the limited trust, of people with the same faults.

If Brunetti now understood correctly, Beni was here to blackmail the police, who hardly needed even the possibility of scandal. All that remained was to find out the price. Not wanting to waste more time on the likes of Beni, Brunetti smiled across at the lawyer and asked, 'What did you have in mind that we could do to resolve this situation?'

Cresti smiled again, trying to make himself look nervous, perhaps even embarrassed. 'I'm afraid it's a bit too soon for that, Commissario. I haven't told you everything.'

Ah, thought Brunetti. It's time to pull out the short knives. 'And what have you forgotten?'

'Oh, it's not that I've forgotten, Dottore,' Beni said, with a new tone of seriousness, something floating towards respect. 'It's more that my sense of . . .'

Into Cresti's fraudulent hesitation, Brunetti was tempted to supply the word 'modesty', or how about 'decency'?

'. . . Propriety . . .' Cresti said, and Brunetti silently complimented his choice, '. . . is so shocked that I thought I would lack the ability to speak of it, even to you, a police officer.'

Brunetti wanted to praise his halting speech, no doubt the better to prepare Brunetti for the shocking news.

'I must confess that I am left without words to express my shock at what happened.'

Oh, merciful God, Brunetti thought, not this one. 'And what was that, if I might enquire?'

Cresti lowered his eyes and his voice as he said, 'Your colleague made certain suggestions to the boy, saying that she knew a place where they could be alone. It seems, as well, that she said she'd give him not only her scarf, but something else to keep him hot, not warm.'

'Why hasn't he come here to make a formal *denuncia*?' Brunetti asked, cutting him short.

Cresti tossed up his hands as a sign of his indignation. 'How can you ask such a question, Commissario? The boy's only fifteen.' From the way Cresti pronounced the number, Orlando might as well still have been in his perambulator. 'Think of the shame he would feel to be viewed as a sexual object by an adult, to have a stranger, and what is more, a stranger in a position of authority, make a sexual advance to him.'

Brunetti could do no more than lower his head, as though this were the first time he had ever heard of such a thing, and mutter, 'I understand.' He considered his choices for some time and then looked across at Cresti and asked, 'What do you suggest we do?'

The now-and-again lawyer pursed his mouth and looked across at Brunetti, as if surprised by the question. 'Well, I haven't given that much thought, but surely we can come up with some sort of amicable solution.' With a twirl of his hand that indicated he was about to make a suggestion, Beni said, 'Perhaps a kind of DASPO might be issued to Commissario Griffoni?'

'Aren't they usually issued to sports fans, to ban them from approaching the fans of rival clubs?' Brunetti asked, though he knew perfectly well what they were.

'I'm using the term in a broader sense,' Beni said mildly. 'To keep any person away from another one.'

'Isn't there usually a fine if the person who is given the DASPO violates the rules?'

'Yes,' Beni agreed with a broad grin.

'And what sort of fine could we agree on, do you think?' Brunetti asked. 'The law asks three hundred euros of the sports fans.'

'Good heavens, Commissario,' Beni said, a maiden caught naked in her bath, scandalized, shocked, insulted. 'I could not even think of imposing such a fine on a commissario of police.' Brunetti wondered if he were going to ask how he could live with that guilt. Beni did indeed continue, 'I could not . . .' but stopped, perhaps hearing the echo of the last time he used the phrase, '. . . as I said, even think of such a thing.'

'How can you be sure, then, that Commissario Griffoni will keep her part of any bargain you might agree upon?'

'Ah, I'm very glad you asked me that, Commissario. I wouldn't like to have forgotten to tell you the idea that has come into my mind,' Cresti said, giving his briefcase an affectionate pat. 'I just happen to have it here.' He disturbed his briefcase, then opened it, and started looking around for something.

The smile on Beni's face as he hunted for whatever was in his bag gave Brunetti the strange feeling that he had somehow been manipulated and outmanoeuvred, and the other man knew it.

Beni's hands stopped and he looked across at Brunetti, one hand still inside the briefcase. 'Oh, I do have a piece of news.'

'And what is that?' Brunetti asked.

'My brother-in-law's just been given a job on the *Gazzettino*.' When Brunetti did not comment, Beni said, 'You must remember the column "*in breve*" from years ago.'

Brunetti did. 'A collection of unusual stories from all over. Only two or three sentences for each story?'

'Oh, I told him people would recall it. I'm so glad you do, Commissario. He'll be so happy to know that people do remember.'

He looked down into the briefcase again and, sure enough, he had finally found what he was looking for. He pulled it out and held it up. Brunetti could see that it was a photograph. A real photo, on paper. Beni leaned forward and extended his arm, but somehow he could not manage to reach Brunetti, who had to lean forward and then finally get to his feet and stretch across his desk in order to receive the photo.

It was a photo of Griffoni in the bar in Castello, a picture of her and Orlando that captured the boy's lovelorn state perfectly, the soft eyes and half-open mouth that showed powerful emotion. And Griffoni, tough, lovely, had an ambiguous smile on her lips but not in her eyes.

'I think they're going to let him use photos in the column,' Beni said, his delight audible, as was, for the first time, his intense dislike of Brunetti.

'That certainly would grab more attention, more readers, for the column,' Brunetti said, not bothering to disguise his contempt for the lawyer and his brother-in-law.

Beni, despised and rejected of man, lost all control for an instant and smiled a very ugly smile, then added, 'Of course, the boy will have told his father all of this.' When he saw the effect of this information on Brunetti's face, his smile softened and became a real response to pleasure.

'Now,' Beni said, regaining his composure, 'let me tell you what I had in mind, my own personal DASPO for the Commissario, as it were. Or, more correctly, the new rules.' He paused here and smiled, but the smile was now devoid of any meaning save threat. Brunetti was sure he did it to prolong the pleasure he was taking in the scene. Brunetti chose silence.

Beni chose, instead, a new voice: cold, austere, precise. 'DASPO:

Forbidden to Attend the Game. She is not to go within a hundred metres of the boy.' Although Brunetti had given no sign of wanting to speak, Beni held up a hand as if to stop him. 'Nor phone him, nor accept any phone call he might make.' He stopped there and forgot about his smile, which slowly evaporated. He waited some time, but Brunetti said nothing. Finally, impatience won, and Beni asked, 'Well?'

'I'll discuss it with Commissario Griffoni,' Brunetti said.

'I think there's nothing to discuss,' Cresti responded in a voice now grown icy. He remained silent for some time, obviously preparing for Brunetti's refusal.

'That's why I came to you, Commissario,' he began in a softer voice. 'I believed – and still believe – that a person who has been with the police for as long as you have understands the importance of having an unblemished reputation. And so you might be able to persuade your colleague to follow the path of good sense.'

Brunetti wished now that he had turned on the tape recorder in his desk: what fortune he would have in being able to play back a recording of Beni Borsetta himself speaking of the importance of having an unblemished reputation.

Cresti allowed a long silence to intervene and then said, 'The results would be devastating to her career.' He got to his feet, and Brunetti thought he had finished. But Beni, like the person who could not resist the last portion of dessert left in the bottom of the serving bowl, added, with a minimalist smile, 'Regardless of the truth, or otherwise, of the accusation.' Saying this, Cresti wiped a crease out of the leather of his briefcase, tossed the photo onto Brunetti's desk, saying, 'I have more,' and left the room.

Well, Brunetti told himself, you certainly made a mess of that. He retrieved the photo. This was, more or less, the size it would be in the *Gazzettino*. He had no idea if either of the two people in the photo would be recognizable to someone who did not know them. The boy, probably not: his head was turned a bit to the side, so not all of his face was visible.

Griffoni, however, was a different matter. Because the photo was in colour, her blonde hair, looking like it had been pulled back carelessly as she got out of bed, gave silent witness to any character a viewer chose to attribute to her. The fact that the photo had been taken in a bar, with her sitting at a table with a man – Brunetti recognized the back of his own head – was perhaps less a testament to her suitability as a defender of law and justice than the average *Gazzettino* reader would accept. Or desire. Nor would her notoriety be pleasant to her police superiors.

He picked up his phone and dialled her extension. The phone rang four times before being transferred to her *telefonino*. She picked up on the seventh ring, saying, 'Is that you?'

'Yes.'

'You're in your office?'

'Yes.'

'What is it?'

'I need to talk to you.'

'This isn't?'

'Isn't what?'

'Talking to me.'

'No.'

There was some delay. He heard another voice, a man's, and then Griffoni said something he couldn't understand.

Then she was back, asking only, 'Trouble?'

'Yes.'

'I'll be there in twenty minutes.' She was gone.

# 19

Brunetti refused to look at his watch. If Griffoni said twenty minutes, then however long it took, it would be, to him, twenty minutes. He looked at the file he had stopped reading for lack of interest and failed to find the energy to return to it. It was not that he did not understand the words or the sentences: they were perfectly clear. But he didn't care about what they recounted.

He went to the window and stared at the vines that had started their yearly pilgrimage up the inside of the fence around the house on the other side of the canal. As spring advanced, it would creep over the top of the fence and head down towards its real object, the water of the canal, only to stop ten centimetres above it, once again deceived by the intoxicating smell of water into forgetting that it was salty and thus poisonous. Grown too long and thus too heavy to retreat, the vine would remain suspended there, waiting for rain, needing rain, shrivelling from the lack of rain, watching pieces of itself fall into the water, blessed water, cursed water, and slowly float towards the *bacino* or away from it until run over by a boat or killed by the water or the sun, sinking down to mingle with the arsenic, mercury, cadmium, and lead that lay sleeping on the bottom of the canals.

He heard a noise, and Griffoni said, '*Ciao*, Guido,' as she came into his office. Not smiling, she asked, 'Should I close the door?'

'Yes,' he told her and went back to his desk.

Griffoni came over to sit in front of him. She studied his face and posture for a moment and said, 'It looks bad. Tell me.'

'I had Beni Borsetta in here an hour ago, asking what you and that boy got up to when you were walking him back to Castello to deliver him to his family.'

'Was that Beni's phrase, "got up to"?' she asked.

'Words to that effect. I was so surprised when he showed up here that I didn't think of recording what he said.'

She shrugged. 'What else did he ask? Or say?'

Brunetti was uncertain how to repeat Cresti's information to her. 'He's got it into his head . . .' he began. 'No, he's got something else in his head, but this is his first step, to make it look like you are to be the Whore of Babylon, seducer of young boys.'

Griffoni crossed her legs and placed her elbows on the arms of the chair, hands folded in her lap. 'And how is he going to do this?' she asked.

Brunetti cleared his throat before saying, 'It seems he's already started.'

Griffoni froze; Brunetti saw her hands tighten. 'What does that mean?'

'He says that the boy told—'

'His name is Orlando, Guido.'

'That Orlando has suggested you made advances to him when you were taking him home from San Marco.'

'Advances,' she repeated in a dead-level voice.

Brunetti could not think of what to tell her. 'You gave him your scarf,' he said, aware as he said it of how ridiculous it was but unable to bring himself to say more.

'Anything else?' she asked.

He was surprised at how calm she managed to look. Only her locked hands betrayed her. He was stalling and knew it, but he had no idea how to tell her about Cresti's last threat.

'He also has a photo of you with the boy that he says he can get published in the *Gazzettino*. It shows the boy giving you a lovesick look.' He stood and leaned over his desk, this time handing the photo to Griffoni, who glanced at it and tossed it back on his desk without comment.

'It's the same scarf he gave you, isn't it?'

'It was six in the morning, and we were walking along the *riva*, and there was wind.'

'So you played San Martino and cut your scarf in half and gave it to the starving beggar.'

'Something like that,' she said.

'Beni kept harping on the fact that you and he left together and took about two hours to get to Castello.' She nodded but did not speak. 'And told the people in the bar that you were his mathematics teacher.'

'I told you before, Guido. I didn't want these men to know – they're his neighbours, for God's sake – that I was with the police and he'd been detained as a member of a baby gang.' As her voice grew louder, her face flushed and her hands put a death grip on the arms of the chair.

'Because it would ruin his reputation?' Brunetti asked sarcastically. 'With those old men in Castello, drinking white wine in a bar at seven in the morning? In Castello, what else would they be drinking, for God's sake?'

She offered no defence beyond a shrug, said only, 'Clever bastard, Beni. He's already got us fighting, hasn't he?'

Brunetti's spirit darkened at what he had to say. 'There's another thing.'

She looked up, curious.

'He told me that the boy – Orlando – told his father that you'd made . . . suggestions to him.'

She half rose from her chair, her eyes flashing to the papers on his desk, to the window, to his joined hands, then to his face. ' "Suggestions"?'

'Sexual suggestions,' he answered, unable to look at her when he said it.

Rough-voiced, she demanded, 'What did he tell you the boy said? What were his words?'

This time, Brunetti did not hesitate at all. 'That you had another way to make him hot.'

After taking a few very deep breaths, she asked, 'Orlando told his father this?' and lowered herself back into her chair. They sat in silence for a long time. Brunetti had no idea of her thoughts, nor of his own, not beyond embarrassment and rage.

Finally she said, 'Did the boy say this, or is Beni simply trying to frighten us? It's blackmail.' Then, speaking offhandedly, she added, 'But he's probably done a fair bit of that in his lifetime.'

Brunetti shrugged.

'What does he want?' she said, struggling to find a normal voice.

'The last thing he said was that he wanted you to be forbidden from coming within a hundred metres of the boy.' His anger escaped his control, and Brunetti said, 'As if you were a football thug who'd kicked someone to death.'

Her face sober, she said, 'The only person I'd kick to death is Beni, and it wouldn't be about football.' Then, more seriously, 'What are his conditions?'

'There's not much to Beni's vision. You are not to go within a hundred metres of the boy, nor are you to have any contact with him, in person or by phone.'

'And in return,' she asked, 'the conversation Orlando supposedly had with his father disappears?'

'Not only that. I'm sure Beni will stop trying to make a

scandal of the fact that you were alone with Orlando for two hours.' He came down heavily on those words to show her what he thought of them. 'And that you intentionally disguised your identity by saying you were his mathematics teacher, and the photo of your lovesick Romeo will not appear in the *Gazzettino*.' Brunetti stopped, leaving it to her to consider the accusations he had just named.

'Is there anything else they could use against me?'

'There are your handicaps.'

'I'm a woman and a Neapolitan – you mean those?'

'Yes. You're also relatively young and very good-looking, and in the case of an accusation like this, those are definitely handicaps.' He paused and considered whether he could joke about this, and decided to. 'It's a good thing they don't know how intelligent you are, or they'd put posters up in the city to warn children away from you.'

'I was about to mention that,' Griffoni said. Her face grew calmer and she said, 'That's your opinion as a police officer. Is there any other part of you that sees things differently?'

'As a Venetian,' Brunetti began, tapping himself on the chest, 'I'm telling you not to pay any attention to it. What would happen if people thought about it? Five-thirty in the morning, on the Riva degli Schiavoni, no place to hide from the cold, with the wind coming in from the *bacino*.' Even as he spelled out the particulars to himself, Brunetti found it difficult not to laugh. '*Orlando e Giulietta*?' he asked.

'Then why did he try it?'

'Beni?'

'Yes.'

'Because he's an idiot and because the only thing he thinks about in any situation is how he can make money out of it, so there's got to be someone willing to pay him if he finds a way to keep you from talking to the boy,' he said.

Hearing those words, an idea came to Brunetti. 'I wonder if this is nothing more than jealousy?'

'What?' she asked.

Brunetti had a noisy jumble in his head as he thought about Monforte and his past and his son and the up-and-down nature of his life. Looking out of the window, he said, 'He's a single father, and this is his only child. They live together. He was a hero.' At that, he looked at Griffoni. 'Remember, the President went to his bedside to shake his hand. But now all he has is a job and his boy, and the only one that means anything to him is his son.' He paused and waited for her to comment, but she said nothing.

Suddenly, she spoke. 'But Orlando seems afraid of him.'

'I'm talking about Monforte, what he feels. Not about the boy.'

She shrugged and finally said, 'It's as good as anything I can come up with. Whatever it is, I've got to stay away from Orlando.' She thought about that for a very short time, shrugged again, and said, 'That's easy enough.'

Brunetti remained silent; he knew she wasn't finished.

'What I don't like is being told to do it.'

'The wicked seductress who is trying to steal the attentions of his son for herself.'

'I think you're crazy?' Griffoni said, but smiled as she did.

'Then let's leave it,' Brunetti said.

A moment passed. Brunetti had watched her carefully as he spoke and noticed that her hands had relaxed and a line that ran across her brow was no longer there.

Griffoni surprised him by nodding as if in response to something she'd heard, though there was no pleasure, no joy, no relief to be seen on her face. Acceptance, yes, and even something that could have been humour at yet another example of how people could do terrible things as easily as kind ones, the only difference being the willingness with which they did them.

'Yes, let's leave it,' she said.

Silence filled the room until Griffoni told him, 'How little we know about Monforte. Perhaps it's time I called my landlord, to see what we can find out about him.'

'The cousin who was in Nasiriyah?

'Yes.'

When she phoned, Griffoni's landlord was pleased to arrange the meeting with his cousin, Lino, adding only that it was better to speak to him in the morning. Yes, the following day was fine, but mornings were better. He lived with his mother and sister in the second house in Corte Zappa, the first *calle* to the right coming down from Ponte de Gheto Novo. He'd call and tell them to expect two guests at . . .

'Ten?' Griffoni asked, and so it was settled.

Brunetti got to his feet and said, 'I'll go down and ask Signorina Elettra if she's had more news from her friend in Caltanissetta.' He realized he had pronounced the name of the city the way a religious person might refer to Gomorrah.

As it turned out, he met Signorina Elettra on the stairs: she'd come to tell him – avoiding the use of the telephone, he noted – that she had preferred to do this search on her personal computer and would finish this evening at home and bring the information to work with her the following morning.

It had taken Brunetti years to learn the public face of discretion. He put it on when he replied, quite as though she'd said she practised origami at home, 'Thank you, Signorina. Have a pleasant evening.'

'You too, Commissario.'

As though he were following orders, Brunetti did just that. He had dinner at home with his wife and children. During the meal, a *risotto ai bruscandoli*, he listened to his son announce that he was thinking of changing his studies, abandoning history for marine biology. Brunetti's first thought was, of course, where his son would have to go to study marine biology, but Raffi had already made a search and reported that 'Most of the good schools are in the States and Australia.'

'Nothing here?' Paola asked. Because she was Raffi's mother, she felt no embarrassment about sounding protective.

'Yes. Bologna.'

In case the others didn't see the strangeness of this, Chiara said, 'Landlocked Bologna.'

When the time came, Brunetti wondered, how far would Chiara want to go? For a year, she'd talked of studying Classics, and she'd come to believe that Oxford was the best choice. He was glad there would be little temptation for her to go to Australia or to America. He told himself it was far too early to start worrying about either of them. They'd go where they wanted to go and do what they wanted to do.

Brunetti smiled at his children, ate the last of his *zabaione*, and went into the living room to have coffee with Paola. After some time, she brought in the two cups and saucers, placed them on the low table and sat beside him. She'd put sugar in the coffee, so there was no need for Brunetti to stir it.

He drank it, leaned back and rested his head on the back of the sofa. Paola did the same and took his hand. Sat these two, one another's best.

# 20

Griffoni was waiting at the top of the Ponte de Gheto Novo at 9.50 the following morning; Brunetti, who had decided to walk on such a clement day, arrived a few minutes later.

'I read some of the online newspaper articles about Nasiriyah again last night,' Griffoni said. 'How could they have been so sure that they were safe . . .' she began, but stopped herself and, in a calmer voice, said, 'They were so innocent. Everybody loves the Italians – they give candy to the kids, probably gave local people a lot of their food. No reason to think people didn't like them.'

She shrugged the possibility away and said, 'At least the government, and the military, behaved well towards them.'

'What does that mean?' Brunetti asked.

'One of the articles I read was about a pension that was to be given to the families of the survivors.'

Brunetti, deciding that this was not going to get them anywhere, said, 'Let's do this,' and started down the bridge.

They turned right at the bottom and then into the first *calle*. Brunetti rang the bell for 'Riccio'. It opened quickly. Brunetti pushed the door fully open and held it to allow Griffoni to pass in front of him. A female voice called down from above, 'Second floor.' They started up.

A tall, thin woman stood at the top of the flight of stairs. She wore a brown skirt and a beige sweater and looked to be in her forties. Her hair was pulled back and held in place by two combs made of some sort of horn. The flesh beneath her eyes was dark and pulled tight with lack of sleep or years – old worry. She stepped back when they reached the top and put out her hand, saying, 'I'm Maria Grazia Riccio. It's my brother you've come to talk to, isn't it?'

Griffoni and Brunetti shook hands with her; Brunetti said, 'Yes, it is. And we're thankful to be able to do so.'

'Oh, Lino will be happy to see new faces. Very few people come to visit him.' Her smile was an uncertain thing; her hands held one another close to her waist. 'Now,' she added.

'Oh, excuse me – come in, come in,' she continued, stepping back and holding the door to the apartment wide open. There was a small entrance with the usual narrow table and white crocheted cloth and a vase of plastic flowers. On the wall were pictures of dogs and cats that might have been cut from magazines. When Brunetti turned to close the door after them, he saw a plastic crucifix on the wall above it, tucked behind it the not-yet-withered olive branch from Palm Sunday, the month before.

A second woman, white-haired, older, face worn thin in the same manner as the other's, appeared at the door to what Brunetti could see was the kitchen. She introduced herself as Lino's mother, shook hands tentatively with both of them and said how pleased she was to have them as guests in her home, that they would come to speak with her boy. Brunetti took a quick glance into the kitchen behind her and saw his mother's dream kitchen come to life. The table had thick wooden legs and a marble top. A tall glass-doored cabinet stood against the wall, plates stacked inside in order of size. Many pictures – these of people – had been slipped between the frame and the glass. The gas stove was old and spotless, the same for the plastic-covered chairs.

Maria Grazia had turned down the corridor that led to the back of the apartment, and they followed her. Here, the walls held framed photos of men in the dark uniform of the Carabinieri. There were eight photos: Brunetti found it impossible to judge if there were different men in the photos or merely the same men standing in different places. All their chests carried a few lines of medals and campaign badges in bright colours. The last photo on the right had only one subject: a young man in uniform, the distinctive white shoulder strap running from left to right. He stood straighter than the flagpoles in Piazza San Marco, and even that space could not have contained the joy on his face at being able to wear this uniform. Brunetti passed him by, afraid to ask, even though he knew who it had to be.

She led them into a long, narrow room with two windows that looked out onto the canal and the houses on the other side of it. At some distance was a church tower, but he wasn't sure which one it was, probably Sant'Alvise. At the end of the room, a man sat in a wheelchair, looking out of the window. They saw the back of his head.

Leading the way, Maria Grazia walked down and stopped on his left side. The man remained silent, staring off to the right. 'Lino,' she said, 'these are the people who have come to visit you.'

He nodded but did not look at her. In a soft, very uncertain child's voice, he said that it was very nice of them to come. Still nodding, he asked his sister, 'Did they bring the transport documents this time?' He looked up at her, still half turned away from the two police officers.

'No, Lino,' she said. She leaned down over him to pull the

plaid blanket back in place on his lap and adjust the woollen scarf he wore around his neck.

'Did something happen?' he asked, his voice grown suddenly higher.

'No, no, Lino. They don't have the papers. They're friends. They've just stopped by to have a chat with you and see how you are.'

'I'm fine, I'm fine, I'm fine, I'm fine, Maria: you know that,' he said in his strange voice. 'But I need those transport papers. I have to get back to Mamma. You know I have to have the papers to leave.'

'Don't worry about it, Lino. The transport people are going to come, and then we'll get you home to Mamma, and everything will be all right.' When he said nothing, she asked, 'You know that, don't you, Lino?'

For Brunetti, she could have been walking into a tunnel as she spoke; with every few words, her voice grew more distant, more unsteady.

'Yes, I'll see Mamma and everything will be all right then,' the man said with forced certainty.

She stepped away from her brother and, turning to Brunetti and using a very soft voice, said, 'I think you can introduce yourselves to him now. First names only, please.' That said, she stepped back and Brunetti took her place and finally saw Lino.

Brunetti put out his hand, smiling, and automatically spoke in dialect, diving immediately into the informal: '*Buondì, Lino. Come ti sta?*'

The remaining half of Lino's lip turned up in what was identifiable as a smile, probably the only emotion his face had been left. Brunetti had noticed that Lino's right hand was under the blanket, so he extended his left and took Lino's, holding the three fingers lightly, but moving them up and down just enough to make it a handshake.

'My name's Guido,' he said, finally seeing Lino's entire face, 'and I'm a friend of Maria Grazia's.' He glanced quickly at the sister, who nodded. 'And this,' he continued, placing his hand on Griffoni's forearm and squeezing it as hard as he could, 'is my friend . . .' He stopped there and, to disguise his panic, was constrained to cough a few times. He couldn't remember Griffoni's first name. He'd worked with her for years, but the sight of the man's face had driven her name from his mind.

He felt a hand on his arm, and he allowed himself to be moved aside by Griffoni. She took his place, smiling at Lino, and said, *'Ciao, Lino, mi chiamo Claudia.'* She accepted his offered fingers and held them lightly while she went on, 'You can hear that I'm not Venetian, so we can't speak in dialect, but if you'll let me, I'd like to use *"tu"* when we talk.' She placed her other hand on top of his and said, 'I hope that's all right with you.'

Brunetti turned to look at her and saw the Neapolitan sun shine out from her face, just as he had heard it in her voice. Lino didn't have a chance.

'Oh, how happy, happy, happy you make me. *Sei bella, bella, bella.'* He sounded like a child, but it would be impossible to tell the age of his voice. Brunetti realized that he had used the size of Lino's head to decide that he was an adult, perhaps in his forties, but even that was hardly certain.

Reluctantly, his sister had turned away from his joy to bring three chairs to place in front of her brother; Brunetti was on time to carry the last one. They sat, Brunetti in the middle. He heard a sound and looked back at the corridor they'd taken to get to this room and saw Signora Riccio at the door. He turned to Maria Grazia, but she was shaking her head in her mother's direction, and when Brunetti looked again, the woman was gone.

'Do you have the transport papers?' Lino asked Griffoni.

Putting an expression of intense sadness on her face, Griffoni said, 'No, I don't work in that department.'

'You work?' he asked.

'Yes, I do, but somewhere else.'

'But you're too pretty to work.'

Griffoni laughed and leaned forward to touch Lino's arm. 'Oh, thank you for the compliment, but I like to work.' Then, brightly, she asked, 'Don't you work, Lino?'

He gave a swift glance at his sister and said, 'No, I don't work any more.'

'But you did?' Griffoni asked encouragingly.

'Oh, yes. I was a brigadiere.' It was a new voice that said this: strong, free, potent.

'Really?' she asked, voice warm with curiosity, the way a younger sister would sound hearing that her brother was a brigadiere. 'In the police?'

The side of his face with skin darkened and he said, 'No, not the police. The Carabinieri.'

'Oh, wow. How wonderful. Here, in Venice?'

That confused him for a moment. He looked at his sister, who smiled, and that seemed to start his head shaking back and forth, back and forth, reminding Brunetti of children's toys that would repeat a motion until the battery ran down.

But Lino stopped himself and said, 'No, not Venice.' He leaned forward and rested his fingers on her leg. 'I was over there. That's why I have to get the transport papers. So I can come back here.'

Griffoni leaned back in her chair, opened her mouth, and nodded in complete understanding. 'Oh, so that's it. Now I understand why it's so important that you get those documents.'

He smiled: both his mouth and his eye reflected his happiness at finally being understood.

Griffoni glanced towards Brunetti, giving him the chance to take over. But he crossed his legs and made the slightest of motions towards her with his chin.

'What did you do while you were in the Carabinieri?' Griffoni asked, her interest audible.

He lowered his head, perhaps trying to hide the smile that had flooded across his face. 'That's a secret,' he finally said.

'But we don't have any secrets, do we, not after you told me you were in the Carabinieri?' Her smile broadened as she said, 'And a brigadiere, too.'

He raised his head at this and said, 'Of course, of course,' as though he'd been persuaded by some higher rule. The blanket slid lower on his knees as he moved in excitement, perhaps at the memory of his time with the Carabinieri.

He raised his fingers and waved her closer. Griffoni leaned forward, and he said, 'I made a lot, a lot, a lot, a lot of money,' and his lips moved in what they remembered was his smile.

Griffoni laughed and clapped her hands. She leaned forward and set his plaid blanket straight, and moving it farther back in his lap. 'Oh, clever you.' Then, leaning forward again, she asked, 'How did you do that, Lino?'

These words drove Maria Grazia to her feet, her face frozen. 'Can I . . . can I . . . get you anything to drink?' she asked.

'I'd love a coffee,' said Brunetti, who had already had two that morning.

'I would too, if it's not too much trouble,' Griffoni said, and smiled at the woman, who was unable to do anything but smile back. She excused herself and went back towards the kitchen.

As if there had been no interruption, Griffoni asked, 'How did you make all that money, Lino?'

'I was in another place,' he answered. 'The one I'm trying to get home from.' Both Brunetti and Griffoni nodded in understanding.

'I worked with transport then.'

Griffoni let out a sigh of surprise and leaned a bit closer to him.

'So I could send things there,' he added.

'Where?' she asked.

'To Italy,' Lino explained.

'Of course, of course,' Griffoni said. 'Were you in charge?'

'No,' he said and shook his head at least a dozen times. 'I wasn't the boss. That was the Maresciallo Capo. My job was to fill out the papers, and then the things went to where I told them to go.'

'Where was that?'

'Venice.'

'Oh, how perfect.'

'Lots and lots of things. Bags and suitcases, and boxes full of things. And books, lots of books.' His face didn't change: it was difficult, now, to know what emotions stood behind the mask of skin his face had become. 'But I couldn't read them – scribble, scribble, scribble.'

'If you couldn't read them,' Griffoni asked with real concern, 'why did you transport them?'

'Because the Maresciallo Capo put them in with the other things. He told me that some people could read them.'

So evident was their interest in this phenomenon that Lino pulled what was left of his other hand from under the blanket and waved it in the air, careful to go from right to left, as though he were drawing *'Alif, Bā', Tā'*, in the space between them.

'And even though they were in those crazy letters, people wanted the books.' He looked back and forth between Brunetti and Griffoni, as if to ask them to comment on how very strange the world was.

It was at this point that Maria Grazia came back from the kitchen, though empty-handed. 'I forgot to ask you if you'd like anything, Lino,' she said and looked across at her brother. He ignored her. 'Lino,' she said, straining to be calm. 'It's time for—'

'It's time for me to talk to my friends. I never have any friends to talk to alone,' he said. Because his face no longer had more than one expression, he could not express his irritation that way, but there was plenty in his voice. 'I never get to talk to my friends alone.'

Ignoring what Lino had said, Griffoni looked around and chirped, 'Oh, what a good idea. Let's all have a coffee together.' She turned towards Maria Grazia and put a look of confusion and sympathy on her face. The other woman nodded.

Lino started to nod: the motion seemed to drive Maria Grazia back towards the kitchen.

In a more sober voice than she had been using, Griffoni said that they were interested in his experiences in transport between Italy and Iraq and would like to hear more.

'We were told we couldn't talk about it. The Maresciallo Capo told us.'

Sounding confused, Griffoni said, 'I don't understand how that could be a secret. People wanted the things and bought them, so certainly they'd talk about them.'

When Lino said nothing, Griffoni asked, 'That makes sense, doesn't it?'

# 21

After what seemed a long time, Lino said, sounding puzzled, 'Yes. It does.' Then, after a pause and growing more insistent, he asked, 'So I can talk about it now?'

Griffoni smiled and said, 'You can talk about everything, Lino. Now that we're here.' Turning to Brunetti, she asked, 'What do you think, Guido? Lino and I think he's got every right to talk about it now.' Then, risking it, she added, 'Especially after what happened. To him.'

'I agree with you,' Brunetti said, striving to sound thoughtful. 'And, as you said, especially now.'

With a bright smile, Griffoni said, 'I'm not going to ask about money, Lino. That's none of my business, but I do congratulate you for being clever enough to conceive the idea.'

Lino lowered his head and muttered something.

'Excuse me,' Griffoni said. 'I didn't hear.' She gave him the most convincing of her smiles.

'It wasn't my idea,' he said, very softly, as though he did but did not want her to hear him. 'It was the Maresciallo Capo's.'

'Well, then he's the clever one. But you had to fill out the papers and oversee it all. So it seems to me he couldn't have done anything without you.' Griffoni had hiked up her voice, as one does when boasting about one's friends. Or defending them. Suddenly, she gave a snort of laughter, then another.

After the third, Lino asked, 'What's so funny?'

Swallowing her laughter and slapping her forehead with her right hand, Griffoni said, 'Here I am thinking you could just go down to the post office and send the package off anywhere you chose.'

Lino continued to stare at her in confusion.

'But it was coming by plane, wasn't it?' she asked, and Lino nodded, happy that they were talking about when he worked.

'Something like a private courier, not the mailman,' Griffoni said. 'So you must have needed a place for them to land. I'd sort of forgotten about that,' she said in perfect imitation of the foolish woman who could not understand much of anything.

'Oh, that was easy,' he said. 'We always landed in Aviano.' When he saw her confused look, he explained. 'The Americans have a big base up there and we used it, too. That's where we brought the men who were coming back.' He pressed his fingers against the side of his mouth and said, 'The ones who had finished their tour.' His eyes scurried for a way to continue, but all he found was 'Or the ones who were ... hurt.' Brunetti thought it must have taken him a great deal of courage to pronounce that word.

Griffoni nodded and asked, in a low voice better suited to solemn matters, 'Did many come back that way?'

Lino had to think about this for some time, but finally he said, 'In the beginning, not many. And usually because of accidents or riding in a vehicle that went over a landmine.' Lino stopped here and was silent for at least a minute before he said, 'A friend died that way.' Then he repeated, 'Died, died, died, died.'

After a moment, he gave himself a shake and said, 'That was

a bad thing.' Like a child, Lino pulled out his mangled hands and began to press them against his thighs and then raise them five or six centimetres in the air before lowering them again, creating a silent rhythm.

It was all a bad thing, Brunetti said to himself but remained silent and motionless, sure that Griffoni knew what she had to do.

'Was the work difficult?'

Lino shook his head five or six times before saying, 'Not in the beginning. But then we had trouble.'

'What happened, Lino?' Griffoni asked in her real voice, and the Neapolitan warmth of it must have struck him, for his hands dropped to his lap.

'To me or to us?' he asked in a strikingly calm voice, as though he'd had enough hiding and could come out now.

'To the group of you.'

'Someone was stealing.'

'Stealing what?'

'The best things.'

'Who decided what was best?'

'One of us had a book.'

'What sort of book?'

'Art. It showed the things that were in museums or that were the most famous.' He looked directly across at her. 'If they were in a book, then things that looked like them had to be valuable, too, right?'

She nodded.

'But then the Maresciallo Capo discovered that some of what he called our best pieces were gone.'

'From where?'

'We had a room in one of the buildings.'

'Where?'

'On the base.'

'Nasiriyah?'

Lino's eye ran around the room for almost a minute, as though he'd seen a snake on the floor, or a bomb. 'Yes,' he finally said, and then tried with what remained of his hands to shoo the name away.

'What happened?' Griffoni asked, entirely fascinated by the story he was telling them.

'The Maresciallo Capo discovered that one of the other people in transport had been issued a key.'

'To that room?'

Brunetti looked at the man and thought of a person trapped in a speeding car, no longer in control of the steering wheel. The brakes had failed and someone else's foot was on the gas pedal. The doors were all locked from the outside, and there was no way to stop.

'Yes.'

'What happened?'

Brunetti heard a noise behind him and turned to see Maria Grazia at the door. Then Lino saw her and said, loudly enough to shock them all, 'Go away. I'm talking to my friends.'

Brunetti had to turn away from the look that crossed her face. She left, and he heard her soft footsteps going back towards the kitchen.

'The day before it happened . . .' Lino began, and Brunetti had no doubt that he was referring to the attack, the explosion that had left what remained of him, '. . . we were moving some things into our room, and . . .'

Lino raised his hands again and returned to his rhythm, though this time he tried to turn his hands upside down once in a while, as if he wanted to calm himself.

Brunetti couldn't remember how long his patting went on, but finally Lino stopped, and both hands scurried under the blanket and were still.

'And then?' Griffoni asked.

'The Maresciallo Capo – he was our leader – told us to grab him.'

His left hand struggled itself free of the blanket and moved the forever straight fingers close to his mouth. He stared at it. Brunetti wondered if he were thinking about the word 'grab'.

No words with which he could set the other man free came to Brunetti's mind. He would not risk a glance in Griffoni's direction. He could only wait.

With no urging, Lino returned to the past and said, 'He was stupid enough to have the other key in his pocket.' His voice tightened. 'So we knew he'd been robbing us, maybe for months.'

'And then?'

'We stayed in the room and asked him where he kept the stolen things.' Brunetti noticed how indignant the man sounded about the other man's dishonesty; he wondered what 'asked' meant.

'And after he told us what he'd been doing and where the things were, the Maresciallo Capo told us to put him in the back of a van, and we drove into the middle of the city.' He stopped here and looked at Griffoni and then at Brunetti, before looking carefully around the room. He grew calmer, having seen there was no one there, lurking, listening. 'Valeriano was wearing his uniform.'

'And what did you do to him?'

'The driver stopped the van. I think only he knew where we were. It's a big city.'

'And then?' Griffoni prodded again.

'We opened the back door, and the Maresciallo Capo gave him a kick and he landed outside, on the street, and we drove back to the base.' There was a very long, very dead silence, then Lino said, 'I never saw Valeriano again. And the Maresciallo Capo made us all say we'd never tell anyone. On our honour. As Carabinieri.'

He stopped, and Brunetti thought he was finished, but apparently he still had one thing to say. 'And the next day, it happened.' He said no more.

Before the silence could grow longer, Brunetti got to his feet and said, 'We should go back to the office now, I think.' He bent towards Lino, shook what he told his mind to call his hand, and thanked him for his time. Griffoni stood and leaned forward to put her hand on Lino's shoulder. '*Ciao, Lino. Tante grazie*' was all she could find to say before her voice broke.

Maria Grazia came and led them back down the corridor. A few steps before the door, Griffoni leaned towards Brunetti and grabbed at his shoulder, rebounded away from him and fell against one of the chairs in the small entry hall.

Maria Grazia was at her side in an instant, pushing her back in the chair and trying to hold her upright. Griffoni's head fell back and smacked against the wall. She remained like this, eyes closed, mouth fallen open.

Lino's mother came out of the kitchen with a cloth, which she used to wipe at Griffoni's forehead and cheeks, and then Maria Grazia was there with a small glass of water, which she held to Griffoni's lips. She took a small sip, then another, and then she opened her eyes and looked around her. She said, 'Oh, I'm sorry. Excuse me, excuse me,' and she grabbed Brunetti's hand and tried to pull herself out of the chair.

Maria Grazia turned to Brunetti and said, 'Let's take her to the sofa. She'll be more comfortable there.' Without waiting for his answer, she put one arm around Griffoni's shoulder and helped her get to her feet. Brunetti was immediately at her other side and tried to take even more of her weight. The mother opened a door and led them into a tiny sitting room, where there was barely enough room for them all.

They settled Griffoni, who never stopped excusing herself and begging their pardon, on the sofa and pulled a chair for

Brunetti in front of her. Because there was only one other chair, Signora Riccio sat next to Griffoni on the sofa, and Maria Grazia next to Brunetti.

A minute passed, and then another. Finally, Griffoni leaned aside and took Lino's mother's hand in hers and said, 'Signora, I have no words. Nothing and nothing. I'm so sorry for your son and for you both and that this terrible thing happened.' She looked around the room: small, with only one window and water damage running down the wall from it.

'I hope they treat you well, considering all that was taken from you,' she said to the other two women.

'Who are you talking about?' Maria Grazia demanded angrily.

Griffoni was confused by the question and its tone.

'The government, the Carabinieri.'

Griffoni looked at Maria Grazia's face; her anger had wiped it clear of anything else. Recalling what she'd told Brunetti about the pension, she explained, 'The special pension that was given to the survivors – surely that's helped you all these years.'

'What are you talking about?' Maria Grazia asked impatiently.

Griffoni immediately backtracked, afraid she might have fallen into that deepest of traps: believing what she read in the papers.

'I don't know what you're talking about,' Maria Grazia insisted. 'There's no special pension. We get the standard amount that goes to men who leave because of injuries.' They watched her try to stop speaking, and they saw her fail. 'It took them seven years to decide how much to pay the families of those who died, and even that's not settled. Imagine how long it will take them to decide on what to give us.'

'My mistake,' Griffoni said awkwardly.

After a moment, Brunetti turned to her and asked, 'Are you all right now, Claudia?'

She smiled and released her hold on Signora Riccio's hand,

placing it palm down on the cushion, which she gave a few soft pats. 'Thank you both. I'm sorry to have disturbed you, and then to make it worse by being such a weakling.'

She stood with her usual smooth grace and took a few steps towards the open door, Brunetti beside her. Maria Grazia opened the door for them, silently. They stepped into the hallway and turned back towards the two women. Signora Riccio looked at Griffoni and gave a small, brave smile. The exchange of pleasantries was strained. They left together.

Griffoni kept her right hand on the railing as they walked downstairs.

Years ago, working on a case with Brunetti, she had pretended great emotion in order to trick someone into speaking. Brunetti had not forgotten his response when he realized that her behaviour had all been a cold-blooded scam, performed to elicit information. She stopped walking and propped her hands on the brick parapet that lined the canal of the Misericordia.

Brunetti turned and leaned against the parapet, waiting, thinking she'd prefer not to have him looking at her when she said whatever it was she had to say.

'That was real, Guido. You know I'm a snake and a liar, but that was real. That's too much for anyone to have to suffer.'

'Which one do you mean?'

'All of them,' she said and continued to study the play of light on the water in the canal.

# 22

'Why didn't they throw us out?' Griffoni asked as they started the long walk to the Questura. 'What I did to him was terrible,' she said. 'And she just went to the kitchen as if I'd commented on the weather.'

Remembering the crucifix, Brunetti said, 'God knows. Maybe his sister believes that confession brings forgiveness.' He was surprised that he would think of such a thing.

'Why isn't he in a hospital?' Griffoni asked.

'Have you ever been in a military hospital?' Brunetti asked neutrally.

'No.'

'It would make you understand why they keep him with them.'

They continued walking. In her time in Venice, Griffoni had learned of the absence of public transportation between the Ghetto and the Questura. They emerged on Strada Nuova for a short time, although long enough to feel enveloped in the bodies of people going in both directions. Brunetti gave the job to his legs, and they slipped through the masses quite easily, adjusting speed, pirouetting around stalled suitcases, slowing on top of bridges because of the photo-taking crowds on both sides, stopping completely when necessary.

It was only when they slipped past the newly planted tree in Campo Santa Maria Nova that they could enjoy the convenience of walking side by side and talking.

Brunetti thought of the soldier kicked from the van and wondered if he had survived the day. The Iraqis would have smelled him within minutes: uniform, boots, well-cut hair, clean-shaven, padded zip-up jacket. Poor devil. They might as well have pasted a target from the firing range on his back.

'Do you think it's true?' Griffoni asked.

Momentarily confused, Brunetti asked, 'Which, the soldier or the pension?'

'The soldier,' she answered instantly, adding, 'The pension's entirely possible. There's always trouble.'

Brunetti nodded in agreement. 'Look at the way they live. No special money's going there.' With no change in his voice, Brunetti continued: 'I believe him about the soldier, though. He was there, no question.'

Griffoni nodded in unspoken agreement, then asked, 'Would a judge believe it?'

'Wrong question,' Brunetti said.

Griffoni missed a step, stopped, and asked, 'What?'

'Is there any evidence?' he asked. Their glances met, and each watched the signs of thought in the other, able now to read a great deal of it.

Griffoni continued towards the Questura. After a few minutes, she said, 'And who would accuse the Hero of Nasiriyah?' There was no response Brunetti could make, so they walked in silence until they stopped at the front door of the Questura.

'Patta called me again,' Brunetti told her.

'You have any idea what he wants?'

'To talk about Bocchese, I imagine,' Brunetti answered.

She turned towards the door, which was opened by the officer on duty. She went in first and together they started up the stairs. Brunetti peeled off at Patta's floor, and Griffoni continued up towards her office.

Signorina Elettra was not at her desk, so Brunetti crossed to Patta's office and knocked on the door.

Patta's '*Avanti*' seemed to lack all authority, or perhaps Patta was simply tired of shouting. Brunetti went in and found his superior at the window, staring at the façade of the church, his hands again stuffed in his pockets, a loss of formality to which he had seldom treated himself before. He turned at the sound of footsteps and, seeing Brunetti, waved to the two chairs that stood in front of his desk, went and sat in one of them, then indicated the other to Brunetti. 'It's safe, Commissario,' Patta said. Did he mean the chair or the conversation they were about to have?

Brunetti walked over and sat, lowering himself into the chair with the help of his right hand. 'Sorry, Dottore, but I'm feeling a bit . . .' Brunetti left the sentence unfinished.

'I can understand that, Commissario,' Patta said, using Brunetti's title with no ironic emphasis. 'I've spoken to the doctors. What they've told me is reassuring.'

'In what way, Signore?' Brunetti asked.

'They've excluded a stroke or a heart attack, in fact, almost all medical possibilities, and they believe he was the victim of an assault and nothing else.' Then, seeing that Brunetti was interested but perhaps not persuaded, he added, 'There was an act of vandalism, as well.'

'The statues, Dottore?' Brunetti asked, recalling what he had seen. 'I saw them.'

'The photos are horrible,' Patta said, 'Thousands of euros' worth of damage. I don't know if they can be fixed – the arms put back on. Or the heads. The crushed faces . . .' He was clearly upset by the vandalism, but what, for him, was lost – beauty or value?

Asking a question about insurance would surely have forced Patta to clarify his view on this matter, but Brunetti did not want to know. According to a message Rizzardi had sent him very early that morning, Bocchese was in fact doing well.

'The crime squad found three statues the vandals must have overlooked in shopping bags hanging on the back of the kitchen door,' Patta said.

Brunetti flashed surprise across his face, and Patta added, 'Perhaps these can serve as the basis of a new collection.' He could not have sounded more pleased if this good fate had befallen him.

For a moment, Brunetti was tempted to stand, kick over his chair, and start shouting, 'These were things, for God's sake – objects, possessions, chattels.' But he knew that if he started, he was bound to say something about the IWC watch, and he knew he'd start raving and saying that it was all stuff, stuff, stuff: have it, don't have it; it's all the same, and sooner or later, no one will want it.

To preserve his sanity, and most likely his job, he remained silent until the Vice-Questore was finished and then asked, 'Did the doctors give you any details?'

'Anything to the head is dangerous, especially when a person is his age,' Patta said with Solonic seriousness and quite as if he and Bocchese were separated by at least a generation. 'The doctors told me that head wounds bleed terribly, as his did, but, thank God, they weren't serious wounds.'

Brunetti thought of his own bloody trousers, sent off in this morning's garbage collection, and the long shower he'd gone home to take yesterday. Yes, head wounds bleed a lot.

'Any other injuries?' Brunetti asked.

'He must have hit his nose when he was knocked down.

There was a lot of blood on the front of his jacket, but most of it came from a cut on the side of his head. His jaw is badly bruised, and two of his teeth were loosened. But beyond that, nothing.'

Patta gave him a long look, as though evaluating how much he could trust Brunetti. 'One of the doctors said it looked like the sort of beating the Mafia gives as a warning.'

'Warning,' Brunetti repeated.

'We're more familiar with this sort of thing than you people up here in the North. A beating like this isn't meant to hurt you, at least not badly – it's meant to warn you. So the after-effects are more mental than physical.'

In all these years, Brunetti had never paid so much attention to anything Patta had said or done. His interest must have been visible to the Vice-Questore, who went on without having to be asked. 'It's a warning for you to change your current path in life, to abandon the one you've taken while there is still time.'

Resisting the impulse to observe that Patta sounded very approving of the technique, he said only, 'You seem very certain of that, Vice-Questore.'

'Oh, I am. I am,' Patta said.

Then, as though he'd finally heard what he was saying, Patta suddenly changed course and, in his best portentous voice, said, 'Dottor Bocchese is a man of vast learning.'

'Dottor Bocchese?' Brunetti asked in open surprise.

'Yes. I looked at his file, the original application he made to the police. Decades ago.'

'Is he a doctor of medicine?' Brunetti asked, recalling Bocchese's familiarity with medical language and the ease with which he read autopsy reports.

'Art history. Florence, almost forty years ago,' Patta said. 'I've had a long career, Commissario, and I've worked with many technicians, but never one like this. Such precision.' Patta pressed the tips of his fingers against his mouth.

Brunetti had noticed that, as Patta spoke, his Palermitano accent had grown more and more apparent. He hoped this would not end up as one of those ridiculous scenes, like a cheap television comedy, of two men speaking their dialects and neither understanding the other.

'I've decided to give this investigation to you, Brunetti. You're a friend of his, as well as a colleague.' He paused, but Brunetti was too surprised to speak.

'You'll have complete control. I'll have one of the magistrates sign off on anything you need. And you're free to choose whom you want to work with.'

Patta took a breath, and his face flushed with anger. 'I will not allow anyone to harm one of my staff.' His face grew even redder, and there was sweat under his eyes. He stopped abruptly, leaving it to Brunetti to speak.

'Thank you, Vice-Questore,' Brunetti said. 'I've already begun to collect information, and—'

'Use any source you can,' Patta interrupted. 'Have her get in anywhere and find anything that might help,' he added, leaving it to Brunetti to understand whom he meant. 'Tell her to let me know if she meets any opposition from the Ministry of the Interior.' He paused a moment, then added, 'Or from Lieutenant Scarpa.' Patta stared at him until Brunetti was forced to nod in understanding and acceptance. 'Do what you want and tell me the results. I have no interest in the methods.' The Vice-Questore paused again. 'I repeat, Commissario: I leave the methods to you. Entirely.' Patta remained silent for some time and then opened his mouth, as though he wanted to continue, but stopped. Brunetti was still too surprised to think of anything to say.

Always attentive to the real meaning of Patta's every word and gesture, Brunetti was instantly curious about what this would be building up to, what the price of Patta's offer of solidarity – however temporary – would turn out to be.

Brunetti thought he'd risk playing for higher stakes and said, 'I have reason to believe that there is a connection with the baby gangs, Dottore. So I thought I might take a look – a very gentle one – at the parents of some of the boys who are involved in them. The father of one of the boys seems to have been in the Carabinieri, but I'm having some trouble accessing his files.'

Patta gave him a long look, and Brunetti watched as his superior made his calculations. Finally Patta nodded and said, 'That might well prove helpful, and I'm sure she'll be very discreet.' As his superior spoke, Brunetti was conscious of how carefully the Vice-Questore chose his words. Even if spoken in front of a judge, there was no way what he had just said could be interpreted to be of criminal intent.

No sooner had he thought it than Patta decided. 'Tell Signorina Elettra if she has any trouble getting . . . access to the Carabinieri files, to try the password ATTAP with them. All capitals.' Having said that, he added, 'And be sure you spell it that way,' and gave a small, very clever smile. The Vice-Questore suddenly got to his feet and walked behind his desk. 'Thank you for coming in, Brunetti,' he said in dismissal, sounding like his real self again.

Brunetti stood, thanked Patta for his frankness, and left without saying anything further.

Signorina Elettra was at her usual place, even though Brunetti felt that the world had just been turned upside down. He was a killer hawk let free of its cage, a Rottweiler let loose at an open gate, a boa told to slip into the empty sleeping bag.

'He said we're free to use anything, do anything.'

'He said that?' she asked, then stood transfixed, no doubt already making plans.

'Yes. Anything. He'll keep Scarpa away from us.'

'Maria Vergine,' she whispered. Returning to the world of the practical, she held up a file of papers and offered them to him.

'This is what I managed to find out with a bit of help from Caltanissetta last night.' She considered this for a moment and then said, 'There were a lot of places I was afraid to go, even to think about going.' She smiled, 'I hate loud noises, and some of those sites had major ordnance piled in front of them.'

'His surname in caps, but spelled backwards, is the password to all of the files of the Ministry of the Interior, so you can try again,' Brunetti said. She looked at him as though he'd brought abracadabra home for lunch. 'It will open the door to everything, he told me. He said to use it,' and then, to remind her, 'All in caps, and backwards.'

Signorina Elettra joined her hands at her breast and looked off to the corner of the ceiling, her expression suddenly taking on an odd resemblance to that of Santa Teresa d'Avila in rapture. 'The password to the Ministry of the Interior,' she pronounced with reverence, as though naming the decade of the Rosary she was about to recite.

Then, looking at him no less solemnly, she said 'Commissario, I swear to you that I will use this only for things to which I believe we should have legitimate access.' After that, she gave herself a small shake and pulled back without explaining whose judgement should be used to define 'legitimate'.

'I don't think it's necessary to swear anything to me, Signorina. I trust you.'

'That's not why I'm doing it, Dottore.'

He raised his eyebrows in honest confusion.

'It's because I don't trust myself.'

# 23

Brunetti had no sooner sat at his desk than he felt the sudden return of his good sense. Heroic Patta, wanting to be the one who throws his body between looming peril and his colleagues? Valiant defender of the staff of the Questura in pursuit of the person who had dared to attack one of his own? A selfless Patta?

What's wrong with this picture? Does the resplendent archangel carry a plastic sword? Does the wolf at the door to its den smile because it is looking at its lunch?

He went to the window and checked the vine, which was closer to the water today, or else the tide was higher. He folded his arms and leaned one shoulder against the wall beside the window, letting his gaze wander off to the rooftops and the lingering television antennae and dishes.

What troubled him was Patta's casual familiarity with Signorina Elettra's cyber excesses and the profound and mutual distrust between himself and the Vice-Questore. Patta had given him full powers in the investigation, but Brunetti saw no reason to believe him.

By putting Brunetti in full charge, Patta had created a titbit he could toss to the press whenever circumstances required. Commissario Brunetti had exceeded his powers, or he could just as easily have shirked his duty – this, of course, would only be suggested – should the investigation into the attack on Bocchese prove unsuccessful.

Brunetti went downstairs and found Signorina Elettra's door open. He entered without knocking and saw her in what might have been a parody of his former pose: arms crossed, looking out of the window, though fewer rooftops were visible from her office. When she heard footsteps, Signorina Elettra turned to see who it was. 'I'm sorry, but il Dottore has left.'

Brunetti nodded and smiled. 'Probably better.' He paused so that she could comment, and when she did not, asked, 'Have you tried it yet?'

She glanced at him and then returned to gazing out of the window. 'I was tempted, Dottore, but I couldn't find the courage to do it.' She gave him another quick look, then went back to the vines, which she could also see.

'My hands didn't want to put in that password,' she said, as if her words surprised her. 'I thought of the consequences should it trigger a warning and somehow give them access to my computer.'

'You think it's a trap?' Brunetti asked.

She gave this a great deal of thought. Had she been a robot, strange noises would surely have come from her head. Finally, she said, 'The simple fact that both of us consider that possibility is interesting, isn't it?'

'You've entered their files before,' Brunetti said, still unable to pronounce the proper word, 'hacked'. 'But there must be layers of information that are far more . . .'

'Sensitive?' she offered. 'Is that the word you're looking for?'
'Exactly.'

'I've been wondering about them,' she said very softly.

'Who? The Carabinieri?' Brunetti asked, half fearing that her presence had been detected and trouble was on the way.

'Yes.' She must have seen his reaction, for she said, 'I don't think there's anything to be nervous about. Well, not if you take a longer view, or a deeper one, of what might be going on.'

'I'm afraid I don't understand, Signorina.'

After a very long silence, she said, 'They're doing their jobs, Commissario, and we're doing ours. But they are not our enemy. He betrayed them and betrayed his oath. But he's walking around, free, alive, and apparently he's in no danger.' She glanced at him, her expression serious, but then she gave a small smile and said, 'I think we should bear this in mind.'

Brunetti followed her back to the computer and saw that the screen showed two Carabinieri in uniform, instantly recognizable by the red stripe running down the outside of their trousers. He glanced at her and saw that her smile was small, almost as if it were meant for herself alone to enjoy. 'Do you recognize his style?' she asked, tapping on the shoulder of one of the Carabinieri in the photo.

'Style?' asked Brunetti.

'Of the jacket,' she explained.

Brunetti took a closer look at the jacket but saw nothing amiss. 'What am I looking at?' he asked.

'It's Valentino.'

'The saint or . . . the couturier?'

'The stylist. These new uniforms were the first things I found when I put in "Carabiniere". They've done a rebranding.'

'You're talking about the uniforms?'

'Yes.'

She wiped the officers off the screen. She typed for a while, and different pages appeared, quickly changing each time she requested further information. After a minute, perhaps more, a page with a large red STOP sign appeared, requesting the password necessary to continue.

'PATTA, all capitals,' Brunetti said, 'spelled backwards.'

In a moment it was done, and a notice appeared on the screen: '3G clearance approved'.

'Where do I begin?'

'Nasiriyah.'

'When?' she asked.

'Start when we first sent troops: anyone working for the quartermaster.'

She looked up at him in surprise. 'Everyone?' she asked.

'There can't have been many – we weren't there long. Take a look at disciplinary actions, demotions, investigations, loss of rank. Even suspicions.'

'Until?' she asked, still typing.

'Until we left,' he said.

For the next few minutes there was only the sound of her fingers clicking the keys as she entered the requests he had given her. When the screen went blank, she asked, 'Anything else?'

'No. Thank you.'

She stared at the screen that flashed official documents in front of them, as if they were the trailer for a silent film. Very often, a document had large areas of red lettering; in a few cases, entire paragraphs were blacked out, with what appeared to be a synopsis printed below.

The papers suddenly stopped appearing, and Brunetti, who had lost count of the pages, thought they were finished. But then there was a sudden motion on the screen and six entirely black pages passed across it, after which appeared a long list of mixed numbers and letters, both upper and lower case. And then there was another series of documents, and then nothing.

She leaned close to the screen and studied the disclaimer that preceded the six dark pages, then turned to him and explained.

'The person making the request has to give the password again, and the redacted pages will be seen only after the requester's identity has been confirmed.'

'How long will that take?' asked an impatient Brunetti.

'I've no idea,' answered a tight-voiced Signorina Elettra. Alerted by her voice, he realized what it might mean for them if the identity was not confirmed. Neither of them liked the possibilities, one of which was that Patta would surely lie to protect himself.

But Signorina Elettra had already entered the name, all in capitals, after which she turned to Brunetti and said, 'I'll bring the pages to you when they arrive, Signore.' As she spoke, her normal voice returned and she asked, 'Would you like them on a stick or would you like them printed out?'

'Printed, please,' he answered, hoping to bolster them both. 'Can you make a copy for Claudia?' he asked.

'Now?'

He looked at her computer and asked, 'Is it safe in there overnight?'

Her face went blank and remained that way for some seconds. Then she gave a small cough, which allowed her to turn her head away. When she turned back, she said, voice calm, 'Yes, it will be put in a safe place. I'll print yours out for you now, Signore, and I'll take Claudia hers tomorrow.'

It was quickly done, and she went over to the printer and brought the pages back for him.

He thanked her and flipped through them to the last one. 'Twenty-eight pages,' he said.

'I had no idea it would be so long.'

'Could it be because of the higher clearance? They permit you to see more?'

'Perhaps,' she said, then added, 'I think the highest clearance is 3J, but I'm not sure.'

'Why would he have such access?' Brunetti asked in a puzzled voice.

'God knows.'

'He's only a vice-questore, after all.'

'Only?'

Brunetti wondered if Signorina Elettra was going to defend Patta. To avoid even the possibility, Brunetti held up the papers and said he'd go and have a look.

In his office, he flipped through them. Signorina Elettra had not printed the black ones, victims of her relentless attempts to save paper. He'd give it ten pages and then think about going home for dinner.

By page three, Brunetti was so intrigued by what he read that he began to take notes. He read little fiction, but he had devoured novels when he was a young man and had come to enjoy the aching fear that the protagonists would finish badly. Reading the Carabinieri reports filed before the Nasiriyah massacre created in him the same response. This time, as with *Oedipus Rex*, he knew what was coming, and it caused him only sick terror.

The chronological reports made him familiar with some of the characters: the major in charge, his lieutenant, the men in A Squad, in B and in C, all referred to only by surname. They drove out on patrol, returned from patrol. Brunetti read 'consumed less than the calculated quantity of ordnance' and eventually understood that it meant they had used fewer bullets than planned. 'Maintained proper distance between vehicles' meant they were careful to move as separate targets. 'No enemy fire' explained itself. It was 'IED' that puzzled him, for – whatever it was – it killed a lot of civilians and more than a few soldiers. Brunetti finally had to look on Google, where he discovered that it referred to an improvised explosive device, of which there were many, usually buried at the side of the road.

Was it Tacitus who wrote, 'They make a desert and call it

peace'? Brunetti wondered. In this case, they had had no need to make a desert: it was already waiting for them. But peace, alas, was not.

His attention had wandered from the report, and he had to retreat a few pages. He looked at the date: the fifth of November. Only a week left.

Things were calm. The happy locals were civil, sometimes even friendly with our boys with the red stripes down their legs. Occasionally things disappeared from the mess hall – once, an entire side of beef. Had it regrown its other legs and walked away? A slaughtered cow might have the red stripes down its legs, too. A few machine guns failed to show up for a surprise inspection of the armoury. 'These boots were made for walkin'.' So, too, were those kept in the quartermaster's storeroom, for at least a dozen pairs a week didn't show up for roll call. Gasoline and oil trickled through the fingers of anyone sent to see how much was there, how much was used, and how much was left. To do them credit – something Brunetti would happily grant them, given what was coming in four, three, two days – the Carabinieri did not interest themselves in the disappearance of food or blankets but simply sent orders back to Italy that more and more and more be delivered. It was November, and these people had nothing.

One comment to his superior from a soldier named Merizzi was reported: 'We have food. They don't. We have shoes. They don't. We eat. They don't.' Infantryman Merizzi was warned that the next time, he would be charged with insubordination.

Brunetti, already familiar with the names of the soldiers who had been burned to death, knew that Merizzi no longer had reason to fear a charge of insubordination. Even a conviction.

Brunetti looked up from what he was reading, knowing he was incapable of continuing. He knew. He knew that within days, these young men – women had been allowed to enlist only four years before, and none had reached Nasiriyah – would walk across an open courtyard and find not a coffee in the bar, not their fresh laundry on their bed, not news from a colleague that he was being rotated back to Italy the following week. Nor would Brunetti find the following week.

He closed the file and went over to his closet to find his briefcase. To assure no one else saw the papers, he'd take them home, although he well knew he would not look at them, not with what he knew was coming.

When he reached the apartment, he put the briefcase to sleep by the door and listened to the silence. He remembered Paola had told him the kids wouldn't be there, but he hadn't been paying attention. There was no scent of food, so he went back to Paola's study, where he found her on the sofa, reading. He stopped himself from asking what was for dinner until he had bent down and kissed her forehead.

'We decided to go out for pizza,' she said, lowering her book to her chest. 'While there's still time.'

'Time for what?' he asked.

'I told you this morning,' she said, with a wife's heavy sigh. 'Time before the summer, when every pizzeria in the city will be filled with tourists and we won't be able to eat pizza, not unless we want to eat at six or at eleven.'

'There's always takeout,' he said.

'Remember last summer?'

'No.'

'They hired a second cook, and he was lousy. You wouldn't go there any more.' She gave him a long look.

'Yes, I remember. I ordered a Margherita – nothing's simpler than that – and it was inedible.'

Paola covered her face with her hands and asked, 'You don't remember what we agreed to this morning, yet you remember a pizza you ate last summer?'

'I remember it because I didn't eat it, my dove,' Brunetti said quite pleasantly. 'That's why I remember.'

He got to his feet and held out his hand to her.

'You can talk yourself out of anything,' she said, smiling, and pulled herself up with the help of his hand.

# 24

Brunetti got to the Questura at nine exactly, disappointed that Patta was not there to see him arrive on time. He stopped in Signorina Elettra's office on the way to his own, where she told him she'd used Patta's name a second time and had passed unquestioned into the possession of the six completely redacted papers. She had noted Brunetti's briefcase with obvious approval when he came in. Handing him the papers, she suggested that the briefcase might well be the best place to keep them and that he might give a thought to not leaving them lying carelessly about.

When he reached his office, he returned to the papers where he had stopped reading them, still two days away from the attack. When he resumed, things were still normal, whatever that meant in a country in chaos: men went off on patrol every morning, and in exchange for leaving the population alone, they were left alone themselves and returned to the base safely.

Planes took off to go to Italy, carrying back the troops who had fulfilled their mission in Nasiriyah, whatever that was. They were large transport planes, and there were seldom more than twenty men going home on them. Sometimes as few as seven men were on the flight to Aviano. Brunetti found copies of cargo manifests filled with inventories of the items that came and went. Many items departing from Iraq were listed as 'souvenirs', a word that forced Brunetti's attention away from the page long enough for him to understand the choice of the word in this context.

The previously blacked-out pages, when he got to them, consisted primarily of secondary documentation: receipts, bank records, witness statements. Its six pages had been prepared by a Major Massimo Fede, who served in the 'Office of Internal Investigations', and concerned the behaviour of Maresciallo Capo Dario Monforte, the quartermaster.

The Maresciallo Capo had first come to the attention of Major Fede because of the inordinate amount of material that disappeared from shipments sent to the base. Boots, socks, even uniforms arrived from Italy and were registered, as were bags of rice, sugar, pasta and other commodities, but the quantities for which believable receipts were provided by the units where they were meant to have been delivered seldom equalled the quantities that had arrived.

Major Fede, who had spent time in the Middle East and who was generous of spirit, decided to close an eye to the disappearance of food, blankets, and clothing, and explained to his superiors that this was in essence a common goodwill payment that helped to ensure the safety of the base and its personnel. In this, Major Fede was telling the truth, and since it was widely understood that the Americans would ultimately pay for what was stolen, no one much minded.

The second part of his report, however, was greeted in an entirely different manner by both himself and his superiors, for it revealed the disappearance of a considerable amount of armaments and munitions. A list of missing – referred to by the quartermaster as 'misdelivered' – materiel, chiefly machine guns, pistols, grenade launchers and grenades, was attached to Major Fede's report, which also contained the names of witnesses – both Italian and Iraqi – willing to testify that the missing materiel was the work of the quartermaster.

When the quartermaster was asked about this, Monforte explained that he could not read the invoices from the Iraqis who received the goods because they were written in Arabic, and he had no choice but to obey his orders and believe in the integrity of the people he was told to work with. Major Fede noted in the margin here that this seemed a reversal of the miracle of the loaves and fishes: Monforte had but to lay his hands upon equipment or weapons for them to disappear into the hands of the enemy.

As to the souvenirs, Monforte remembered sending carpets, women's silk veils and a photo portrait of Saddam Hussein, the sort of things 'all my friends were sending'.

Two days before the explosion, it was decided by the authorities in Rome, who had read Major Fede's dossier on the activities of Maresciallo Capo Dario Monforte, that the Maresciallo Capo would be arrested on 14 November and returned immediately to Rome. The charge was profiteering from the theft of the cultural heritage of Iraq, at that time a favourite topic of the international press. His arrest could surely serve as an example of the purity of the motives of the Western powers whose troops were serving in Iraq, and as an example of what the Western allies would not tolerate. No mention was to be made of the theft and probable sale of weapons to the enemy, and in no way could his behaviour be made public.

Brunetti paused here and, for some time, sat rubbing his fingers against his bottom lip while he considered this latest information.

He set the six pages aside and returned to the original document. This contained the names of those who were scheduled

for duty in the Italian headquarters on 12 November: Giovanni
Andreoli, Giuliano de Rossi, Lino Riccio, Alessandro Cagnassi,
Matteo Marcon, Daniele Campi . . .

He stopped at that name and set his memory to find it. Months
ago. One of the islands, he thought. A fight. No. Something violent, though. He looked out of his window, an old friend who
had helped him remember many things. Over the years, he'd
developed the technique of focusing his eyes on the most distant point and concentrating only on that, to the exclusion of
all else.

That was it – a mugging in broad daylight. On Murano, of all
places.

He returned to his chair and keyed in the crime logs for the
city, found Murano and found the name: Daniele Campi. The
report was brief. Five months ago, late in the afternoon, a man
returning from work saw an attack taking place on the *riva*.
Recognizing his neighbour as the smaller man lying on the
ground, he shouted, unable to do more. The larger man turned
towards him, then ran off, disappearing into the first *calle*.

The man on the ground had fallen against the low brick wall
between his house and the canal, and his bleeding lip was
already beginning to swell. The neighbour helped Campi to his
feet, found his keys in his pocket and helped him into the house,
then accompanied him on the boat to the hospital and waited
while three stitches were put in his lip and the wound on his
forehead was cleaned and bandaged. A nurse told him to come
back in ten days to have the stitches removed, then handed him
the police form to fill in to report a crime.

No serious harm had been done; therefore, no one from the
police had been sent to talk to him, although the attack was
listed as a mugging, one of the very few ever registered on
Murano. Hence Brunetti's memory of the place, not of the name
of the victim.

Without thinking what he would say, he called the number given in the report. It was answered on the third ring, a man's voice, deep. 'Campi.'

'Signor Campi, this is Commissario Brunetti. I'm calling to ask about the incident some months ago.' Campi said nothing, so Brunetti continued. 'Did one of our men ever come out to interview you after the attack?'

His voice a little less deep, Campi said, 'No, no one did. But it doesn't matter. Whoever it was didn't take my money or my documents.'

'I'm happy to hear that,' Brunetti said, using his amiable voice. 'Sometimes the process of getting things replaced is worse than the theft.'

Campi began to say something, but his voice was devoured by a deafening rumble that sprang up from nothing, then roared so loudly as to drown out everything, before slowly disappearing as though something were chasing it away.

'What was that?' Brunetti asked.

'EasyJet to Gatwick. Right on time.'

'You're at the airport?'

'Where else should I be? I work here.'

At the airport, Brunetti repeated to himself, and then, making himself sound uninterested, just keeping the conversation going, asked Campi, 'Doing what?' and waited for him to say it.

'I'm in charge of baggage handling.'

'Oh, how interesting,' Brunetti said in a tone that blared out that it was not interesting at all. 'Let me tell you the truth, Signor Campi,' he said, and continued without waiting to hear a response. 'Our rules say that all victims have to be interviewed. I realize that this is a bother for you, but we need to do it or we have trouble.' He allowed himself a resigned snort of laughter and added, 'And our bureaucracy is a good deal worse than the one that handles lost documents, believe me.'

'Can't we do it on the phone?' Campi asked.

'We need a signature, and one of us has to go and talk to the victim.' Before Campi had time to protest, Brunetti said, 'If it will make things easier for you, I could come out there, talk to you for a few minutes, you can sign the paper, then I take it back to the archivist, he registers it, and that's the end of it.'

'Out here?'

'Yes, I can get a car at Piazzale Roma and come out, and on the way back,' Brunetti began and lowered his voice, as though he thought someone near him might be listening, 'I could stop at Panorama and get an air conditioner. I think this summer's going to be a killer, and this is a way to get it home without having to organize a car. If I wait until it's hot, there won't be any left. To buy.'

'And after you get back to Piazzale Roma?' Campi seemed unable to stop himself from asking. 'With an air conditioner?'

'I'll have a launch to return to work, and the pilot will take me home first. Nothing easier.'

'It certainly sounds it,' Campi said and made a noise that resembled a laugh. 'When would you like to do this, Commissario?'

'As soon as possible.'

'To see me, or to get the air conditioner?' Campi asked and laughed, the new best friend of a police commissario.

'Could we do it this afternoon? Three-thirty? That way I'd get to Panorama after the rush of the lunch break and save time.'

'You'll have a police car?'

'Unmarked, but with a driver in uniform.'

'Good. I'll tell you where to go.'

And so Campi did. Brunetti called the station at Piazzale Roma and said he needed a car and driver for a few hours that afternoon and would be there at three. In the past, he would have asked if he could have a car, but Patta's promise put muscle in his voice, and the car was his for the asking.

Brunetti returned to the papers on his desk and continued reading, although he had already read – what was it the Americans called it, 'the spoiler'? – and was well aware of what was lurking in the following pages.

About three hundred kilos of explosives in a tank truck filled with flammable material. Ten-forty in the morning; everyone at work at the headquarters. In the midst of this grotesque possibility, the Lord had raised his hand and prevented the truck from entering the courtyard; it blew up at the entrance, sparing how much more death and pain?

Among the list of the wounded, he found the names of three Venetians, all still resident in that city: Daniele Campi, Lino Riccio and Dario Monforte. The writer of this document was made of the stuff of scholars: there were footnotes, referring the reader to pages 27 and 28. The notes on page 27 told of the triage practised by the doctors and nurses who were there, while those on page 28 gave the names of each of the wounded, their original prognosis, and, as expected in cases of burns, the time spent in various hospitals before their release.

Lino Riccio had spent almost two years in a number of European burn centres – Graz, Zurich, and Hanover – in all of which he had been treated for psychological as well as physical damage: Campi had spent three months in Bergen, and Monforte three months in Barcelona and another three in Copenhagen. During the first two years after the attack, four of the other men sent to burn centres had died there, while another was believed to have committed suicide.

Brunetti forced himself to read the initial diagnoses of the three men. A handwritten note at the top of the page stated that photos had been omitted, out of the charity of either the original compiler or Signorina Elettra – he cared not which. There followed written descriptions. Riccio's was the worst, his legs as devastated as his hands, which had been rendered 'useless'.

Campi had been burned on his right leg and back, his buttock saved by the body of another soldier who had been blown against him. Monforte had been extensively burned on his arms, chest, and back. Brunetti found that difficult to believe, given the facility with which Monforte had moved and the easy physicality of his presence. But then Brunetti remembered the red dots that walked across his forehead and into his hair.

All three had ultimately been offered, and had accepted, medical retirement, the terms of which were not given but were different for all three, factoring in their years of service and the extent of their physical damage. They were granted the right to use military hospitals for the rest of their lives. Given that many services would be performed in civilian hospitals, which already provided free medical services to all citizens, they had not been treated, it seemed to Brunetti, very generously.

Neither Riccio nor Campi, both Northerners and both subordinate to Monforte, had attracted the attention of the investigating team.

Brunetti turned back to the first page and straightened the pile of papers on his desk, thinking about the questions he might put to Signor Campi, and then decided to go home for lunch.

At the table, both Raffi and Chiara were jerky-spirited with the arrival of spring. They fidgeted in their chairs, failed to listen to anything that was said at the table, served themselves large portions of pasta with *puntarelle* and then ate only half of it before complaining that there was no dessert, which neither of them was in the habit of eating at lunch.

After they'd both left the table, forgetting to ask permission or at least announce that they were leaving, Brunetti turned to Paola and asked, 'Is it too late to sell them?'

Busy gathering up the plates the children had failed to take to the sink, Paola asked, 'Would you buy a used teenager?'

Brunetti grabbed a few plates from the table and stacked them in his hands. He carried them over to Paola and set them down on the counter, then went back and picked up all the knives and forks, careful to point them all in one direction. He set them on top of the plates.

Shaking her hand in the water to move the bubbles around, Paola said, 'If this weren't lunch, I'd give you a grappa to reward you for bringing those things over to me.'

'I've got to get back,' he said, deeply sorry that he could not spend the afternoon in the company of his wife and the Marquis de Custine.

'There's San Pietro for tonight,' she said.

'You make me your slave,' Brunetti said, and went to get a heavier jacket to wear to the airport, where it was often cooler.

## 25

It was some time since Brunetti had been to the airport – perhaps as much as two years – and he found it new and utterly confusing. The place seemed to be a shopping mall with an enormous parking lot and a few runways. The driver said he had no idea of the layout, so Brunetti called Campi, and as Campi gave directions, Brunetti repeated them to the driver, who seemed to make sense of them. Within a few minutes, the car pulled up to a man standing at an open gate. He waved them in and pointed at some sort of command sensor at the gate, which slid silently closed.

Campi was fair-skinned, short and stocky, and wore a bright orange jacket, his name printed on the breast pocket. He appeared to be in his fifties and walked with a slight limp. He braced his hand on the door of the car, leaned in the back window the driver had opened, and asked, 'Signor Brunetti?'

'Yes,' Brunetti answered. 'Where do we leave this?'

'Park it over there,' Campi said, indicating a row of cars on the left.

Brunetti got out and told the driver to wait for him.

Campi approached and put out his hand. Brunetti took it. It

was an exchange of courtesy, not a fight for domination. Campi led him into a transitory-looking building and down a long hall. At the end, he opened a door and led Brunetti into a windowless office almost as small as Griffoni's that somehow managed to house a tall filing cabinet and two chairs on either side of a table whose surface was stained but clean and half covered with folders and loose papers. Luckily, the upper half of the door was glass, although it gave no view better than a long corridor with windows on the right.

'This is the best place, I think,' Campi said. 'It's mine. They'll call if they need me, so we might be interrupted.'

He walked over to the table, turned and rested against it. He put his hands in his pockets and said, 'I've had time to think, so I'd like to know why you're really here.'

'It's about the attack,' Brunetti said. He repented the half-lie immediately and told himself to be as honest with Campi as he wanted him to be, and so added, 'At least in part.'

Campi smiled and revealed a different, less suspicious face. 'I'm sure it is. But your story about having to fill out papers and get my signature is . . . well, there are vulgar words for what it is, but I'll settle for "unbelievable".'

Brunetti remained where he was but smiled back without embarrassment. 'It is, isn't it, but I didn't have enough time to prepare a better one.'

Still standing, Campi moved behind the table and waved Brunetti to the other chair. 'Now's your chance to tell me a better one.'

'I'm more interested in the attack at Nasiriyah and your boss while you were there,' Brunetti said.

Campi froze. His face flushed, then he grew pale. He sat down in his chair behind the table and put his hands on the surface in front of him, staring at the space between them.

His voice was almost inaudible. 'It's more than twenty years.'

Without being aware of it, Campi put his right hand on his left arm and patted it, as if to see how it was. He looked across at Brunetti, all expression wiped from his face. 'I don't know if I can do this. I used to think about it and wonder how terrible it would be. That the whole thing would come back. The fear of it all.' He half rose from his chair but then sat down again and asked, 'How much do you know?'

Brunetti saw no reason not to tell him. 'I know about the flights from Iraq and what was sent back to Italy, and about the flights to Iraq and what happened to some of the cargo. He was the quartermaster, wasn't he? Packing and sending and delivering – nothing easier.' Brunetti paused, waited for Campi to say something, and when he did not, went on: 'I know the material coming here passed safely through Aviano and I suppose it got passed to antique dealers who knew the market.' In the face of Campi's continuing silence, Brunetti said, 'I also know about the weapons that were sold.'

Brunetti stopped and then, in a far different voice, said, 'All of that is the concern of the art police or the army's police.'

'Then what are you interested in?'

'Monforte's son. A colleague of mine helped the boy, and since she did that, we've encountered Signor Monforte's name a number of times, and I think he's behind a threat that's been made to my colleague.'

Campi nodded but remained silent.

'And now,' Brunetti went on, 'his name came up when we were talking to someone who was at Nasiriyah.'

'Lino?' Campi asked.

'Yes,' Brunetti said, and then, almost involuntarily, 'Poor devil.'

'Yes, he is,' Campi agreed in a voice so soft as to be almost inaudible. 'He got the worst of it.' Having said that, Campi looked at the wall in front of him. 'What did Lino tell you?' he asked.

'About the shipments to and from Italy and the way you and he and Monforte ran them as a private business.'

'You've forgotten someone.'

'Who?'

'If you spoke to Lino, you've heard about the fourth man, Valeriano Anzoletti.'

'Yes,' Brunetti said, though he was hearing the man's surname for the first time.

'He was a good friend of Dario's.'

'Until he wasn't a good friend of Dario's.'

'Exactly.'

'Were you in the van?'

Campi failed to hide his surprise that Brunetti would already know about that. 'We were all there,' Campi said roughly. 'The difference is that Dario was the only one who knew where we were going.' Campi saw Brunetti open his mouth to speak and rode right over him. 'You don't have to believe me, Commissario, but you do have to listen to me.' He waited until Brunetti nodded before continuing. 'Dario found out about it – that he was stealing from us.' Campi grinned at the verb.

'We got in the van. Dario said we were going out to the airport. We were all in uniform. But the van went towards the centre of Nasiriyah. Dario spoke some Arabic, so I suppose he told the driver where he wanted him to take us.

'Dario told him to stop the van in front of the entrance to the souk. I assumed that Dario wanted to buy something, although we had everything we needed.

'I didn't ask him why we were there. Dario didn't like to be asked questions, not about anything.

'He and Lino were in the back with Valeriano. Valeriano and Dario had obviously had some sort of argument before they got in the van, but I was busy paying attention to the people around us, so I never had a chance to talk to Valeriano. The van was white and was an easy target, so I just wanted to get out of there. But suddenly I heard them – Dario and Valeriano – start shouting, and then the door on Dario's right opened – he was in the middle, between Lino and Valeriano – and when I turned around to look, I saw Dario kick Valeriano out onto the ground. Both feet – he almost flew out. He fell on his face, and Dario poked the driver in the shoulder and told him to go back to the base, the other maresciallo wasn't coming back with us.

'And that's the way it was. We drove back to the base, and I didn't look back. I didn't want to see anything or know anything. We went back, and this is the first time I've spoken about it since then, though I think about Valeriano all the time.' Campi stopped for just a few seconds before continuing with the Eulogy of Valeriano, the accused thief: 'Poor devil.' Then he added, in a far softer voice, 'He didn't die there.'

'He made it back to the base?' Brunetti asked, almost ready to believe in divine intervention.

Campi stood and walked into the corridor to look out of the window there. He saw cars, trucks, planes, people, buses. After a time, he came back into his office and looked across at Brunetti. 'Did you read the list of victims of the bombing?' he asked Brunetti.

'Quickly, yes.'

'Do you remember reading his name?'

'That's not likely, is it, not if Monforte kicked him out of the van in the centre of town, wearing an Italian army uniform.'

'No, he'd have no chance.'

Brunetti waited for Campi to say more; he was tired of the back and forth, yes and no, but decided to wait.

'His name was on the morning roster,' Campi finally said.

'But you said he wasn't there,' Brunetti reminded him.

'I said he didn't *die* there. Someone else did.'

'I don't understand.'

'There were . . .' Campi stopped speaking and ran both hands down his face. Brunetti noticed only now that his face was covered with sweat.

'There were pieces.'

'*Oddio*,' escaped from Brunetti.

Campi had run out of words and stopped speaking as suddenly as he had started. He waved a hand in the air to demonstrate horror or monstrosity or futility or waste, or all of them together: it really didn't matter.

'A friend told me, but this was months later, that in some cases, there was no way to tell who . . . So they used the roster.'

Whatever either of them might have had to say was drowned out by the roar of another departing plane. Brunetti feared the walls would blow in at them from the noise or the force or the wind, but nothing happened. The sound gradually diminished, then disappeared. Campi smiled, but it was an uncertain smile.

'Why did Monforte attack you?' Brunetti suddenly asked.

The question surprised Campi. After some time, he said, 'He told me he was thinking of re-establishing the business. He wanted me to join. He said it would be like old times.' After a lapse of a few seconds, he added, 'That's what I was afraid of, so I told him I wasn't interested.'

'Business?' Brunetti asked.

'Business. It's the word he used.' Campi went silent for a time and then said, surprised at what he had just realized, 'He must have needed money.'

'But you said your money wasn't taken when you were attacked.'

'He'd never steal such a small sum,' Campi said, his voice stopping just short of indignation.

'You refused him,' Brunetti said.

'Commissario, I'm older, I'm married, I have a wife and two kids, and I don't do things like that any more.' His voice had the sound of truth. He opened his mouth to continue, paused and studied Brunetti's face, then said, 'Suffering does no one any good, Commissario. But dying – as I should have done – and then coming back, that can.'

Before Brunetti could speak, Campi went on. 'It's a second chance. And I don't want to waste it doing the things I did before the bombing. That was my life before, but now it's different.'

'Tell me,' Brunetti asked.

Campi gave him a long look and said, very softly, 'You're the only person other than my wife who's ever asked me to.' He sighed and looked down at the back of his hands, and it was only then that Brunetti noticed the colour and texture of the skin on the back of Campi's right hand.

'For six days, when I got to Bergen, I was in so much pain that I cried and screamed all the time, no matter what they gave me for the pain, and they had to put someone in the room with me all night. Suicide watch, that's what they called it.' Campi stopped speaking, and for a terrible minute Brunetti feared that he would expose an arm or a leg to show him the reality of his burns.

Instead, he pushed his chair back a bit and stretched out his legs. 'It's the truth and, yes, twenty years ago I would have been embarrassed to confess to crying like that.'

Light is not really a tangible thing, is it? It allows us to see other things, but it's not as if we see light as a separate entity: we just see the things it illuminates. Brunetti thought this as Campi's voice began almost to glow when he said, 'But then my wife came into the room – I'd never seen her before. Her brother was on the same ward – and she asked me if I could perhaps not scream because he couldn't sleep when I did.

'I'd never seen her before, not once in my life, but when she asked me, I wanted to help her and help her brother, so I told her I'd try. And I did, but it took me time to stop, it was so bad.

'On the third day, I went the entire night without screaming, not once. I grunted and moaned, I suppose,' he said with a small smile, 'but I did not scream. And before she went back to her hotel that evening, she came into my room and thanked me, said her brother had slept most of the night and the whole day.

'And she touched my hand with hers, and I started to cry, and she thought the pain had come back, and she said she'd give me a five-minute pass for screaming if I needed it, and I laughed because she meant it as a joke, and I knew that.

'And I got better. I don't mean the burns – they were still . . . bad. But inside I was better because I could want to do something good for someone else, and that had never been anything I had wanted to waste my time on.' He stopped.

'I see,' Brunetti said. He did.

Believing now that this man would tell him the truth, Brunetti said, 'I'm here because what I know about him doesn't make any sense.'

'For example?'

'How did he become the Hero of Nasiriyah?' Brunetti asked.

For a moment, he thought Campi was going to laugh, and then he thought he was going to try to spit something from his mouth. At last he said, 'Luck, perhaps.'

'Are you joking?' Brunetti asked when it became obvious that Campi didn't want to answer.

'No. There's nothing to joke about. But he *was* lucky.' Then, the volume and the passion of his voice increasing as he spoke, Campi said, 'I was there, on the other side of the courtyard, getting ready to go out on patrol. I'd just come downstairs and was still inside the building, behind the wall of sandbags we'd built, waiting for the armoured car we used.

'I forget who I was talking to . . . anyway, to someone . . . and he said he heard the armoured car coming, and because he liked to sit in the back seat, in the middle – because that was the safest seat – he started across the courtyard. Then I heard the engine too, but when I looked down, I saw that one of my boots was untied – I can't remember any more if it was the right or the left.' He stopped there, and for a moment Brunetti thought he was trying to remember which it had been.

Campi looked at Brunetti and shook away the idea. 'Probably doesn't matter, but it was important then because if you don't retie it, you'll eventually trip and fall, and that's not a good thing if there are people around who want to shoot you.'

He looked at Brunetti for confirmation of this simple truth, and Brunetti nodded.

'So I leaned my rifle against the wall of bags and bent down to tie it. But it wasn't the car. It was a truck, and it rolled closer, but I was bending down and didn't see it, and then I heard an explosion and some sort of power wave knocked me sideways and I lost my balance and fell.'

Campi's breathing had grown faster; he closed his eyes and took a few deep breaths. When he was calmer, he opened his eyes and held a reassuring hand towards Brunetti.

'When I opened my eyes, I saw fire in front of me, and all I could think about was getting away from it. I tried to push myself up, but my left arm and shoulder felt like they'd been electrocuted. So did my right leg, but only the back of it because I was lying on my stomach. And something was on top of me.

'It wasn't until I tried to push it away that I realized it was a man. Well, his body, because he must have been dead.

'And it was hot all of a sudden. I pulled myself up by grabbing on to the bags. The wall was almost as high as we were, but I could see into the courtyard.'

Campi stopped speaking and looked at Brunetti as though he'd never seen him before, then said, quite casually, 'I know I'm not there. But when I start to think about it, it's almost as if

I'm there again. The pain comes back, too, that's the strange thing. But only if it wakes me up. If it's like this, things are fine, and I know I'm not there.' Suddenly a look of tremendous uncertainty passed across his face and he leaned towards Brunetti and asked, 'We're not there, are we?'

'No,' Brunetti said, putting his hand on Campi's shoulder and giving it a light squeeze. 'We're not there. We're safe.'

As if Brunetti had not said that but had asked for more, Campi went on. 'That's when I saw Dario. He was running towards me because I was standing at one of the openings we'd left in the sandbag wall. Behind him the truck was burning, and there were smaller explosions. I could see that the back of his uniform was on fire. He kept batting at it with his hands – over his shoulder and then with his hands behind his back.

'All of a sudden, Lino was beside him, beating at his back. That's how Lino lost his hands, I think, not that they ever tried to figure those things out. Then someone else started running beside them – I didn't recognize him because he really didn't have much of a face any more. He still had his eyes, though, and he saw the opening in the wall and was running for it, like Lino and Dario, as if it was some sort of race.' He stopped here and started to examine the palms of his hands. This was the first time Brunetti had looked at them; he turned his eyes away.

'They kept running – but it wasn't running, just staggering and screaming – towards the gap in the wall, right towards me.' Then, as if trying to make sure his story was accurate on all counts, he said, 'The opening was small. We always had to turn sideways to fit through it. The man on Dario's left – I don't know who he was – stumbled and started to fall forward. And Dario took his arm and pushed him away.

'The strange thing,' Campi said in an entirely conversational voice, 'was that they were staggering around like drunks. In fact, Dario lost his balance when he pushed the other guy away, and if Lino hadn't grabbed him and pulled him up, he would have fallen.

'They finally got to the wall, and Dario did it again. He screamed and pushed Lino aside and came in first, and then Lino got through and then there was another explosion and another blast, and the three of us ended up in a heap on the ground.'

He looked at Brunetti and said, 'And that's how the Hero of Nasiriyah was born.' He smiled then, a very weary smile.

'I don't understand,' Brunetti said.

'He ended up on top of us, and he had an arm around each of us, as though he were trying to protect us. Nothing more heroic than risking your life for others, is there?'

Then, in a voice as cold as ice, Campi continued. 'We had a disaster on our hands. No one had bothered to put barrels of cement at the entrance; no one tried to block it. So the truck kept moving towards us even after the guards shot and killed the driver.

'I was unconscious, so I have no idea what happened to us, who found us, what they did for us, where they took us, how they got us to a hospital, or to Europe, or anything. If I woke up, I screamed. If they drugged me, sometimes I stopped.'

For a while, Campi remained silent, but then he asked, 'Did you ever see the photos of those people who died in Pompeii?'

Confused, Brunetti said, 'Yes.'

'I saw them when I was in school, and I wondered what they had been doing when they fell down and died. Our teacher said they died instantly from the gas that came with the eruption. But I always wondered who they were and where they were going, and were they alone.'

Because he didn't understand what Campi was trying to say, Brunetti didn't know if he was expected to speak or not. So he chose to remain silent, a wise choice because Campi started speaking again. Looking directly at Brunetti, he asked, 'And what's better than a hero? It's what every disaster needs.'

He suddenly got to his feet and went out into the corridor to take another look at the airport, as though it required his frequent attention. Things must have been in order, for he came back and sat opposite Brunetti.

'He called me soon after I was promoted here,' Campi said, waving a languid hand to encompass the entire airport. 'We met for a drink, and he asked me if I'd like to go back to making the same sort of money I'd been making when we worked together before. He'd heard that I was in charge of cargo, but he didn't really want me: he wanted access to the cargo holds. There are no direct flights yet. He says he's planning ahead.'

'And you turned him down?'

Campi nodded and, speaking mildly, said, 'He's not accustomed to having people say no to him.' He rubbed his hands together, then began to turn his wedding ring round and round with his thumb.

'So he attacked you in front of your house?'

Campi smiled, and Brunetti thought of the many statues he'd seen of the Buddha, that same eternal smile in the face of good or evil. Finally, Campi said, 'Not really.' Then, seeing Brunetti's face, he added, 'He shoved me, and I tripped over my own feet.'

'But why did he shove you?'

'Because I reminded him of what really happened and that there was no treasure to be found.'

'I'm afraid I don't understand,' Brunetti said.

Campi covered his eyes with his hands. 'We didn't have much success. Dario believed his own bragging.' He took his hands away and looked at Brunetti. 'We sold a few things, piece by piece, and we made some money in the beginning, but not much. Then Dario decided to keep everything there, on the base, and send it all back in one shipment, when he could be sure there would be no interference, no inspection.'

Campi stopped, as if he had said all there was to say.

'I still don't understand,' Brunetti admitted.

'It all burned in the fire. The entire base was obliterated: the buildings, the trucks, the weapons . . . the men.' Campi paused a moment and added, 'So there was no treasure left. There was nothing to sell.'

It took Brunetti some time to think of something to say. 'What will he do?' he finally asked, wondering if Campi had put himself in greater danger by refusing him.

'Oh,' Campi said, as if it were a subject of little importance. 'Probably nothing. I told him I'd left a letter with my lawyer, in the event that anything happened to me.'

'Did you?'

Campi laughed. 'Do I look like the sort of person who'd have a lawyer?' Before Brunetti could speak, Campi shrugged and said, 'It doesn't bother Dario to hurt people. It's not that he likes it particularly, but it would never stop him from doing something he wanted to do, and he thinks it makes people obey him.' He glanced at the door. 'That's the essence of Dario, Commissario: he needs to be obeyed.' Then, in a more reflective voice, he said, 'I left the war, but Dario never did.'

'You aren't afraid?'

'Don't forget the make-believe letter,' Campi reminded him.

In the silence, Brunetti realized there was nothing else he could learn from Campi. He stood and thanked him for his time and his help. 'I hope this is the end of it for you.'

'So do I,' Campi said and smiled.

'You seem very calm about it.'

Campi started to speak but stopped himself and stood, mouth

half-open, his attention caught by something that was not in the room with them.

'What were you going to say?' Brunetti asked.

'If you've been in hell, Commissario, everything else is very calm.'

# 26

On his way back to Venice, Brunetti thought about Maresciallo Capo Monforte and the way Fate or Destiny had transformed him from a soldier selling weapons to the enemy into a national hero. The ease with which Brunetti accepted the possibility unsettled him. What came next, one day as a lion?

Surely, he knew, there had been witnesses to what had happened, but witnessing it had brought death to most of them. And time would have brought forgetting or confusion.

The report Brunetti had read was compiled by the rescuers, and all they had to go on was what they saw. When Maresciallo Capo Monforte was found, he was stretched atop the two men who lay beneath him, one arm around each of them. He might have carried the men out of the range of the still-burning truck and dragged them into the space behind the protecting walls. Or not. By the time the two men lying under him were in any state to answer questions, the story had been told.

The name of Maresciallo Capo Monforte was the first to rise, phoenix-like, from the smoking ruins of the Carabinieri compound in Nasiriyah into the ears of a grieving country. *Forte*, strong indeed, in his extraordinary bravery, in his scorn for danger when duty summoned him, and in the courage with which he endured the terrible price he had to pay. Surely, Monforte had within him the stuff of heroes.

Only an act of spectacular heroism such as his could have distracted attention from – perhaps somehow minimized – the debacle of Nasiriyah. The official report noted that repeated warnings from the secret services had been ignored, but that truth could easily be overlooked for – or replaced entirely by – a tale of personal valour and sacrifice, for that remained longer, and more comfortably, in the individual and national memory. Had not the Twelfth Battle of the Isonzo – though it cost three hundred thousand Italian lives – come to be viewed as yet another jewel in the crown of the military prowess of General Cadorna? If not, why were so many streets named after him?

When the officer who was meant to initiate the case against Monforte learned of the radio and television broadcasts and their use of the word 'hero', his first thought was that they had to find two more. As the only hero of Nasiriyah, Monforte would be – alas – forever untouchable: better to find two more and dilute the glory a bit.

His superiors rejected the idea, saying that they needed a single figure in whom national pride could be concentrated. They could show one man – three would complicate things terribly – as a model to children, adults, the old. Besides, many of the badly burned weren't presentable, and some of them were not certain to survive. Three days had already passed, and it would seem strange if they discovered new ones now.

Again, Brunetti recalled the President of Italy at the side of Monforte's bed. He saw that his hands were shaking.

Brunetti never remembered how long he sat in his office,

thinking about patriotism and loyalty and who and what our leaders are, and who gets to make up the rules about what a person can and cannot do.

To break this mood, Brunetti called Signorina Elettra and asked what information there was about Bocchese.

'The last I heard was from his doctor, who said they found a note on his pillow this morning saying he was bored and was going back to the Questura.'

'Has there been a sighting downstairs?' he asked.

'No one's told me they've seen him.'

Still battered by what he'd read, Brunetti thought he'd go down to the lab anyway and see if Bocchese was there. Not pausing at the entrance, he went directly across to Bocchese's open door and knocked on the frame a few times. Bocchese, who had been in the process of opening a cardboard shoebox, looked up in surprise and said, 'Ah, Brunetti, it's good to see you,' then returned his attention to the box.

Brunetti studied the other man's face and saw the signs of deep bruising around his nose, though the swelling had already begun to disappear and the colour was returning to normal. A bandage covered about three centimetres directly above his left ear and was taped to his shaved skull at both ends and along the edges.

Bocchese's high-wattage lamp was on his desk and turned on, pointing into the box, so the total illumination in that area was unpleasantly powerful, more than 200 watts, and was painful to Brunetti's eyes. As if sensing this, Bocchese switched the lamp off.

'Enzo,' Brunetti said, his store of patience suddenly run out, 'are you going to tell me what happened, or should I go back to my office and mind my own business?'

After a long pause but with his eyes on whatever was in the

box, Bocchese said, 'I've had enough. It's as simple as that. Enough.'

'Enough of what?' Brunetti asked, taking a step closer to the desk.

'Of that bastard and his parents.' He pulled the cardboard box closer and opened it. He reached in, slowly, slowly, and pulled out the statue of Hercules, safe inside in a pillowcase that he opened carefully. The hero's club was wrapped in a small square of plastic packing material and taped to his back.

'You saved him?' Brunetti asked.

Bocchese shrugged the question away. 'I found him. Lying on the floor, his nose pressed into the carpet and, as you see, his club snapped off. But otherwise he's all right.'

'And the club?' Brunetti asked, honestly curious.

'I think I can get it back into his hand, but only with glue, so the break will show.'

'He's a fighter, isn't he?' Brunetti asked rhetorically. 'So he's probably used to broken bones and weapons. And scars.'

'Yes, I'd thought of that,' Bocchese said. Then, eyes on the hero, he added, 'Thanks for finding me, and for your help.'

'It was nothing,' Brunetti said. 'Hercules and I work as a team, and it was my turn.'

He was standing beside Bocchese, so all he saw was a small motion of his mouth. It was enough. 'What are you going to do?'

'I've already made a formal *querela* for assault and vandalism. I did it downstairs, the way any citizen would.' Before Brunetti could ask why he hadn't requested his help, Bocchese continued: 'I didn't want to involve anyone I know, didn't want it to look like favouritism. I told them exactly what happened and signed the transcript: he pushed past me when I opened the door to my apartment, and when I tried to stop him, he hit me and knocked me to the floor, and then he went to the back room, where the collection was, and began to throw the pieces around.

I followed him and tried to stop him, and he hit me in the face and I tried to get away from him. After that I don't know what else he did.'

Brunetti was stunned into silence by the viciousness of the attack.

A very small smile formed on Bocchese's lips, and he said, 'His fingerprints were on everything, and I can testify that I saw him. The case is a magistrate's dream.'

Brunetti nodded grimly. Bocchese said, 'I also collected all of the receipts I have for the statues – when and where I bought them, how much I paid, even including the tax.'

'To claim damages?'

'Not to *claim* them, Guido. To *get* them,' Bocchese said hoarsely. 'His father is never going to hear the end of this.'

Brunetti made no effort to disguise his pleasure at what Bocchese said.

Bocchese held up his hand and told Brunetti, 'Your Venus is all right.'

'She wasn't hurt?'

'When he was tossing them around, she ended up under the sofa, so he never had the chance to hurt her.'

'You realize how many years it might take to settle this?'

'This is Italy. Of course it will take years.' Bocchese, in the heat of the moment, pulled the chain on the table lamp and turned it on and off a few times before saying, 'I don't care what it costs or how long it takes.'

It was then Brunetti realized that Bocchese was beginning to sound like his old self. His nose was still bruised and swollen, but his spirit was eager for battle.

'What about the other statues? Will you still sell them?' Brunetti thought to ask.

'I called off the sale,' Bocchese said, his relief evident. 'I don't know what I was thinking when I agreed to sell them.' After a long pause, he said, 'I'm going to keep them.'

'Good for you,' Brunetti said. He reached out and patted Bocchese's shoulder.

The technician surprised Brunetti by saying, with sudden earnestness, 'It's time to change things, Guido.'

A mixture of surprise and something like fear stopped Brunetti from speaking for a long time, and then the best he could think of to say was 'Give yourself time, Enzo,' not at all certain what he meant.

'I've already started.'

'Started what?'

'Another job.'

'What?' Brunetti demanded. 'You've been in the hospital. What other job could you have?'

'It's not final,' Bocchese said. 'There's no contract yet. But it's real.'

'What is it?' Brunetti asked, honestly curious to know what job a police technician with years of experience with drugs, weapons, blood-soaked clothing, and a long list of unpleasant objects, a man around the age of retirement, could possibly offer a new employer.

'I told you, Guido – a new job.'

'Doing what?'

'Working with bronzes,' Bocchese said. 'As a kind of curator and technician.'

For a moment, Brunetti hardly understood what he was hearing. Bocchese? Curator? Without diplomas and letters of recommendation? Without an academic career or years of work in a gallery? Would he simply walk into a museum and say he was reporting for work?

Brunetti saw the smile on Bocchese's face, so he softened his tone and, in what he tried to make a calm, normal voice, asked, 'Tell me about it.'

The smile moved around Bocchese's face: eyes, mouth, even his nose had begun to look happy. 'You know Eugenio Pavan, don't you?'

'The banker?' Brunetti asked.

Bocchese's nod solved the mystery.

'"The collector" would be more appropriate, I suppose?' Brunetti asked.

Bocchese pulled his lips together while he thought about what to say. 'I've been doing some work for him. For years.'

'Work?' Brunetti asked.

'Oh, stop it, Guido,' Bocchese said, but with a grin. He went on in a friendlier manner. 'He has an important collection of bronzes, and he's got in the habit of asking my opinion when he's not entirely sure about whether he should bring one home.' After a moment's pause, Bocchese added, 'And he's asked me to repair some that have been badly treated or abused.'

It came to Brunetti to joke with Bocchese and point out that he spoke of the statues as though they were human. He decided, however, to keep those words to himself and said, instead, 'Tell me more.'

'He's been asking me for years to work for him.'

'Doing what?' Brunetti asked.

'Pretty much the same things I'm already doing, but not only on weekends or when I can find time.' Then, his face growing serious with what Brunetti recognized as pride, he added, 'And he needs someone to research the whole collection to see if anything in it is stolen.'

'It sounds like a full-time job,' Brunetti said.

'I hope it will be,' Bocchese said.

'And this?' Brunetti asked, waving his hand around Bocchese's office and towards the back room, where his crew worked.

'It's time, Guido,' Bocchese said, giving him a serious look. 'I don't want to do this any more. I want to work with beautiful things.'

A long silence fell between them, and Brunetti tried to remember how many years he'd worked with Bocchese, trusted Bocchese, respected him.

He pushed himself away from the desk and said, 'I wasn't ready for this, Enzo.'

'I am,' Bocchese said, and Brunetti knew he was right.

# 27

Spring burst upon them the next week and beat everyone over the head with sun and bright colours and the desire to be outside. The change in weather was registered by the police: pickpocketing, in imitation of the dandelions, was absent one day, full-blossomed the next; domestic violence now moved out of the confines of the home and took place outdoors, in parks, *piazze*, open-air restaurants and bars; even vandalism grew more popular, since the bulk of it was committed outside.

In April, chaos unleashed itself in Mestre one balmy Tuesday night when two gangs of minors, one from Venice and one from Mestre, met in Piazza Ferretto a little past midnight in order to . . .

Had any of the police who answered the call been asked to finish that sentence – or the parents of the boys or even the boys themselves – they would have failed, for the baby gangs had no reason for what they did to one another, at least no reason they could explain to an adult.

There were comments, usually in the form of boasts made on social media: 'We're tougher than they are.' 'We have more likes on Instagram.' 'The kids in the neighbourhood look up to me.' 'We protect one another.'

No, they didn't want to steal anything. No, they didn't know any of the kids in the other gang. No, they didn't dislike them or want anything bad to happen to them. But they were there, and so were the others, and so they had to fight it out. They all knew themselves to be tougher than the others. As to just how this was measured, no one had an explanation but everyone seemed to agree on the final verdict.

This was incomprehensible to Brunetti and frightened him not a little. The gangs went in search of an emotional response: fear, admiration, respect, emulation. The gangs were not in search of profit or acquisition, those two sacred cows of capitalism. They had no desire to strip their victims bare, pillage their homes, stick their heads on pikes and exhibit them.

Instead, they made videos of the fights and posted them wherever they could, glorying in the sudden increase in the number of followers that resulted from every encounter with a rival gang. They preened at their prowess in inflicting pain and in winning, whatever that meant.

Their rewards were equally evanescent: someone ticked 'yes' or 'like', perhaps even devoted a word or two of approval for their attack on some other gang that was equally concerned with the aftermath of battle and hoping for the same votes. Did they hurry home to read their reviews?

Spring continued, as was its wont, and things grew quiet in Venice, at least as far as crime was concerned. The tourists continued to arrive in ever-increasing numbers, but since they did not come to steal but to be stolen from, any influence they might have had on crime statistics was in augmenting the numbers of the victims of pickpockets.

During the last week in April, the same Roma woman who

had been arrested so often as to have become a legend at the Questura was apprehended three separate times for pickpocketing on the vaporetto from the station to Rialto, apparently her favourite workplace. Each time, she pulled out the copy of her correctly dated ultrasound exam that showed her to be pregnant; consequently the best the police could do was take her to Piazzale Roma and send her back to her home on the mainland, hoping she would go there and not immediately back to the Number One vaporetto, that was almost her place of business.

For a day or two, a rumour circulated in the Questura that the officers in the narcotics section had begun a lottery at five euros a ticket: guess the number of times she'd be arrested before the end of June and you'd win it all. Lieutenant Scarpa, who was aware of this rumour, apparently before it started, posted a notice saying that such levity was not to be tolerated and anyone found trying to buy a ticket would have that fact entered in his or her personnel file. Interest in the lottery increased, but it had not been a reality and never became one.

It did not rain. It had not rained since Easter, and that was more than a month ago. The streets bore witness to the absence of rain, and the plants and trees in the various gardens, public and private, began to show signs of their suffering. The Church called for prayer; the Comune advised against wasting water; and the *Gazzettino* revealed the shocking percentage of water reported to leak from the underground pipes even before reaching the cities towards which it was meant to flow.

The temperature declined, and the subject disappeared from discussion and public concern. And still it did not rain.

It grew hot again as spring concluded and passed the temperature to summer to see what sort of number it could conjure up. The heat appeared to have affected the baby gangs, for nothing was heard of them for weeks. Young people, however, still continued to do stupid things: on the mainland, they raced their scooters into traffic and broke their arms; in the city, they dived into the Laguna from the Ponte Panada at Fondamente Nove and were sick for days from the water; they imitated the French boys who had introduced parkour to Venice and came to the city to jump over narrow canals and climb up the façades of the buildings on the other side, sometimes to the third floor. In short, these foreigners took risks and took films of themselves taking risks to send to their friends back home, who were taking even bigger risks. The Venetians upped the ante and tried to climb to the fourth floor, and, when they found it, the fifth, believing they would always be lucky enough, if they fell, to fall into a canal.

Until one of them, after climbing to the third floor of a house along Rio di Santa Sofia, thought he'd try to make it to the next and then to the roof. He would surely have succeeded had the hinge on the open shutter on the fourth floor not been rusted through and had it not given way when he set his full weight on it and raised his hands towards the roof.

His friends had always told him that if for some reason you started to fall, push yourself as hard as possible away from the façade of the building you were trying to climb, twist like a top, and try to go head first into the water of the canal. The friends who were climbing with him that day, one of whom had made it to the roof of the same building two weeks before, saw him fall and thought he'd remembered. He had, but he had forgotten to add to his calculation the fact that there was no *riva* on the southern side of Rio di Santa Sofia, and thus the north side had a slightly wider *riva* than was usual. His head missed the pavement, but his shoulder hit it with the accumulated force of the fall and all but ripped it from his body.

His friends were in the water in seconds, and he was dragged out before he'd taken more than a few breaths. He screamed at the pressure against his shattered ribs and then continued to scream for the twelve minutes it took the ambulance to get there. And was dead from shock and loss of blood by the time he got to the hospital.

*Il Gazzettino* had time to publish the story on the front page of the regional editions and to elaborate on it in a full page of the local, which also provided a quickly thrown-together history of parkour, explaining that it had been invented in Paris, city of lights, by young activists who wanted Paris to be the city of fewer lights, at least between midnight and six in the morning.

With the end of the school year, the police concerned with the baby gangs feared that things might worsen during the months the members would be left to their own devices. Instead, the gangs seemed to have gone on holiday, for there was no trouble with them until the third week of June, when two classrooms and the principal's office in the Morosini middle school in Venice were discovered to have been vandalized. The computer classroom was a triage clinic, with bits and pieces, shards and debris covering the floor, all of the screens smashed with perverse efficiency. The natural science classroom next to it had suffered similarly: all of its exhibits were scattered around the room, the microscopes and measuring instruments not locked away for the summer were shattered, and all of the records of the experiments students had made that year were tossed onto a pile and kicked around until they were rendered incomprehensible. The principal's office was in no better shape: its computer was smashed, his secretary's as well.

The school had been closed for weeks, and the janitors and painters had been inside; that part of the third floor would have been next. It was only two phone calls from people living near the school who had heard noises during the night that had encouraged the police to investigate, although they did that three days after the calls were made.

The element that most perplexed the police who came to see

the wreckage was the message left on the only surviving black-board: 'From the Lions of Lido'. Only those officers working with the baby gangs recognized the insult to the Lions of Venice, made worse by the fact that it had taken place on their territory.

The morning after the discovery of the vandalism, Brunetti went up to Griffoni's office to talk about the school invasions, as the *Gazzettino* had begun calling them.

'Lions of Lido?' Griffoni said, and risked falling off her chair as a result of making what Brunetti thought of as her 'crucifixion gesture', a wild and potentially dangerous thrusting of her arms to both sides as an indication of the loss of any remaining patience with humanity she might have had. 'These kids are fourteen, fifteen, and they think of themselves as lions?'

They sat in silence for some time, each of them following the same thought and not liking what they saw. 'None of my sources knows anything,' she said, always reluctant to use the word 'informer'.

Brunetti rubbed his fingers against his jaw, something he did when he was nervous or knew he was going to have to do or say something that would embarrass him.

With no introduction, he asked, 'Orlando?'

'I haven't heard from him since that time we met his father. And there's been no trouble from his gang since he said there was going to be something big,' she added with jeering sarcasm in the last words. Then she asked in a half-angry voice, 'For God's sake, why did they have to choose such a stupid name?'

'They're teenagers, Claudia,' Brunetti said, thinking of some of the things Raffi had said when he was that age. Or, even worse, some of the things he himself had thought and said when he was fourteen.

'It's strange,' he added after a pause. 'Even what that Roma woman does makes more sense.'

When Griffoni made no reply, he continued, 'She has a family to support, so she steals money from strangers.' He knew most people would give him odd looks if he were to say something like this to them, especially if they knew he was a policeman.

Griffoni nodded. 'And the baby gangs make no sense?'

'Only to adolescents.'

'What about Sant'Alvise? Did that make sense?' she asked, referring to a fire a few weeks before in a garbage pile in a garden near the church. It had spread quickly in the dead bushes and grass. The firemen had extinguished it easily and at no peril to themselves, leaving it to the likes of the *Gazzettino* to mention the possibility of arson.

'Has your nephew heard anything?' Brunetti asked, returning to the original topic.

Griffoni, not bothering to inform anyone except Brunetti, had contacted her nephew, Antonio, who was completing his doctoral work at the University of Naples in something called the Sociology of Communication. He had recently begun research on his dissertation, 'The Theory and Technique of Adolescent Communication', which Griffoni had construed to mean, 'Helping Aunt Claudia to Understand What Teenagers Write on Social Media'.

She had, in flagrant violation of the laws protecting the rights of minors, given him instructions from Signorina Elettra on how to 'access' the social media accounts of all known members of the Lions of both Venice and Lido and had asked him to alert her if he ever read a message to or from any one of them that might suggest gang plans for violence or confrontation.

She revealed to Brunetti that, yes, she had feared Antonio would refuse. Who, after all, would submit to reading the posts and chats of more than twenty testosterone-crazed teenagers? Instead, after much thought and a discussion with his thesis adviser, Antonio had gladly agreed, for his professor had found

the subject so interesting that he suggested he change his dissertation topic and study the language of micro-criminality.

'Up until now, he hasn't found anything we can use,' Griffoni
continued. 'He said there was no increase in traffic – ah, how
easily I've learned the jargon – at the time of the fire at
Sant'Alvise, and none of them posted photos of it. But he did
say there had been a barely detectable increase in what he's
started to call "pre-combat and post-combat boasting" on the
part of the Lions of Lido just before and just after the discovery of
the damage at the Morosini.'

'Why didn't he tell you before?'

'He did, but he said that it might as easily have been spring
fever or something like that, the increase was so small. It was
only after he read the self-congratulations that he called me to
say that something very strange seemed to be going on.'

'What?' Brunetti asked, to whom all of the communications
were strange.

'Some of the congratulations seemed to come from members
of the Lions of Venice and showed no signs of antagonism, at
least in what they posted.'

Brunetti groaned in exasperation. 'They carry on as though
the feud between them has been going on since the Middle
Ages. Next it'll be a treaty: the prince will marry the princess,
and they'll all live happily ever after.'

With that, they left it.

## 28

But then things started to move. A sixteen-year-old boy from Lido who had decided to go and visit a friend in Pellestrina was deliberately knocked from his bike by another cyclist who passed him at speed. The second cyclist, who was wearing a white helmet and sunglasses, reached out his right hand as he passed the first one and gave him a shove on the shoulder. The boy lost control of his bike, mounted the kerb and – luckily – crashed into a hedge, where he came to rest, much scratched but with nothing broken.

By the time he freed himself from the branches and stood, a bit wobbly, there was no sign of the other, who could have turned either way at the next intersection. Nor were there any pedestrians within sight. He had no choice but to pick up the bike, miraculously undamaged, and decide what to do: continue towards Pellestrina, do something about the increasingly bloody scratches on his right leg, or call the police.

He opted for the second, and when he told the pharmacist where he went to buy disinfectant and bandages what had happened, the pharmacist took it upon himself to do the third.

The police were there quickly and, as the pharmacist cleaned the worst of the scratches, the officers got almost no information from the cyclist. White helmet, sunglasses, dark shorts, short-sleeved shirt, sorry, I didn't notice the colour, and he wasn't very tall. Yes, it was deliberate. Thank God there was the hedge.

A week later, much the same happened to Ruggiero Orsino, another schoolboy from the Lido, enjoying the freedom of speed offered by Via Sandro Gallo, straight on down to Malamocco and no cars on the road, everyone home for lunch. This time, however, it was two bikes: one passed and cut in front of him, distracting him, while from behind came another, who did the same. One shove and his bike careened out of control, flinging him away to land on the grass, stunned, motionless, until he slowly got to his knees, then stood to see that nothing was broken.

Ruggiero had heard the story of the other cyclist and had no compunction about calling the police immediately to report the same crime.

He had barely noticed the first cyclist, the one who had passed him, and he had been so afraid of falling that he had paid no attention to the second.

The only crime the police could think of was 'assault', and as such it was put into the records. The recording officer, therefore, had no choice but to name the 'weapon' as 'bicycle'.

Two days after this, Antonio called her and said that there was increased messaging on the part of the Lions of Venice, one of whom boasted that he had sent a false lion into the under-growth, a remark that made no sense to him, although it did to her.

The messaging increased and grew more cryptic, with refer-ences to revenge and repayment from the Lions of Venice, a name she still could not take seriously.

Griffoni had forwarded the messages her nephew sent her to Brunetti and went down to talk about them with him. She scrolled the messages back to the top and then counted as she quickly went through them. 'There might be a hundred, and I can't make any sense of them – who's sending or to whom? How do they understand one another?' she asked, shaking her phone as if hoping to force it to answer. 'They've decided to spell things as they please, and it sounds like they've substituted new meanings for words.'

Before they could continue, Antonio called to tell her that it had taken him about five minutes to penetrate what both the Lions of Venice and those of Lido surely thought was an impenetrable wall of cyber protection.

Griffoni broke in here, saying, 'Antonio, stop boasting and tell me what they're saying.' She nodded to Brunetti and turned on the loudspeaker.

'Which ones, Venice or Lido?'

'Both, if possible,' she answered.

Antonio let a moment pass, then saved time by asking: 'Would you like me to send a bilingual text? What they write, and what it means in our language?'

'So long as ours is Italian,' she said, absolutely serious.

'It might take me some time to do the translation, but there's no hurry.'

'What do you mean?' she asked.

'You'll understand as soon as you get the translation,' he said and hung up.

As good as his word, Antonio sent many pages of translation into standard Italian about a half-hour later, but it did not happen that Griffoni or Brunetti understood everything.

Each of the more than twenty boys used a pseudonym, they all used emojis, and many words were spelled differently by those who used them. After reading through the first two pages, Griffoni wrote to Antonio and asked him for a summary of what was said, reminding him that her single interest was what the gangs were planning to *do*, and where and when. *Basta*.

When Griffoni and Brunetti finally translated the various messages into a story they could understand, they learned – or at least believed they learned – that on Thursday night, at the previously agreed time, the two gangs would meet at a place yet to be agreed upon. And they would settle things.

Antonio explained that most of the exchanges were very much in the fashion of Viking warrior boasts that the boys had learned about from a television series. Before battle, warriors spent a great deal of time listing their powers, their past battles, their victims: thus the Lions of Venice and Lido could convince themselves that they were something more fearsome than a bunch of kids who could think of nothing better to do that night.

Griffoni put her hands to her face and said, from between her fingers, 'When I was fifteen, I had to be in the house before ten, and my mother wouldn't let me get my ears pierced.'

Brunetti glanced at her and, ignoring her last remark, said, 'They've already given us the day, Thursday, and sooner or later they'll tell us when and where.' Before Griffoni could question this, he added, 'Adolescents have no patience.'

'You sound so certain,' Griffoni said.

'I live with two of them.'

# 29

Brunetti was to be proven right. Antonio did his part by keeping an ear to the communications among the *telefonini* of more than twenty adolescent boys. Before agreeing to do that, however, he had designed a programme that rejected anything referring to clothing, shoes, television series, sports, girls, fast cars, or computers. From the remaining communications, he deciphered the vocabulary they used in planning their group movements and read only the ones that made reference to that, thus reducing the number of messages and postings he actually had to read.

Late on Tuesday afternoon, Griffoni received a message from Orlando confirming that something BIG – he used capital letters – was planned for Thursday night, and adding that he was going, followed by three happy yellow faces. He ended with *See you there?* followed by the same happy faces, but these had their tongues sticking out at her.

Thursday night, but where and when and who? Through all of this uncertainty, Brunetti remained calm. Adolescents cannot keep secrets, he repeated, as though it were a law of nature: the temptation of attention conquers all. It had been true for him and for his friends, and it would be equally so for the baby gangs.

Not only did Brunetti struggle to convince his colleagues that they would find out the plans of the gangs in time, he also tried to persuade Patta to authorize sufficient manpower to stop the boys before anyone was hurt. All previous promises forgotten, the Vice-Questore grudgingly agreed to assign two extra officers to Thursday night's shift, convinced that all of this was 'rumour and exaggeration'.

Nothing was discovered during the next two days, save that Antonio reported that the number of messages between the boys chatting about Thursday's event – still not described in any particulars – was increasing. Brunetti insisted on staying at the Questura on Thursday evening, certain that the boys would not be able to keep this secret much longer. Griffoni, not from hope but from loyalty, remained as well, and Foa said he had nothing better to do that evening and would stay. The two supplementary officers were in the squad room, playing cards, while Vianello was in a small village near Torino for his father-in-law's funeral.

At ten-thirty, Brunetti and Griffoni were still in his office. Conversation was desultory or non-existent. Finally, Griffoni said, 'It's the not knowing that troubles me.' And then, as though one thought followed the other, 'I've got some sandwiches upstairs.'

It didn't sound like an invitation to Brunetti, so he said nothing, and she didn't move. He looked at his watch and was surprised to see that it was almost eleven. In the past, the gangs had always met one another before midnight.

A message pinged out from Griffoni's phone. She read it but said nothing.

There was another ping, and then another, and a fourth. She held up her phone, read the rest of the messages, and said, 'It's Antonio, and he knows where they're meeting.'

After a moment, the phone pinged again. She looked at it and looked at him. 'Giudecca' was all she said and she closed her eyes in frustration. Before Brunetti could speak, she added, very softly, 'Antonio's Neapolitan, so that must sound like enough information to him.'

A few minutes later, they heard another ping. After reading the message, she said, 'Antonio. Get ready for *this* news.' She sounded exasperated, not excited.

Brunetti looked up but said nothing.

'They've signed a peace treaty.'

'The gangs?' Brunetti asked, hoping this was true. No one would be hurt, and he could go home and go to bed.

Looking at her phone, Griffoni passed on Antonio's information. 'The leader of the Venetians offered a truce to the ones from Lido, saying the gangs on the mainland would have more respect for them if they were bigger, and they'd have more fun working together.' Before Brunetti could ask, she said, 'Yes, "fun".'

'God help us all,' Brunetti muttered, leaning towards her, as if being closer to the phone would make it easier to understand.

'He also said he had an idea for tonight, a way to celebrate their treaty that would get them a lot of attention.'

Marvelling at the delusional self-importance of youth, Brunetti asked, 'Did he say what it was?'

Griffoni shook her head. She looked over at Brunetti, who remained silent. 'Come on, come on,' she whispered to her phone.

Brunetti watched her hand on the *telefonino*, rocking it lightly as if trying to keep it awake. It responded with another ping.

'They're on their way,' she said and pushed herself to her feet, as though it were imperative that they join the boys who were in motion.

'Who?' Brunetti asked.

'The Lions of Lido,' this time treating the name seriously.

'There's ten of them. Two have boats, so they don't have to take the vaporetto.'

'Where are they going?'

'It's near a place on the Giudecca called Fondamenta de la Rotonda,' she told him, then waited for him – he was a Venetian, after all – to tell her where it was. Brunetti, however, had only a vague idea: down towards Sacca Fisola somewhere.

'There's an abandoned factory,' she said. One of the few things Brunetti knew about that part of the city was that it was full of abandoned factories and workshops, left behind decades ago when the work, and the workers, migrated to Marghera and Mestre.

'Nothing else?' he asked.

'It doesn't seem . . .' she began and was again interrupted by her phone. She looked at the screen, and her expression froze. She looked away from the message and over at Brunetti.

'What's wrong?' he asked.

'The spokesman for the Lions of Venice told them he hoped they'd have some extra fuel in their boats.'

'Foa will know where it is,' Brunetti said, grabbing his jacket and starting towards the staircase. He emerged on the landing of the floor below and shouted off to the right, 'Foa! Foa!' There was an answering shout, then two more. After a moment, Foa and the two officers emerged from the doorway, all wearing dark clothing, and came quickly to join the others running down the stairs.

At the door, Brunetti and Griffoni paused while he told the man on night shift that they were going to the Giudecca, nothing more.

Outside, Foa already stood at the wheel of the Questura's unmarked electric boat; only the ruffled water at the back gave any indication that the motor was running.

The two uniformed men were already down in the cabin.

Griffoni went and stood to Foa's left, Brunetti to his right. 'Fondamenta de la Rotonda,' he told the pilot. 'There are some abandoned factories behind it.'

Foa nodded, as though Brunetti had pointed to something on a map. 'There's some, but they've been empty for years – fifteen, twenty.' He was silent then, considering the route. Decided, he turned to Brunetti and said, 'We can take Rio di Sant'Eufemia.' He turned from them and pulled the boat silently away from the dock.

As he arched the boat in a wide turn to the right, Foa said, 'There are two factories with a common courtyard. The first made bricks.' There followed a long silence as Foa rooted around for whatever else he could recall. 'The other one made paint, I think. Or solvents. But they went bankrupt: It's all been empty since the factories closed.'

Foa increased their speed up the Canale della Giudecca, almost devoid of traffic at this time of night; the gathering speed made the hull slam down harder on the water, but no sound came from the mute motor. After a few minutes, Foa slowed the boat and swung it to the left and into Rio di Sant'Eufemia. He cut the speed, and they slithered through what at this hour served as a parking lot, with a long row of boats moored to the right side of the canal, leaving barely enough room for other boats to squeeze past them. Some houses backed onto the canal; then came a long section on the right of a vine-devoured wall before the houses resumed. Soon after, Foa pulled the boat to the right and stopped. A sign on the wall read, 'Calle Storta dei Squeri'. Putting his hand on Brunetti's arm, he whispered: 'Go straight ahead, first left, and you'll run right into the brick factory. Behind that, there's a courtyard and the paint factory is over at the end of it, right on the Laguna.' Griffoni and the two officers stepped onto the embankment:

'Where will you go?' Brunetti asked.

'Out into the Laguna. There's a place I can hide. When you finish – or if you need me – send me a message: I'll be there in two minutes, no longer.' Without further talk, the pilot engaged the soundless engine and moved off towards the Laguna Sud.

The four of them did as Foa had advised, Brunetti leading them, but not before they had all turned their phones to silent and lowered the light on the screens to the minimum.

The streets were preternaturally quiet: Brunetti thought he would be able to hear a cat's footsteps. To the end, left, under the underpass, and there it was. He saw and heard no one. They followed what might have been a path where the trash and undergrowth had been ignored for years and some of the bushes were now almost as high as a man. Their dark clothing made them all but invisible if they were in front of the bushes, completely so if they backed into them.

One of the officers moved ahead a bit, then waved at Brunetti to come closer. When he did, the officer whispered, 'The wall down there has crumbled.'

Before Brunetti could say anything, a message slipped into Griffoni's phone, faintly illuminating the screen. She read it and told them, 'The ones from Venice are almost here, but from what Antonio's heard, they got off the vaporetto at Sant'Eufemia and are coming on foot.'

Another dimness of light, and Griffoni looked again. Brunetti saw her shoulders stiffen as she read the message.

'What?' he asked, thinking that perhaps he should not.

'It's from him. He's with them,' she said.

He knew whom she meant, but he still asked. 'Orlando?'

She nodded.

'What does he say?'

She passed him the phone, and he read: *My father's a hero and risked his life to save people.* Brunetti turned his head towards

Griffoni and raised his eyebrows. Her face remained impassive, so he read the rest of Orlando's message: *Tonight everybody will see how brave we are.* No sooner had he handed her the phone than another message arrived. This time, she merely tipped the screen towards him. *It will be really BIG*, he boasted.

Brunetti was saved from having to think of something to say by the low purr of a small boat and the sound of voices coming from the direction of the Laguna.

Because the moon was full and the courtyard of the factories was illuminated by street lamps the city had not bothered to remove, they had the advantage of being able to see what was happening while remaining hidden themselves.

Signalling the others to stay where they were, Brunetti followed the young officer towards the end of the wall, where part of it had disintegrated, raining rubble on both sides. Through a hole, Brunetti saw a group of young boys, perhaps a dozen of them and surely not long into their teens, already waiting in front of what Foa had said was the paint factory, their heads raised and turned towards the noise of the small motor approaching.

The sounds drew closer, closer; there were a few thumps and hissed commands of '*Silenzio.*' More noise. Someone laughed. Suddenly the motor died, the sound replaced by voices and more hisses to be quiet, then the noise of feet on gravel. The noise stopped for a moment, and then sounded out even louder. A few words were shouted. One voice started out deep, gruff, masculine, but, at a certain point, it rocketed into the feminine register and stopped. There was laughter and some yelling, but no aggression in their raised voices.

Suddenly they went silent and then, one by one, appeared at the top of the wall that separated the factory from the Laguna. Brunetti assumed they'd tied up at a landing place on the other side of the wall. The Lions of Venice ran over and offered their hands to help their former enemies as they jumped down into the courtyard.

Brunetti felt a grip on his arm. Surprised, he moved to try to shake it off. The hand was gone and a low voice said, 'Should I get the others, Commissario?'

He nodded and gave the officer a gentle shove back towards the others, and the young man drifted into the darkness. After a short time, Brunetti heard something resembling a bird's call. Silently, as though they were children playing at war, Griffoni and then the two officers, bent over and walking as quickly and quietly as they could, reached him. Most of the noise they made was drowned out by the voices in the courtyard.

The assembled boys, if they heard anything, didn't bother to turn to look, so fully taken were they with the arrival of the lions, either their own or the ones from the other part of the city.

The four of them, granted invisibility by the wall, heard another boat approaching. It arrived with no trouble, but then thudded against the embankment and was greeted with shouts, but moderate, amused ones.

Within minutes, a line of back-slapping, excited boys filed into the courtyard. Brunetti, even from where he stood, could feel the energy radiating from them.

Suddenly Brunetti noticed the old, multi-pastel 'PEACE' flag hanging limply from a window of the abandoned paint factory – torn, ragged, faded – and tried to remember how many years ago that eruption of hope had taken place. On the ground beneath it, successive high tides and many *acque alte* had washed up against the front of the building, leaving waves of abandoned cartons and newspapers, broken bottles, even a cut-open mattress that had spewed gobs of padding on top of decomposing garbage bags.

Three of the newly arrived boys entered in step, clenched fists raised on straight arms a bit higher than their heads, chanting,

'Lido, Lido, Lido,' and a ghost passed over Brunetti's grave at the sight. He had never seen it, but here it was again.

At the front of the boys from Venice strode their bull-like leader, a tall blond young man who looked to Brunetti to be too old to be playing at these silly games.

The boys from Lido cheered their common leader, and then so did his own followers. There was a great deal of hard back-smacking and even harder chest-punching from which no one dared flinch. The blond boy-man did not pause in front of them but passed through the splayed doors of the factory. After a minute or two, he emerged two floors above the entrance on a small balcony, its guard rail and glass doors broken and lost decades ago. All the windows of the building's façade were missing, and many of the roof tiles had fallen or been tossed to the ground and left there: broken, useless, out of fashion, as now were the men who had once worked here.

Both prides of lions stood below the balcony, some with their arms around the shoulders of a friend or new friend. They talked in their normal voices, no shouting, no threats. They were a group of boys from the same city, discovering that they had friends and relatives in common.

The boy on the balcony raised both his arms and succeeded in capturing the others' attention and silencing them. Into this new calm, one of the boys at the back of the group shouted, 'Gianpaolo, Gianpaolo, Gianpaolo.' It took the other boys only seconds to join in the chant, which swiftly changed to 'Porpora, Porpora, Porpora,' a name Brunetti recalled from the doorbell of Bocchese's neighbours.

Gianpaolo, suddenly judging it sufficient praise, took a step forward, closer to the railless edge of the balcony, and raised his arms. As soon as the noise stopped, he began to speak with full confidence.

Voice deep and decisive, he said, 'Because we're in Venice, I'll be the host, so welcome to all of you, especially to our new friends from across the Laguna, the Lions of Lido.' He paused here and waited for the cheering and whistling to end.

'Now that our numbers have doubled, we should begin to make our presence better known in both Venice and Lido.' He leaned forward and looked down at the assembled boys. Pointing at one standing among the Lions of Lido, he asked in a peremptory voice, 'Right, Marco?' Instead of speaking, the boy pumped his hand in the air. The boys standing below shouted and stamped, encouraging Marco to call out above their noise, 'Let's show them what we can do.'

Suddenly Brunetti saw Monforte appear from around the right side of the building. The boy on the balcony saw him, too.

Looking down at the group, Gianpaolo stepped back and shouted into the crowd, 'Hey, Orlando, your daddy's here. Come to get you?'

Ah, thought Brunetti, what a genius for politics this young man has: as soon as you have a potential group of followers, create an enemy; even better, create two. As soon as you can set your followers loose against an enemy, any enemy, they are yours to do with as you please.

Orlando screamed, but no one could hear him, or wanted to hear him. Gianpaolo raised his arms, commanding silence. He turned in the narrow space of the balcony and looked at Orlando, perhaps ten metres from him. 'Are you still with us, Orlandino?' he shouted, more for the boys than for his victim. 'Or has your daddy changed your mind for you?'

From below, the boys, who had no idea what Gianpaolo was talking about, started to call out. 'Answer him, Orlandino.' 'Why isn't your Mommy here, too, Orlandino?' 'Afraid of the Lions, Orlandino?' Hearing them, Brunetti realized how the use of the diminutive strengthened the case – whatever it was – against Orlando. Then one last question floated up: 'Going to show your *papà* how brave you are, Orlandino?'

Gianpaolo silenced them with another gesture. 'What do you say, Orlando? Do you have the courage to show how brave you are?' The boy on the balcony looked towards Orlando and, keeping a sing-song rhythm in his voice and deliberately pitching it high, asked: 'But you'll still have Daddy, the hero, to protect you, won't you, Orlandino?' The crowd turned towards Orlando.

Strangely enough, the boys did not call out more questions at Orlando but gave him silence into which he could speak, perhaps even the chance to show his bravery.

Brunetti raised his head above the wall to see how Monforte reacted. Slowly, the boy's father started along the front of the building, the boys unwilling to stop or challenge him, either because of the lack of an order from Gianpaolo or at the mere sight of Monforte's bulk.

'I'm not a coward,' Orlando shouted up at Gianpaolo, but there was little power in his voice, and his remark was greeted with whistles.

'Prove it,' the boy on the balcony shouted down and then turned it into a chant: 'Prove it, prove it, prove it.'

The boys, already stamping out a two-note chant, moved to encircle Orlando, and then the order came again from above: 'Prove it, prove it, prove it.'

Brunetti could almost weep at the predictability of it all: insult him and then set him an impossible task; it was the same technique the bullies in his class had used, years before, and was meant to provide sure proof of Orlando's cowardice. It would also prove who was in control here, who was the leader of the pack.

Like a ripe plum, Orlando fell: 'Tell me what to do, and I'll show you how brave I am.' Like one of the minor characters in a bad film, he broke through the circle of boys surrounding him and stopped alone below the balcony.

As soon as Brunetti saw the boy on the balcony open his mouth, he knew the whole thing had been a set-up.

'What do I have to do?' Orlando asked.

Brunetti watched Gianpaolo and saw his smile. It had all been so easy. No, Orlando wasn't a coward. But he was still a boy.

'Come up here with me and I'll show you.'

Orlando walked towards the door to the building. From behind him, Monforte called his name, but the boy ignored him and disappeared inside.

A minute or two later, he appeared at the side of the speaker and shouted at him, as if he could silence him that way. 'What do I have to do?'

As though he'd been waiting for just this, Gianpaolo asked, 'Did you see the liquid on the steps coming up here: paint and solvent and . . . benzine?'

Orlando looked down at his feet and nodded.

'Do you have it on your feet the way I do, Orlando?'

'No,' Orlando said in a voice that suggested he had just failed the test of bravery.

'But you're brave, are you?' Gianpaolo asked, turning away from Orlando and playing to the audience.

'Yes.'

'Are you this brave?' he demanded, pulling a cigarette lighter from his pocket.

There was a collective gasp from the boys and a far deeper one from the man standing in front of them. Orlando took an involuntary footstep back to be farther from the lighter.

'You seem frightened, little Orlandino,' Gianpaolo said.

Orlando stepped towards him and held out his hand.

'Let's see about that,' Gianpaolo said and raised the lighter over his head. He pulled a piece of paper from his pocket and set it ablaze, then turned to Orlando and asked, 'Are you brave enough to throw this on the floor?'

Without a moment's hesitation, saying nothing, Orlando grabbed the paper and threw it on the floor behind them.

Three seconds passed in terrifying silence, and then some of the empty windows along the left side of the building were illuminated one by one as the flames spread and slipped along the wooden floor, under the doors and down the wooden steps, following the sloppy trail Gianpaolo and two friends had made earlier in the evening, carrying up jerrycans as well as cans from the abandoned storeroom on the ground floor. Thus was to be created the BIG THING they wanted to offer the city as proof of their prowess.

The flames from the jerry cans and the cans of paint that had been left behind when the factory was closed decades before took possession of the building with frightening violence, as though eager, finally, to pay someone back for having kept them in hiding all these years.

Within seconds, the wooden stairway was a tunnel of flame, and only then did Gianpaolo, the king of the Lions of Venice, bother to go and look for another exit.

# 30

In the courtyard below, fear reigned. As with animals in the presence of fire, the boys' instinct was to flee, so that is what they tried to do. When they reached the wall where they'd jumped into the courtyard, they discovered two uniformed officers in front of them. Trapped, they had no choice but to obey the officers and follow one of them over the wall and down to the boats, where they were told to sit. Almost immediately, Foa arrived, and the remaining boys obeyed the second officer and followed the others down to the landing and onto the third boat. When that was done, the officers – Venetians and thus at home in any boat – jumped aboard. Flames behind them, Foa took command and led them out into the Laguna and towards the Questura.

Brunetti and Griffoni had observed it all and saw that neither Orlando nor Gianpaolo had been among the boys, nor was there any sign of Monforte.

Griffoni and Brunetti decided to separate and check both sides of the factory for another place of entry that might prove a place of exit. As he turned the corner of the building, Brunetti saw Monforte bent towards one of the windows on the ground floor, its wooden shutters lying at his feet. His hands were wrapped around two iron bars, and Brunetti could hear him gasp as he tried to tear them free.

Brunetti grabbed him by the arm and hauled him away from the window. Behind it, the fire had gone wild and was lurching ever closer to the windows and the oxygen that would add to its power.

Brunetti all but dragged the man, stiff with shock, farther along the building; up ahead, he saw a wooden door hanging inwards on one hinge. He propped Monforte against the building and stepped closer to the door. He kicked at it, and then again. Something moved, but the door did not open.

Monforte was still leaning against the wall of the building, his arms tight around his chest, eyes closed. Brunetti grabbed him by the upper arms and shook him. 'We've got to get in,' he shouted at the other man, who looked at him blankly. Still holding on with his left hand, Brunetti brought his right hand from behind him and slapped Monforte twice across the face, as hard as he could.

The man's eyes opened and he yanked himself free. He pulled his arm back and made a fist just as something enormous crashed behind the door: Monforte forgot his fist and snapped into life again. He pushed Brunetti aside and ran at the door, smashing against it with the entire force of his body concentrated in his right shoulder. He took a few steps back and tried again, and this time the door moved inwards a few centimetres. He backed off and once more hurled himself against it, like a creature immune to pain.

In the midst of this noise, Griffoni appeared and ran towards Brunetti. He yelled to her and told her to call the *pompieri* and tell them to send at least two boats, then call the Questura and tell them to send Foa back as soon as he got there. His voice disappeared under another thunderous crash from inside the factory, then he shouted, 'And an ambulance.' She nodded and moved away; Brunetti turned back to the building.

The door hung open, but there was no sign of Monforte. Brunetti gazed into the room, astonished, for it looked like it was getting ready for a giant costume party. Captive in a six-surfaced Pollock, Brunetti saw strips and whirls and overlapping splotches of red, yellow, white, orange, blue – every colour he could imagine. Over the years and with no plan, cans had exploded and splashed over the ceiling, walls, and floor. Some of the empty cans from which the paint had burst – from heat or age – were stuck with serendipitous artistry in puddles of conflicting colours; others lay in careless poses, drowned in their own viscera. Some of the creations had gathered wrinkles and cracks that often enhanced their beauty. Some, instead, were covered with mould.

Brunetti smelled the burning wood, but it was the sharp chemical odour that worried him more. He heard something slam on his left, and he turned towards the noise. Suddenly, filling the doorway with his mass, Monforte appeared, surrounded by a haze of yellow smoke. Jove the Conqueror.

Brunetti tensed his body for attack, but the other man slammed the door behind him and came over to Brunetti, pointing as he said in a newly raspy voice, 'Nothing down there. Just empty rooms and cans of paint. Too much smoke.' There was a sudden noise from above – it could have been a voice – that pulled Monforte's attention away from Brunetti. Both men froze.

It came again, above and from the right, sounding more like a voice this time. Both men ran to an iron safety door: behind it they found a narrow metal staircase. Monforte launched himself upwards with the speed and agility of a monkey, taking the steps two at a time and using the handrail to haul his weight up faster. Brunetti followed close behind him. He grabbed the rail but pulled his hand back with a gasp.

At the top of the second flight, they paused to listen and heard the voice again. They both ran towards it, and Monforte yanked open the first door they found.

Heat engulfed them, and the horrible whoop of fire, but they saw no flames. Even above that noise, they could hear the high-pitched voice screaming, *'Aiuto. Aiuto,'* only to be drowned by an eruption of noise from another part of the building.

Monforte was through the door in seconds, Brunetti close behind. The noise fell on them: roaring, snarling, boasting of what the fire was going to do to anyone it caught. The voice came from someone on the floor. From the size, Brunetti knew it was Orlando and not Gianpaolo. The boy lay face down, crying and screaming, his right leg bent below the knee in a way it should not be bent.

When he saw them, he howled, *'Papi, Papi, aiuto.'* He pushed himself up and dragged his left knee forward, hauling his weight onto it, then heaved himself towards his father, away from the fire, still screaming. Brunetti suspected it was from terror as much as pain. As if to show Brunetti how right he was – and how prescient the boy – the fire rushed through the door behind the crab-like figure and hurled a burning panel teasingly close to his legs.

Brunetti turned and saw Monforte bent over, immobilized by coughing. In an instant, Brunetti was beside the boy, grabbing the collar of his jacket and trying to pull him away from the burning part of the building. He heard heavy steps and was roughly shoved aside by Monforte, who picked up the boy as though he were a far younger child, draped him over his back in a fireman's carry, and, ignoring his son's cries of anguish, started for the landing. At the bottom of the stairs they had used, the fire, having finished devouring the tins and barrels of paint, had settled itself into the slower and more decorous consumption of the main course – furniture, the frames of doors and windows – and then, for dessert, a walnut credenza filled with files.

Brunetti had no sense of where they were in the building. He had seen it only from outside, and when he'd been chasing sounds up the stairs and down the hallways he'd paid no attention to direction, only speed. He saw a door on the other side of the landing and opened it: the passage led towards light at the other end that must come from the street lamps.

He turned and cried to Monforte, 'This way.' Brunetti set off running towards the end of the hallway, realizing as he ran that, ahead of them, nothing flickered, nothing flared.

When he reached the stairs at the end of the hallway, he turned to Monforte and the boy. Then, when Monforte paused for breath, Brunetti ran ahead of them down the steps. One flight. Two. At the bottom he was stopped by an iron security door. '*Oddio*, grant me this,' Brunetti heard himself whisper. Later, he was unable to remember whether he had spoken out loud or only to some spirit of mercy in which he didn't know he believed.

He reached out and turned the handle: the door swung open to the loading dock behind the factory, as if doing no more than aiding a worker stepping outside to have a cigarette. The night air seemed almost chilly.

Monforte came up beside Brunetti, then walked away from the building, closer to the wall of the Laguna. Cautiously, shaking with the effort, he went down on one knee, then the other, and slid the boy slowly down and across his chest, then even more slowly onto the ground. Orlando lay there, motionless, almost gelatinous, one shoe missing, clothing and body unsinged, no sign that he had been near a fire. No sign that he had, for some time, breathed in chemical-filled smoke. Brunetti glanced at Monforte, who knelt next to his son. Instinct warned him not to go near them.

It was Monforte who moved first. He pushed himself totteringly to his feet, and no one seeing how long it took him to do so would recall the strong, healthy man who had gone into the building. He coughed, then coughed again, violently. He spat on the ground. Thick, red. He glanced at Brunetti, who had also seen it.

Brunetti walked closer and stopped a metre from the other man. 'An ambulance is on the way' was the only thing he could think of to say. Ordinarily, confronting a parent with an injured child, he would offer some bromide: looks all right, breathing is fine, good hospital, chief doctor very competent. But with Monforte – and remembering the force with which he had attacked the door – that fact was all Brunetti would risk conveying.

Suddenly Griffoni was beside him. She looked at Monforte, her glance level. Keeping her eyes on him, she moved her left hand slowly and unbuttoned her jacket. Her right hand moved a bit away from her body.

Monforte saw her motions, looked down, and closed his eyes. He shook his head a few times, but with no more energy than someone who had missed a bus.

He looked up, straight at her, and asked, 'You know about Nasiriyah?'

'Yes.'

'Everything?'

'Yes,' she said and lowered her hand.

He started to sigh, but coughing cut it off and left him bent over, all but helpless. This time, some of the red fell on his shoes.

He jerked himself upright. 'Don't tell the boy. Please.'

She looked at Monforte. Only now did she see how ash and smoke had coloured him as though he were the only person there who knew that Carnevale had begun and it was time for costumes.

A siren sounded, then drew swiftly closer. Foa, who had returned, switched on his searchlight and pointed it into the sky for a moment, then lowered it to the brick stairway on the outside of the low wall leading down to the water. The ambulance approached, slowed to a stop, and two uniformed attendants hurried up the steps, one carrying a rolled-up stretcher.

Monforte commanded, 'Here.' Nothing more, but the certainty of the command brought the two men running to Orlando's side. The boy, conscious now, turned his head to see them. The one without the stretcher knelt and put a stethoscope to the supine boy's heart, took his pulse, and, giving every appearance of ignoring Monforte looming above him, grabbed the end of the stretcher and set it on the ground, parallel to Orlando, close to his standing colleague.

They had both seen the angle of Orlando's leg, so they began by sliding the stretcher under his shoulders and left leg. The one in charge took Orlando's right thigh and leg, holding them as motionless as he could, and placed the right leg beside the left. Orlando moaned but no more than that. He kept his eyes on what was happening.

They lifted the stretcher and turned towards the ambulance, but Monforte stood in their way.

Griffoni appeared from behind the men from the ambulance and walked up to Monforte as casually as if she'd seen an old friend. She nodded but did not smile and placed her hand on his arm. They exchanged a few words, stopped speaking. After some time, Monforte spoke again, but only a few words. She nodded. Monforte walked over to the stretcher, bent down and touched the boy's cheek.

'Help my friend, *Papi*,' the boy said. 'Please.'

Monforte smiled at him, then stood back and moved out of the path of the attendants.

Griffoni followed the two men to the ambulance, waiting

while they stepped down into the back and slid the stretcher into place, then strapped Orlando's chest and thighs securely. She moved to the front of the boat and said something to the pilot, who stepped back to let her come on board. The pilot engaged the engine and turned towards the way they had come. Griffoni did not look back.

As soon as the boat had disappeared, Monforte turned to Brunetti. When he saw the other man's face, Brunetti thought it would be wise to prepare himself for an attack, something he had been taught when he first joined the force. It had something to do with keeping your body agile and ready, but all Brunetti could bring himself to do was to rise up a bit on his toes and keep his knees loose. Given that someone had just been carried to the hospital, and he was standing in front of a burning building, he did not think it made much difference what he did with his knees.

'Where are the firemen?' Monforte exploded.

'I don't know. My colleague called them.'

'Useless bastards,' Monforte said, then stepped aside and, ignoring Brunetti, studied the burning building.

A moment later, they heard the sirens of two fire-boats announce themselves from a distance, then they both all but leaped into the Laguna from Rio del Ponte Longo, the only canal leading to the Laguna that was wide enough for them. The apparent chaos of roaring motors and shouting firemen was all quickly revealed to be part of a strict discipline. Within a minute, both boats were tied to the stanchion at the back of the building, the ends of three hoses were dropped into the water, and the pumps started working. By the time the firemen, slowed by the weight of their protective uniforms and the difficulty of carrying the hoses to the factory, had got close enough to the building, water was already streaming out of the hoses with such power that it took two men to hold each in place.

Two more men leaped from the boat to the pavement and joined the others. They must have decided to ignore the lower floors and pointed the hoses at the windows of the third. It all seemed, however, to make little difference. Small explosions were to be heard, and occasionally a heavy crash sounded from inside the building. As the water power intensified, the firemen braced themselves and waited for the command for where to aim.

All of a sudden, one of the firemen raised his arm and pointed to the right, to the part of the building where the flames seemed less fierce. The three streams followed his motion, all crowding around and into the same windows.

Behind Brunetti, the pumps of the fireboats roared back at the flames, and the water streaming into the building smashed into the walls and tried to drown the floors.

A light-haired head appeared, seemingly from nowhere, in the last window to the right. Mouth open, the boy shouted something no one could hear, not that it made any difference. The crew holding the middle hose faltered at the sight of him, and their stream of water veered down for a moment, smashing against the wall of the building. Things quickly righted themselves, and the stream returned to where it had been. Either by instinct or by training, the men on the right lowered their hose and ran the stream through the broken window under the one where the boy stood, then played the water into the window on the other side of him. Again the boy shouted, and still no one could hear what he said.

Brunetti sensed motion to his right and turned to see Monforte stumbling from the deck of the larger fireboat, something that looked like a silver box in his arms. He straightened up very slowly; two men shouted at him; he ignored them, although whatever they said was lost, anyway, in the collective noise of machines and pumps and water and men screaming incomprehensibly. By this time, there was also the noise of an audience of neighbours standing on both sides of the canal and a few boats out in the Laguna, trying to help by turning their spotlights at the façade of the burning building.

Monforte clutched the object to his chest, shuffling forward. Brunetti forced himself to move and stood in his path. A burst of coughing halted Monforte in his tracks; he pushed his face down into what Brunetti could now see was a fire-retardant blanket. He continued to cough, then stopped for a moment, sank to his knees and gasped, begging for air with his lungs, then coughed again: rough, violent, loud, red. Suddenly he stopped coughing as though he'd been commanded to and struggled to his feet.

Brunetti raised his hand to try to stop him, but Monforte slapped Brunetti's arm away as though it were an insect. Brunetti looked up at the window of the third floor, but the boy was no longer there. He thought of the flames he'd seen, the heat that had singed his jacket. All of a sudden – as if this were a card game and noise had been declared trumps – they all heard a thunderous crash as part of the roof at the other end of the building fell in upon itself. Brunetti had turned at the sound, and when he looked back, Monforte was almost at the door through which he had carried his son.

At the door, he halted, turned back to Brunetti, shook open the blanket with both hands and wrapped it around his shoulders. Eyes on Brunetti, he shouted, 'He thinks I'm a hero.' He took a step closer to the building, stopped and reeled back as though he had walked into a wall.

Monforte bowed his head, then raised it, and in a motion that was strangely feminine, wrapped one loose corner of the blanket around his throat and tossed it gracefully back over his shoulder. And staggered into the building.

# 31

From: Maggiore Massimo Fede

To: Generale di Brigata Filippo Lauria
    Colonnello Roberto Bisso
    Tenente Colonnello Sara Minella

*Signori,*

*In response to your mail dated yesterday, I submit the reasons we should treat the case under consideration as a normal, however lamentable, event: the death of a former Carabiniere in an attempt to be of service.*

*You have seen copies of the report I submitted twenty years ago, as well as copies of the documents upholding my accusations at the time. There is no question about the nature of Monforte's behaviour: had a charge been brought against him, the scandal would surely have provoked a governmental investigation at a particularly delicate historical moment when the very possibility of a charge of treason would have had a devastating effect upon* the entire corps and upon the careers of the officers who were above him in the chain of command.

Those events belong to the past, and must remain there. People remember Monforte, and they remember him as a hero. Thus we must present him as a hero who died in his last act of bravery. The attached report from the coroner who performed the autopsy states that the damage to his lungs from both heat and chemical smoke was so vast that there was no way he could have survived, yet he found the courage and strength to return to the building.

He saved his son's life (attached please find the statement of Commissario Guido Brunetti of the Venice police) and willingly went into the burning building again in an attempt to save the life of another boy, Gianpaolo Porpora. Unbeknownst to Monforte, the boy had already escaped the building by means of a fire ladder attached to the back wall, climbing down to the second floor and throwing himself into the Laguna.

Monforte's acts of bravery have served so far to attract all the attention the press might choose to pay him. A military funeral with full honours will divert interest in his past and serve as evidence that he lived as a hero and died as a hero.

I suggest that a military funeral – with all honours and with a rifle salute – be held as quickly as possible, perhaps by the end of the week, and that he be referred to and mentioned as an example of the bravery that characterizes the entire corps. If you judge it wise, we could also award him some sort of medal; the best would be that for valour.

Most respectfully,
Massimo Fede,
Maggiore